Venom

A Warren Dennihan Novel
by scott wellinger

Cover Art and design copyright © by WWPGroup®

World Wide Publishing Group

Www.WWPGroup.webs.com

Venom

A World Wide Publishing book / published by arrangement with the author

Copyright © 2014 by Scott Wellinger

For information, address: World Wide Publishing Group.

Printed in the United States of America

10 9 8 7 6 5 4 3 2 1

ISBN: 978-0-9899421-4-0

To DJ.

The inspiration behind the fictitious Stubbs. Your heart is as big as the character.

PROLOGUE

THE RED AND BLUE LIGHTS COULD BE SEEN long before reaching the building, or entering the complex for that matter. The road past the main gate leading up to the enormous pharmaceutical research facility was lined with trees and signage which enabled workers and visitors alike to navigate to the appropriate building within the compound. All of which were reflecting the flashing emergency lights from deep within facility.

The property took up nearly one thousand acres just outside of Downtown Charleston, South Carolina. The various buildings which held various research data were dropped sporadically about the premises. The half-blind could have found the building being sought because of all of the lights and commotion in the early morning darkness of 2:00 AM. No signage nor a GPS was needed. A vehicle was approaching the epicenter of activity at triple the posted speed limit of twenty-five miles per hour, as the driver was late to the party.

The sedan made the right turn hardly slowing down, as if it were on rails. The blaring music of Miranda Lambert's *Crazy Ex-girlfriend* could be heard, muffled from outside of the racing vehicle, which ricocheted through the corner. The car raced beyond the large parking lot toward the building to the very edge of the cordoned area designated as such with yellow police tape. The illuminated sign which read 'BIOGENESIS Pharmaceuticals Toxicology and Herpetology laboratories' was lost in the flashing lights of the Charleston Police cruisers, unmarked Homicide Detective vehicles, the Coroner's van, CSU vehicle, and BIOGENESIS security vehicles. The scene was a rave, only previously without music.

The lissome and attractive Homicide Detective, Carina Fischer, exited her air-conditioned vehicle as rushed as she had driven onto the site. She pulled aside the bottom, left, front corner of her blazer, revealing her Charleston homicide detective badge to the sweaty, flat-footed patrolman who was maintaining the perimeter. He lifted the yellow police tape for her.

She nodded to him and said in her Southern drawl, "BIOGENESIS. Isn't that the steroid company that — "

The officer interrupted her, which she hated. " — totally unrelated. I thought the same thing. Somebody is dead but it isn't A-Rod, unfortunately."

She paused on the other side of the police tape, staring the patrolman in the eye. It was hot and humid even without the sun, she wanted to go into the building, into air-conditioning. But not before setting the patrolman straight.

"Very funny. You'd think that they'd change their name. Nobody wants to be associated with assholes. Take me, for example. I'm a cop, but then so are you. Your Momma never taught you not to interrupt people when they were talkin'?"

The Patrolman didn't like to be dressed-down, especially by woman. Even if she was a superior.

"Aren't you a little late? Probably nothing left to investigate at this point. I'm sure you'll take all the credit though."

"What are y'all doing here? Issuin' parkin' tickets?"

She was in no mood for the usual red-neck, sexist crap that was dished out to her regularly. She was promoted because she was good at her job, if the lesser-achieving males have a problem with that then they can just get over it. At thirty-four, she had already accomplished more than the forty-something uniformed cop who was razzing her.

If he had a snappy comeback, he either didn't say it or she didn't hear it. She moved quickly toward the entrance to the building where more personnel were milling about. Their conversations were abruptly halted as she approached them, preferring to gossip and theorize about what transpired inside privately. Once she had reached the main lobby, she was informed that they were waiting for her on the third floor laboratory. The loiterers didn't say who 'they' were, but she didn't need them to. She knew who was waiting because she had taken the late-night phone call from the people requesting her presence.

The ornate yet understated lobby was surrounded by glass, a waterfall fell from the top floor down into the center of the reception area. The falling water hid the side-by-side elevators behind it. All of the appointments were made of glass, wood, stone and to a lesser extent steel, creating a very natural-looking habitat. The tall trees added to the organic effect.

Both of the semi-hidden elevators were being held on higher floors, so Carina decided to take the stairs. Her long legs allowed her to ascend the stairs two at a time despite being in heels. She reached the third floor long before either of the elevators made a bid to drop to the lobby to collect her. The emergency stairs deposited her in the small reception area of the lab on the third floor which was decorated with the same muted, natural colors used in the lobby. A gaggle of people occupied this area, including her boss, the man whom had called her cell at her home. The Captain of the Charleston, South Carolina Homicide Division, Bryan Simms did not look happy.

"Captain Simms, I got here as soon as I could. I wasn't aware that I was on rotation. My desk is full, Sir."

"I called you because it looks like your desk and this homicide are related. We have ourselves a very serious situation."

"Isn't murder always serious, Sir."

He broke free of his entourage, drawing Detective Carina Fischer out of the crowd with him.

"You can lay on that Southern charm can't you? What I'm saying is that we unofficially have a serial killer here in Charleston."

"This is related to my poison cases? Here?"

"I think it will make more sense once we go inside. But before we do, I need for you to know that we are trying to keep this out of the public for as long as we can. At least until we have an arrest. The last thing we need right now is to destroy our prime tourism season with a panic."

"Y'all know this is going to go viral, if it hasn't already. All the people millin' around? I had to get through a half-dozen news crews before I could even get through the main gate." Her Southern drawl was thick.

"They know there was an incident and that a third-shift lab worker is dead because of it, but they know nothing else."

"Then they already know more 'n me."

"Always a wise-ass, Detective. Why can't you act like a lady? You certainly look like one. I let you walk all over me because of your close-rate."

"You wanted to show me the scene, Sir?" She was tired. Tired after having worked all day and then being dragged out of her much needed rest. Tired of the same conversation with her boss.

Captain Simms had overcome some of the same obstacles that Carina had to overcome on her way up the ladder. He gave her a wide berth for that and other reasons. He shook his head and guided her into the secure lab.

A security ID badge had to be used no less than three times to get into the main part of the lab. Simms had been fortified with a magnetized security card, which he needed to slide through the electronic reader. Each time Carina and her boss stopped at another electronic gate-keeper, she noticed that in addition to needing a badge, the entrances were being surveilled by Closed Circuit Television cameras.

"Before you ask, the system that records the security footage for this floor has been disabled and the card that was used to access the lab was assigned to a member of the night cleaning crew. Only that cleaner hasn't worked here in three years."

"They can't all be easy I guess. How'd you know I was fixin' to ask you that?"

"I can read your mind."

They entered the lab which was filled with wall-to-wall laboratory machines. Other than the trays with test tubes resting on the large machine that presumably filled them, Carina hadn't a clue as to what all the equipment did.

Along the perimeter of the lab were glass walls with doors leading to an assortment of desks and computers. They made their way to the back of the room where under the counter of a workstation, a slight man was dead on the floor. The amount of blood that was pooled on the floor could have filled a gallon milk jug. The man's lifeless eyes stared at their shoes, his arms folded in a way which indicated he was dead when he hit the floor. There was obviously no way that he could have been comfortable or tried to move once he had landed there. The Medical Examiner, Spencer, approached behind them to restate the facts that had already been relayed to Captain Simms.

"You cannot see from this angle, but this guy was hit rather hard on the back of the head. He was a tiny man. Judging by the damage, he was hit harder than what was needed to kill him." The M.E. Squatted down under the counter and turned the victim's head so Carina could see the matted, blood-soaked hair. The victim had been struck with such force that the hair and skin on his head had been pulled away from his skull.

"Wow. This little man really pissed somebody off."

"But that's not the best part. It gets weird."

He set the victim's head back on the cold linoleum floor, which was now red from the pooled blood, and pointed to the lumbar portion of the small dead man's back. He lifted the wet lab coat with tweezers the size of salad tongs which revealed what was once a white Oxford shirt. It had already been untucked and lifted, the M.E. pulled it up again for Carina.

"Same bite marks as the other two vics," Carina said.

"Exactly the same from what I can see. I will remeasure and confirm when we get him back to the morgue, but it seems pretty clear that he was bitten just like the others. I'm just not sure which came first, the chicken or the egg. Either one would have done the trick."

"So he could have gotten bit, which would have made him bleed out, then slipped and hit his head on the counter or something, which would have made him bleed out. But either way he never had a chance?"

"There are no clues or marks to indicate that he struck his head on this counter, or any other counter in this lab. All the blood is right here." He pulled a pen out of his shirt pocket and pointed to the bite on the victim's back. The two holes were swollen and purple, still slowly leaking blood. "These are classic snake bites, just like your other two victims Detective. I'm no reptile expert, so it is impossible for me to pinpoint the exact species of snake, especially without finding it, but the bleed-out suggests it is in the Viper family. The colleague that I consulted with on your other two cases said that there are several types of Vipers who's venom has a vicious anti-coagulant component. Meaning that if you get bit, you don't stop bleeding until your dead. Like your victims."

"So where is the snake?"

"Just like the others. Not here," Captain Simms offered.

Spencer continued. "Also there is the issue of not having any bite marks from the lower dentary. If the victim was bitten, there has to be a top and a bottom of the jaw. We only see the top fangs. Granted those two fangs are what inject the venom, but without the bottom of the jaw for leverage? Again, I'm no snake expert but that seems quite odd to me."

"Do we have a time of death, Spence?" Carina was continuing to look over the body while the M.E. was speaking.

"The window is too big right now. The trouble with these killings is that there is normally Petechial Hemorrhaging, spots on the skin, which help us to determine T. O. D. The placement, number and size of the spots on the skin are tell-tale signs. The snake venom prohibits the blood from clogging, or even collecting. Like I said, all of the blood from the vic just flows out of the body instead of pooling. Rigor is another factor used to narrow it down, but lack of blood messes with rigor. I don't think we are going to get a very accurate time-frame unless we look at outside factors."

"Like?"

"Like a time reading on the magnetic badge reader. Data entries on the computer may help as well."

"Makes it hard to nail the bastard, darlin'? If I don't know when they were here, alibis are pretty loose."

"Just like the others, Detective, I will narrow it down the best I can."

"Thanks a bunch." She turned to her Captain. "Who else was here in the lab tonight?"

"Nobody. There was another technician working in another lab on the floor directly below this one. The blood got under the linoleum, soaked through, and started dripping on the lab below. His ID card doesn't allow access to this floor, so he had to call security. The guard saw this mess and called us."

"We have someone on the loose who over the last five weeks has killed three people by unleashing a snake. You say that the ID used to get in here has a high clearance status but hasn't been used in three years?"

"Correct."

"Ain't that lovely."

"It gets even weirder Fish," Simms said as we waved off Spencer, relieving him of his duties with them for the moment. "Carina, take a guess at what they research here."

1

THERE ARE SOME THINGS IN LIFE that you will never forget. Certain people, certain events, are stuck in your mind no matter how much time passes. A smell or a word can trigger those memories to come rushing back like they happened yesterday. I wonder if when I'm eighty, if I make it to eighty, I will still have the ability to recall with such clarity the events that have transpired over the course of my forty years on this planet.

As I sit here with a cup of coffee steaming in my hand, the aroma takes me back to the not-so-distant past. The case wasn't closed yesterday, nor the day before. In fact, it hasn't yet been six months, but this one will be burned into my brain for while. It ripped the heart out of me for good measure. It's not like I live a boring life. So the story that I am about to share with you sticks with me, not because it was one odd-ball story in an otherwise dreary existence. Nope, I have a very colorful past.

I was born in Boston, and raised in Southie. For those that have never watched one of the many Boston movies that have been recently made and become hugely popular, Southie is South Boston. It was, and still is to a lesser extent, a rough Irish neighborhood. Where the Irish mob that Irish cops don't want to mess with. Whitey Bulger was from there.

I made my way through it by boosting car radios. Maybe the occasional car. I still stay in contact with all of my old acquaintances, but most of them have been gentrified out of Southie. But that's another story.

I became a Massachusetts State Police Trooper, which was very boring, but it happened so I'm giving you context. Sitting on the Mass Pike watching the daily commuters struggle through gridlock was like watching grass grow and plucking the odd weed. It sucked. But the powers-that-be had originally sent me through the Police Academy, after my juvie record was expunged, *because* of my questionable past. Meaning they wanted me to rat on my neighbors. They got pissed when they finally realized that it wasn't going to happen. But I had already been through the Academy at that point and passed with flying colors. So they stuck me on the Goddamned Pike.

My memory isn't the only long one, as it turned out. It took forever, but I finally made detective. I don't know what you do for a living, or what your daily life entails, but I can tell you that it probably involves exponentially less bullsh than what I had to deal with. Politics is not my thing. I grew up in a very tough and very poor neighborhood, you call a spade a spade. Mind games and alliances a-la-*Survivor* would earn you a beating. Again, I wouldn't play ball, so everybody in the department knew I was never going to be promoted. I would retire a Detective Junior Grade, which would just be sad.

So I took on some odd-jobs to keep life exciting. One of which was MMA fighting. I was only an amateur, but I had offers to go pro. Technically I was a welterweight (170 pounds), and lean one at that, but I would always cut weight and fight the lightweights. I won more fights than I lost by far. I grew up fighting. That's just what you did in Southie. Even the homos fought, they would scratch the shit out of you. Problems were a lot easier to solve back then. Anyway, I trained with Kenny Florian and learned Brazilian Jiu-Jitsu. No, I'm not name-dropping. Again, I'm just giving you context. I still practice five or six days per week, as time permits. I don't get into the cage anymore, but the skills come in handy for my current career.

While with the Staties, I also took side jobs helping out some friends in Southern New Hampshire with investigations. This would not have gone over well with my superiors, but everybody saw the writing on the wall and anything to grease the wheels of my departure was looked at kindly. I helped out my friends so often that I ended up going into business for myself. I was a licensed Private Investigator in both New Hampshire and Massachusetts. I still am. Life is good now.

I helped out one of those friends in New Hampshire, a lawyer with his own firm, regularly. I saved his life at one point. He had an entirely new perspective on the prison experience.

We don't talk about that though. Not anymore. That was a hum-dinger too. The past is the past. We don't really talk at all anymore, since he moved to South Carolina.

Everybody always says that they will keep in touch when friends move, but they never do. JG and I were no different. Out of sight, out of mind. Life happens. We get busy and one day leads into a week, which leads into 'holy shit has it been that long?'.

I don't have that many true friends. I have a ton of contacts, acquaintances, people to whom I owe favors, people who owe me. But true friends that you can call on when the feces hits the proverbial fan, no matter how much time has passed? No. I ain't got many of them. So I was shocked and stunned when Jacob Grantes called me. Happy to hear from the guy, don't get me wrong, but I knew there was a reason. He needed a favor. Again.

It wasn't JG's ass in a sling this time, but he needed help nonetheless. He needed me, Warren Dennihan, but everybody calls me Deni.

As I sit here drinking my Starbuck's Costa Rican blend, I'm not sure if I should have gone down to Charleston. Hindsight is twenty-twenty. You know who your friends are when they drop everything and come to your aid. So I went. But sometimes a friend in need is a pest. Especially when you don't get all of the facts right away.

"Deni! It's JG. Long time, no see. How are you?"

"Hey. How are you? How is Charleston? You're still in Charleston, right?"

"Yes, of course. I was trying to think of the last time that we spoke. It must have been when Olivia passed."

Olivia Craig was Jacob Grantes's mother-in-law. Well, ex-mother-in-law. But, again that is another story. She was filthy rich. How she got that way is yet another story. I told you that I have a colorful past. I've got lots of stories, but I digress. I had worked with her on the case that freed her only next of kin, as it were, so she left me a decent nest egg. JG was the sole care-provider for her only grandson. Other than a few charities and a couple of other odds and ends, she left them everything.

"Yeah, must be. Sorry I couldn't make it down there. I kinda felt like a heel, especially since she left me money."

I was not expecting it or I would have gone. I really didn't know her that well. But I guess you go to those things for the loved ones that are still alive. I messed up.

"No worries. There were so many people at the funeral that I would have felt bad for not being able to spend much time with you anyway. Hey look, I'd love to catch up but I have some time constraints."

Here it comes.

"I need to speak with you in person. I need your help with something that is going on down here. What does your caseload look like?"

"I've got some things going, JG. I can't just book a flight and pop down to Charleston on a whim."

"Look, I know it's terrible to just call after so much time and needing a favor. But it's important. I have a case that is an absolute mess. I was hoping that I could talk it over with you. Just have you take a quick look. I need you buddy. Name your fee."

Now that my good friend is free and rich, he has become just like some of the people that I can't stand. Money buys them whatever they want. 'NO' doesn't mean 'NO' because everybody can be bought. Then again, I don't know what that says about me because I didn't hang up on him.

"Are you in trouble?"

"Me personally? No. But I have a colleague and friend down here that is being charged as a serial killer. Falsely."

"Jesus, how long have you been down there? You don't have an investigator?"

"I have a few that I use. But none of them are as good as you."

He was playing to my amazing skills as an investigator. He thought that could win me over.

"I can have a private jet waiting at Logan Airport in two hours. Fly down here and listen to the situation. If you don't want to take a look at that point, I'll understand. What do you say?"

He thought he could get me to do whatever he wanted by writing me a blank check, complimenting me on my expertise, and flying me on a private jet.

He was right.

venom

Damned my hubris.

2

I CAN TELL YOU FROM PAST EXPERIENCE that the *only* way to fly is on a private jet. Security, jet-lag, and ears popping cannot be avoided. But you don't have to deal with things like the four hundred pounder that tries to squeeze into coach like he was trying to get in a Yugo. They always pick the middle seat too, have you ever noticed that? You don't have to deal with all of the screaming children, lines at the tiny bathroom, rude flight attendants, baggage claims, and believe me I could go on. None of that. You are now free to roam about the cabin. Drink your fill. For an Irish cat like myself, that is *the* perk. It also may have been my downfall.

When I landed in Charleston, I was buzzed and feeling good. I seemed to be getting on well with the super-hot flight attendant. There was no mile-high club involved, not even a good make-out session, but I still felt the vibe.

I deplaned and JG had a car waiting for me. I'm not usually impressed by such things, but he had a Mercedes Benz *S63 AMG* parked with the door open and a driver waiting. I felt like a million bucks.

The last time I was in Charleston, South Carolina, I didn't have such a great time. I was on a case and chasing a runaway suspect. I was in no mood to appreciate how beautiful the area is. The area around the coast that is. Which is where JG lived. He lived in his ex-mother-in-law's house. It was huge and in the Historic district known as Rainbow Row. These four-storied mansions-turned-condos were juxtaposed along East Bay Street and were varying shades and colors in pastels, which is why it has the nickname. Of course JG and his son Brady were not in a condo. They owned the whole building, which ran one-block deep. Brady had to be the richest six year old ever.

The ride from the airport didn't take long. None of it really took long when you stop and think about it. I was sitting in his home on Rainbow Row on the same day that he had reached out to me.

"Deni, thanks for coming down. I wanted to meet here rather than at the firm. It is a little less formal."

I was happy about that. I didn't want to be around a ton of stiffs because I had added to my buzz by having another drink in the car. Which was stupid.

"Thanks."

"Uncle Deni!"

I turned and saw his son, Brady, running toward me for a hug. He seemed genuinely happy to see me. How he remembered me was a mystery. The kid was always smart, but my gut told me that he had been coached. 'Make the long lost guy I'm trying to persuade to help your dad feel warm and fuzzy,' JG probably had said to his son. Joke is on them. I already felt very warm and fuzzy.

"Hey kiddo. How are ya doin'?"

"Great. Will you be around later? I've got to go for my guitar lesson now."

Yep. He was coached.

"I'm not sure. I might be. Your dad and I have to discuss some stuff."

"Great. Well, I hope to see you when I get back."

I'll bet.

"Can I get you anything before we sit down?" JG was smiling. Everything was to plan thus far, I would imagine.

"You got any Irish Whiskey?" Stupid.

"Of course. Right this way."

We went into a room that could have been an upscale pub. Only it was in my friend's house. Oversized leather seats, dark oak, old looking books that lined shelves library-style. The bar was long and the shelves behind it were stocked. None of the stuff was Well. All of the various bottles of booze were call brands.

"You like Redbreast right?"

"You've got a good memory." I also noticed that he had only one lowball glass out on the bar. "Aren't you going to have any?"

"I don't really drink anymore."

"You have a bar in your house, but you don't drink anymore?"

"Not often. The bar is for entertaining. Besides, I need to be sharp to go over this case with you."

Buzzkill.

"But Deni, feel free," he continued as he handed me my three fingers of expensive twelve year old whiskey that I didn't really need. I felt silly drinking in front of my friend who was abstaining. But I drank it anyway. Partly out of nervousness. Partly because 'why stop now?'. We sat in our respective plush, riveted, leather sofa-chairs. JG began spelling it out for me.

"Deni, it has been a while so let me catch you up on what I have been doing, it will give you some perspective."

I nodded but said nothing. What was there to say?

"When I came down here after the fiasco in New Hampshire, I was not sure that I wanted to practice law anymore. I was able to, I just needed to take the bar exam down here. Jenna and I played house for a while, but my being home all the time was too much. She went back to school and she continually urged me to get out of my funk and do something with my life. I had no idea what to do, so I went through the motions and studied for the South Carolina Bar Exam at the university library that Jenna was going to. Are you with me? You look bored."

"I'm here." Get to the point JG.

"So anyway, I passed the bar, started and expanded my practice with the money that Olivia had left me. It is now the largest law firm in South Carolina. But all of that time that I spent at the university library, kindled a passion for teaching.   So I met a few contacts and now I teach law at South Carolina University, School of Law. In my practice, I am really just a figurehead and take only the cases that truly intrigue me."

"Must be nice to have that option. Why am I here? You are super-rich and can get anybody you want to investigate whatever it is you need to investigate. Why me?"

"I'm getting there.   So South Carolina University at Charleston has an enormous campus. It actually started as a medical school in 1824, which is now the South Carolina Medical University and Research Institute. The Law School and the Medical University are on the same campus. I met somebody there and became very good friends with her. She is the one who has been charged as a serial killer."

"*Her? She?* Here we go, JG. Again? What is it about you that is attracted to crazy killer chicks? Haven't we been down this road?"

"It's not what you are thinking, and she didn't kill anybody."

"What am I thinking?"

"That I cheated on Jenna with a women who is psycho."

"So where is Jenna in all of this?"

"She is no longer in 'all of this', as you put it, because of Sierra.   The woman."

Is this guy for real? Clearly my choice in friends could be better. And sure as shit my decision to come down here was not a good one either. I need to drink less.

"I've had a few adult beverages, so please interrupt me if I have this wrong. Your life in New Hampshire was very close to be ruined partly because you were suspected of cheating on your ex-wife. You get out of that mess and move down here. You miraculously get beyond all that, start a new life and *actually do* cheat on the woman who you were suspected of having an affair with up North? This new woman, the woman down here, being the one who is presumably incarcerated after being charged as a serial killer? What the fuck Jacob?"

"Like I said, it's not what you think. My relationship with the accused, Sierra Byrne, was not .... consummated .... until after Jenna and I both realized that our relationship wasn't going anywhere. She was left with quite a sum of money from Olivia, she will be just fine.

"As far as Dr. Sierra Byrne, even if we weren't together she needs a proper defense. She is innocent. There have been three murders of people attached to the same research facility and/or university where she works. The first death was originally designated an accident. The second was suspicious, so they reopened the first because the deaths were similar. The third was ruled a homicide, no doubt. Three individual deaths with a cool-off period between, in this case over a five week span, is classified as Serial. They needed someone to pin down and quick. A serial killer on the loose in the beginning of summer, prime tourism season, would be murder on the city. Sierra has ties with both SCMU and the research facility funded by BIOGENESIS Pharmaceuticals. They have some circumstantial evidence that they are going to try to make stick."

"So why me?"

"It is getting political down here. Big Pharma, serial killer, government officials trying to save their precious city and tourism .... You aren't part of any of that. I need someone that I can completely trust. Someone who doesn't give a sweet shit about anything and someone without fear. I need to save the woman I love. I need my friend, Warren Dennihan."

"Need, need, need. Want, want, want. It's all you do. Nice speech though. How long did it take you to practice that?"

"A good-long while. Did it work?"

venom

Shit.

3

THE FOLLOWING DAY WAS A REAL TREAT. I was hungover and without a toothbrush. I was also without a change of clothes. I really did think that I was going to be able to go back to Boston, even if I did look into the case. So I didn't bring a bag. I called my business partner in the Financial District of Boston so he would know where I was and that I was generating three times my usual rate down in Charleston. He was as unenthused as I was, apart from the money.

I then called Ryan Wells, JG's former law partner. I needed to let him know that I was going to be out of pocket for the duration of this fiasco. He was fine with it as long as I hurried back.

My wealthy friend gave me a credit card for my expenses. An Amex Centurion Card. The black one with no limit. JG said that I could blow it up if I wanted, he would pay my inflated fee and expenses. I wondered if I bought a Mercedes like the one that I rode there in the day before was considered an expense? I needed transportation. But am not about avarice. I needed clothes more.

For the second time in my life, I went shopping for clothes in Charleston. And for the second time in my life I was taken to the pee-patch. I don't really need designer clothes. I don't really *like* designer clothes. I was just in want of basic jeans, some t-shirts and maybe a jacket in case I need to look presentable. Not in Charleston. My non-skinny jeans were over $300. One pair. What happened to t-shirts under $20? I was looking in the wrong places, because there weren't any. The sport jacket was as expensive as my first car. The one I didn't steal.

After purchasing my new wardrobe and had finally caffeinated away my hangover, JG and I were ready to go over to Leath Correctional Institution for Women. This was the level Three facility that was currently housing Dr. Sierra Byrne. She had been denied bail, which was no shocker. After all, it's not like she was accused of breaking into a piggy bank. This lady was labeled a serial killer and put into protective custody. The ride was long one. Apparently the posh don't like to have their societal refuse too close them. Or to their tourists. I found that odd because the tourists spend hard-earned money on the Haunted Jail Tour of Charleston by the hundreds. But what the hell do I know?

After going through the various gates inside the prison and my new wardrobe being patted down by the butch she-man Correctional Officer, we were led to a private meeting room. It was drab and concrete, but it was private.

Two different female COs tugged Sierra into the room. They took off her ankle chains; the cuffs on her wrists, however, remained in place. She sat down only after the officers left the room, and they only left after informing us that they would be waiting outside if they were needed.

She was a stunner. Very sinuous. Very tan. Or maybe she was milatto or milano or whatever you call those gorgeous women who have the perma-tan. Perfect skin. Her brown eyes were currently wearing the weight of the world in them, but stunning. I could see why JG had given up on what was, at the time, the most beautiful girl I had ever seen face-to-face.

"Jay, I am so glad to see you. It's only been a week and I have no idea how I am going to make it any longer."

"This is Warren Dennihan. Everybody calls him Deni. He is going to investigate your case. I wanted you to meet and maybe you can fill him in."

"Nice to meet you Deni. I wish it was under different circumstances. I have heard so much about you. I am not sure how much Jay has told you."

"I haven't told him much," JG interjected. "The information is privileged and I wanted to make sure that everybody was onboard before we delved into it too far."

"Well, there really isn't very far to go. I have no idea who did this, but I know it wasn't me."

My turn.

"So why do *you* think, that they think, that it *is* you?"

"You're accent is thick. Where are you from? New York?"

"Not a fuckin' chance. Boston. Southie, actually. But back to the point, why are you getting blamed?"

"Because I knew all of the victims in this case. The first was a doctoral candidate that was working directly under me. The second was a lead researcher at our lab at SCMU and the most recent was a lab worker at the BIOGENESIS lab. He ran tests at the pharmaceutical lab. We worked closely with them. I worked closely with all of them."

"BIOGENESIS? Isn't that the steroid company that — "

" — no, Deni. I could see how you would be confused but no. Steroids are not what we do."

"I'm a little behind. Maybe we can share with me what it is you do, exactly."

"I apologize. I thought that Jay might have covered that. I hold three PHDs in Toxin/Toxicology, Herpetology, and Bioengineering. I am also one of the leading experts in Venomology."

I had no idea what any of that meant except that this chick was fuckin' smart. How does one person get all that? Looks and brains? God is cruel.

"Yeah, let's pretend I am not as smart as you and just tell me what you do with all of them degrees and what-not."

"Of course. I teach Bioengineering, among other things, at SCMU. My erudite grad students actually do most of the teaching these days, as my workload is very rigorous. My doctoral candidates assist in the research that I oversee, which takes up most of my time. They benefit from cutting-edge research to complete their respective thesis, while we attract top minds to assist in the work."

"Pardon for interrupting, but did you say what that work is yet? Lots of big words and really just the one question I need answered."

She gave JG a look that I didn't like. I make my living at being able to read people and she just shot a look that told her lawyer that she was afraid that I am not smart enough to investigate a missing dog. Lets face it, I ain't no genius. But I am smarter than I let on. I do that on purpose. People underestimate me. I may not be the best speaker, have the biggest vocabulary, or even have a degree; but I am not dumb.

"Simply put, we create drugs. There are many chemicals found in nature that have a very specific purpose. We study those chemicals and develop synthetic drugs to cure illnesses that align with the original purpose. For example, have you heard of the Nano-bee?"

"Nano-bee? No, I don't think so."

"Ok, well the Nano-bee, just like other bees, sting people to protect their hive. Every bee sting injects a venom, but the Nano-bee is named such because they contain nano-particles in their venom which carry a toxin that has a specific purpose. That purpose is to effect the immune system of the recipient, which has been shown to attach itself to HIV. HIV, as I'm sure you know is the Human Immunodeficiency Virus which causes AIDS. A synthetic drug is currently being tested which was derived from Nano-bee venom that has very few side effects. That drug will cure HIV."

The excitement was back in her eyes. I could see that she loved her work. Curing AIDS. Pretty cool. 'What did you do today honey?' 'oh, nothin'. Just cured AIDS'. What did I do? I took pictures of a cheating wife last week. Who's cooler?

"So you think that these murders are bee-related?"

"No. Not specifically. That was just an example. We have many projects. I say *we*. The university is funded by a huge pharmaceutical company that has many projects. SCMU, the research institute, BIOGENESIS, and the World Toxin Bank work closely together because the work is mutually beneficial."

"Did we go over what the Toxin Bank place is yet?"

"No, probably not. The World Toxin Bank houses the largest collection of natural toxins on the globe. It is the only one of its kind. Think of it like a semi-public spice rack. Or a toxin library. When researchers are looking to analyze a specific toxin, they can obtain a sample from the WTB instead of having to obtain a live specimen from the field."

"Semi-public?"

"Yes. It can get a bit political. Those that contribute to the WTB supply get first priority, along with the largest financial contributors. There isn't an infinite supply, so it has to be parceled out fairly. And while the WTB has over 10,000 toxins on hand, there are an estimated 20,000,000 toxins. Of those 10,000, only about 1,000 are actually being studied at present. The goal is to eventually have a blueprint of every toxin. That is a far-off goal as you can see. In the meantime, the arrangement with the WTB is the best we can do to accommodate everyone."

"Obviously not everyone is pleased. Have the police looked into this World Toxin Bank?"

JG chimed in while fumbling through his files. "The investigating detective's name is Carina Fischer. I had another investigator, Eric Stubbs, look into her. She is a tenacious thing. She looks clean and is very good at her job. Except this time."

Lucky me.

"So our alternate theory is that someone doesn't like this research or WTB arrangement. Who might that be?"

"Take a number. I get threats every day, Jay will tell you. We get some at home …. "

I let it slide that she said *we* and *home* in the same sentence. Clearly JG and Brady were not the only ones living on Rainbow Row.

" …. PETA, other research facilities, other universities, other big drug companies and — "

" — Walk me through that."

"PETA? People for Ethical Treatment of Animals are — "

" — they think bees are pets?"

She looked at JG again. I couldn't quite read what that particular look meant. She probably just continued on thinking about how stupid I am.

"No. No, they don't think that bees are pets. Bees populations are dwindling, but frankly they don't really know what they are talking about. They think that we kill and do drug testing on animals. They make a big noise despite not having any facts."

"OK. What about other universities?"

"This research is very competitive. Drugs are big business and everyone tries to get a piece of the pie. Research brings in dollars. Universities love dollars. The quicker and better the research, the quicker the patents. The patents mean that only those drug companies can produce that drug for the length of the patent. When the patents run their course, generic companies get involved."

"So we have no shortage of people who could have killed these people. All we really know is that it has to be research related, and somebody who had access to all three of the victims."

"That's what makes the most sense."

What had I gotten myself into? This was going to be like trying to find a needle in a stack of needles. As it turns out, I *am* dumb.

I really should have asked more questions.

venom

4

I NEEDED TO LEARN MORE ABOUT THE CRIMES. The latest crime scene was going to be the easiest to glean information from. Which, according to the reports I had attained from Jacob Grantes, meant that I needed to go to the lab. JG made some calls and arranged it for the following day. The lab was on hold until day three.

The rest of my night was free until then. The house was big enough where all of the occupants could be present but not seen or felt. If Brady came home that night, he didn't come to see me. He must have forgotten. Or he was tied up with his mates and stayed wherever he was. It seems like the last was a long-shot though, he was only six. But I am no parent, however. So what do I know about kids and curfews?

With the night free, I wanted to look up Jenna. JG's old girlfriend was a smoke-show. She used to work at this bar, Sully's, in Barstone, New Hampshire. It is conveniently located across the street from JG and his partner Ryan Wells's practice. I still work with Ryan on occasion, as he still has the practice, and I still go into Sully's but with less occasion because it's just not the same without Jenna.

I wanted to get in-touch with Jenna, though it was very much against 'guy code'. It was against the rules because I very much wanted to touch Jenna. You don't date your friend's exes. That is axiomatic. A steadfast rule. But I'm not much for rules. Odd for a former Mass State Police Detective, but I am paradoxical I'm told.

I am not going to say that I didn't try to find her. That would be a big fat lie. I called the old cell number I had for her. Disconnected. I hit up six dining establishments and bars looking for her. I asked everyone who paused to talk to me, and showed just as many people the picture that I had of her on my phone. Only one person said that she looked familiar. I knew the guy was full of shit, because let me tell ya — if you saw Jenna you would remember. She wouldn't just 'look familiar'. She tried to disappear on me once before, and I found her down here. Now that she was through with JG, she had vanished for good.

Could she have been behind this? Tossed aside for another attractive and wicked smart woman was a strong motive to frame said attractive and wicked smart woman. I had suspected her of some shady shit in the past, could she be involved this mess? I would keep it in mind. Or maybe I just had her in my mind and I wanted to find her. Don't judge.

The following day, day three, I went out to BIOGENESIS Pharmaceuticals to check out the lab. I had an appointment with the Director of Operations, the top dog over there. JG had classes that day, so I was on my own. I'm not sure if the driver had the day off, but the Mercedes *S63 AMG* was available for use. I put it through it's paces. That car was as fast as greased-lightning. German engineering at it's finest.

The GPS told me it was going to take 27 minutes to get to the compound. Over the Ashley River, onto Route 17, and North a few exits on Interstate 95, I weaved in and out of traffic. I made it just over fifteen minutes. It would have been faster but I sped past my exit and had to turn around.

The rent-a-cop at the main gate was busy with all of the commotion outside, so it took a minute to get to me. News crews and protesters were congesting the entire entrance. Once I had made it past them without running someone over, which is what I wanted to do, I was told to park in the parking lot off to the left and a Jarod Lynde, the Director of Operations himself, would be there shortly to transport me to the appropriate lab. I was early for my 10:00 AM appointment, so I was made to wait. I spent the time playing with the buttons and what-not in the *AMG*. I also found a cool music channel on SiriusXM, called *Lithium*. Old-school Seattle bands. Nobody makes Grunge anymore.

Jarod Lynde showed up in a golf cart. After introductions he drove about ten football fields over to the Toxicology and Herpetology Lab. The building was still cordoned off, but from whom I had no idea. The parking lot was empty.

"You will have to excuse the mess. We have been cleared to clean it up but with the lab shutdown, it has not been a top priority."

"You aren't getting back to business as usual?"

"Unfortunately no. We have some other …. internal issues that have occurred which has further disrupted what you would call, 'business as usual'."

"Like what?"

"I am afraid that is confidential."

"I am trying to help you find out who killed one of yours. Help me help you, guy."

"BIOGENESIS is a publicly held company under the umbrella of a much larger conglomerate. I simply enforce what has been directed from above me, who report to the Board of Directors, who report to a Fortune 100 Corporation. Stock Prices are volatile, I am only allowed to say so much without lawyers present."

"Then what am I doing here? If you aren't going to answer any of my questions, why did you agree to meet with me? Jacob Grantes, the attorney that I work for, had this all set up like we would be able to work together."

Lynde parked the golf cart, ushering me inside the building after using his magnetic ID card to unlock the door. He led me into a conference room on the second floor, not a laboratory. He waved his hand indicating that he wanted me to sit in one of the chairs surrounding the conference table. I wanted to rip off his arm and shove it up his ass.

"We can chat here for a bit, where I will give you what information I can. You will have to sign some waivers and confidentiality agreements before I can let you see our Lab. Then, and only then, will you be able to tour the third or any other floor."

"Pretty cloak and dagger, wouldn't you say?"

"As I said, we have a very large company to protect."

"Can you elaborate? I'm a bit confused by that."

"What I am about to tell you is public record, so I can. BIOGENESIS is one of the top Pharmaceutical Research Corporations in the world. We have thousands of projects in which we design and manufacture innovative drugs for human illnesses. All of which are in various phases of the process by which a drug is available for sale by prescription. Our revenues last year were close to $100 million US dollars. We are but a cog in the wheel of our umbrella company, PROXER, which is currently *the* number one Pharmaceutical Company on the planet. With revenues of just under half a trillion US dollars last year, they are in the top 100 of *any* company in the world."

"Did you say *trillion*? Maybe medication could be a little more affordable if you greedy fucks would settle for making half-billions."

"I said revenue, not profits. Everybody thinks it is easy to generate these medications."

"You just drove me over here in a golf cart wearing a designer suit that probably costs a years worth of my salary, and you claim to be a low-level Director of Operations. Don't cry poverty, guy. Especially after you just said trillion. You'll make me cry."

"Your quips aside, do you have any idea how much money and research goes into creating a drug?"

"No, not really. But I'm guessing that is what you are going to share with me, instead of the information I came here for."

He ignored the slam, and went on with the *School House Rock* version of how research becomes a drug.

"There are currently forty-nine umbrella companies in the pharmaceutical and biotech industries that generate as low as tens of millions of US dollars per year. Everybody from Bayer to Proctor & Gamble to AstraZeneca and many, many more are all competing for the next miracle drug. We are just the underling of one of these companies. They are all trying to hire the best researchers in the field, from the best universities, to advise them in their research and testing of potential drugs. I say potential drugs because there are millions of dollars that go into a potential medicine before it even gets to a test phase.

"A lab, like ourselves, generates promising data off of a theory. We then submit an Investigational New Drug, or IND application, to the Center for Drug Evaluation and Research. The CDER. Once the application takes effect, clinical trials can then begin. But that application can be stalled by the FDA on a 'clinical hold' for virtually any reason, which is usually political. Kickbacks usually take place to spin the wheels of progress. Clinical trials can last years depending upon the side effects, and the FDA is basically up our ass the entire time about; rules on reporting, specs, methods of analysis .... everything from packaging to distribution. These formulae are patented, but the trials could outlast the term of the patent, which makes the research free game for competitors. Any of these forty-nine huge companies, never mind the smaller ones like us, could swoop in and generate the same medicine with comparatively no research money shelled out. That is *if* the drug even makes it to that point. I can't tell you the number of 'promising data' theories that never make it to the local pharmacy. Millions and millions of dollars are spent with no return.

"We haven't even mentioned pilfering researchers from competing companies to steal research. It is highly illegal, but it is done. It's easier and more cost beneficial to pay a Piracy or Infringement settlement than shell out money for research. By the time our lawsuit gets into the Civil Courts, this lab will have been vacant for years."

Ah-ha. There was the slip.

"So that is what you meant by 'internal issues'? Somebody defected?"

"Oh. No. I was speaking hypothetically. We do need you to sign those confidentiality documents now, if you please."

He handed me a stack of papers with little adhesive arrow tabs pointing to where I needed to put my John Hancock. I didn't even read them, I just signed while I pressed Mr. Lynde.

"OK, so let's speak in hypotheticals. Hypothetically, if some people were to be eliminated from the equation and other key people were to be enticed to bring their expertise to a competing company, that would put and end to the research?"

"Hypothetically, yes. At a minimum it would set the research back decades. By that time the patent would expire, the drug could be released by a competitor, or never get made at all. Millions of dollars lost."

"And millions of people don't get a cure for what ails them. You were studying a cure for HIV correct?"

"No, that is not correct. Who told you that? We are well beyond hypotheticals now aren't we?"

"I must have been misinformed. I thought you were studying bee venom or something to cure HIV."

"You have been misinformed. But even if you were correct, I couldn't say," Lynde said. He was visibly uncomfortable.

"So whatever it was that you *were* researching, who would want to kill it? Or kill for it?"

"Are you kidding? We have thirteen buildings with independent projects all working simultaneously — "

" — I'm not asking about the twelve other buildings, I'm asking about this one. Unless there were murders in the other labs, I don't give a shit about 'em."

"Get in line. Did you see the crowd outside the main gate?"

"The news crews? They have somethin' to do with this?"

"Yes, Mr. Dennihan. The news crews. The news affiliates killed a lab worker and are barricading the complex. Are you mad?"

"Are you tryin' to piss me off? 'Cuz I'll beat the life outta ya in your Italian suit."

"I apologize. It's a trying time and I am on edge, as I'm sure you can imagine. The crowd outside would be there whether there was a legal incident or not. PETA is upset about animal cruelty, religious organizations are incensed about snake venom being the seed of Satan, Unions about outsourcing, fair wages and benefits, doctors, politicians, and God knows who else are outside those gates every day trying to interfere with our work."

"Did you say *snake venom*?"

That's not good.

The tour of the lab was fruitless. The body was gone but the outline of the lake of blood was still present. I didn't see any animals in the lab, and Lynde said that they never have any animals in the labs with the exception of lab mice on certain projects. He would not elaborate on what was going on in that lab, or what was being developed. With all of the equipment in that glass fortress, it could have been microprocessors for all I knew.

For every question I asked, he would respond with statements of confidentiality and me not being a cop. I love the classics, but every once in a while some new material is nice. I was getting nowhere and I was getting there slowly.

Since I was being chaperoned, there was no way to get into one of the other buildings to interview other people who may have known what was going on in the now defunct one. Especially cleaning crews. The report JG had given me said that the last ID card that was used to enter the lab belonged to a member of the cleaning crew three years prior.

I asked for a list of employees and that went over like a fart in church. Square one. The only thing that Lynde said to me, that was of any interest, was about a defector. I needed to know who that was. He also had a quick comment involving snakes. I was desperate to get that out of my mind. I have no interest in them whatsoever.

Outside the gate, I parked the *AMG* in line with all of the news vans. I decided to canvas the crowd. See what I could learn. The reporters and cameras were doing their own interviews and coverage, which gave me an idea of how to approach the protestors. Amidst the crowd was a tall female in a blazer that I spotted as a detective a mile away. She could not be in many crowds and go unnoticed. She had a Natalie Portman thing going on, only taller. She was five-nine or ten. The interview pad she was writing on, the badge, and bulge for her weapon was what made me add 'detective' to the other things that I was thinking about her. The closer I got, the more I liked.

I started doing interviews of my own, but kept her in the corner of my eye. *Let her come to me.* Which she eventually did.

What I learned in those interviews wasn't much. PETA went on about the rights of animals, but had no specific information about the case or the specific lab. A religious group prattled endlessly about the facility being an anathema of God, an abhorrence in the eyes of Christ that will bring about Armageddon. The End of Days were upon us.

Good. I'm more of a night guy anyway.

There was also a unionized group or something that disliked that BIOGENESIS used cheap labor and college students instead of paying a fair wage, but their hearts didn't seem into it. There was a small faction of them that supervised the picketing, while the minions apathetically went through the motions. I found that to be hypocritical, but about right.

"Are y'all at the eighty?"

Here she was. Just a matter of time. When I turned to face her, she was even more beautiful than from afar. Not like high-def TV where the closer the camera gets to the celebrity, the less attractive they become. Her Auburn hair had the slightest of red highlights, which accented the green in her hazel eyes. And that Southern drawl melted my soul. She was hell on heels.

"Uh. Excuse me?" And apparently my brain.

"Eighty Broad. Crimes Against Persons?"

"Oh. No. I'm with myself."

"Not a cop? Y'all a reporter?"

"No. Investigator. I'm Warren Dennihan. You can call me Deni. And you are?"

"Ah, Lord Almighty. Let me see some ID, hun."

I didn't remember that all Southern women say *hun, honey, darlin', handsome, sweetie* and the like. Even if they can't stand you. I thought she was keen on me. When I see a pretty girl, I do what I always do. I flirt.

"You can see anything you want."

"Just your ID will be fine." The way she said 'fine'? I was in lust. I broke out my driver's license and my Private Security and Investigation licenses for both Massachusetts and New Hampshire. I handed all three of them to her.

"You didn't say who you are." My Boston accent is strong. Wicked strong. As strong as her Southern drawl. She picked up on the accent, I'm sure. She definitely did when I said *are*, because they sound like *ah*. I generally don't pronounce *r*'s if they are in a word, and I add one if there isn't one. But my licenses proved what she already knew.

"Missin' a State in here aren't ya there loverboy? I knew y'all were a Yankee. That accent gives you away, darlin'. I'm Detective Fischer, and we got a problem."

"You're damned right we do. I hate the Yankees. I'm a Red Sox fan."

"Great. Follow me." She handed me back my IDs, along with her business card and guided me to her unmarked sedan. With her perfectly shaped buttocks in front of me, I would have followed her anywhere. She stopped at her car and turned around to face me. An even better view.

"Just what are y'all doin' so far from home?"

"I'm looking into the death that occurred here. I work for the attorney Jacob Grantes. He's defending the accused, Dr. Sierra Byrne. I'm helping with the investigation."

"Shit. You're not helping me or anybody else, darlin'. Not even yourself. You can't investigate a damned thing down here. So unless you are down here buyin' souvenirs, you should pack yer shit and head on back to your Red Sox."

Hot as a two-dollar pistol, curses, and feisty. I was ready to propose.

"Not a baseball fan, huh?"

"This is football country down here. Real men play contact sports."

She was killing me.

"But that's got nothin' to do with it," she said. "Things are different down here. I'm gonna cut you a break. Today. I'm gonna help you out and tell you somethin' that your fancy lawyer-boss should have told you. You need to be licensed in South Carolina. These out-of-state PSI licenses don't mean shit down here. Even if they did, PI's in my fine State do background checks, insurance scams, security, infidelity cases and such. No crimes. Cold cases maybe, but only if they are no longer being investigated. This one *is* being investigated. By me. Which means it sure as shit ain't cold. South Carolina Title 40, chapter 18. Might be good readin' on your plane ride home."

"So maybe I'll just get a license down here, beautiful."

"Typical. Yer cute but you don't listen for shit. You can't be anywhere near this case. I see you again anywhere but on one of our beaches, and I'll see you get locked up and fined ten grand. Am I gettin' through that perdy little head of yours now?"

OK. Maybe she didn't dig me.

5

I HAD, FOR ALL INTENTS AND PURPOSES, been kicked in the gift-bag. Detective Carina Fischer intrigued me. Lets face it, we're all friends here, she gave me chest pains. Read into that what you will. I licked my wounds and headed to SMCU. I needed a word with my employer. I raced over there and made it in thirteen minutes, or three songs and a news report on the Rock Station, 98.1 FM. God, I love that car.

Finding your way around a campus that size is a nightmare. Whomever was in charge of the look and feel of that university was far more interested in beauty than function. Flowers and cobblestones everywhere, but find a fucking sign. It took me longer to get to JG once I reached the campus than it did to get to the campus from BIOGENESIS. I eventually had to call him back and have him talk me through it. SCMU and the law school within the university were next to each other but did not occupy the same buildings. I was lost but he got me where I needed to be. Freshman must never get to class at that school.

He was in his office. He was supposed to be having his office hours, where students with issues could go in and talk about what they weren't understanding. But I put an end to that. The two cute undergrads and the nerdy kid had to screw. And they did.

"Deni, you can't talk to people like that down here. They pay tuition and have the right to come see me during posted office hours. You can't just run them off like that."

"Listen, I've had a tough morning because you've been less than forthcoming about what I am able to do down here. Lynde was useless and the hot-as-hell detective chick dressed me down. I'm down here doing you a favor and you feed me to the fuckin' wolves."

"I don't know what you mean by 'feed you to the wolves', but I thought that more doors would open up for you, yes. When I spoke with this Lynde, he gave me no indication that he would be uncooperative. I kinda knew Detective Fischer was a ball-buster, but I had no way of knowing that she would be there. You're a big-boy, I've never heard you whine like this."

"Yeah well, it doesn't matter. According to her, legally I can't do anything anyway."

"That's not exactly true. I have a fix for that."

The door opened without a knock and a tall, blonde, mountain of a man came in through it. I've never been one to be intimidated by anybody. The bigger they are the harder they fall kinda thing. The fights that I have been in, I might not have won them all, but the sons-of-a-bitches knew they had been in a fight. I have literally gone toe to toe with a linebacker.

But this guy was diesel. Huge and muscular. I'm six feet tall, and he stood over me by three or four inches. Imagine if he had a neck? He would have been seven feet tall. We won't even get into how much wider than me he was. His nose had been broken a few times, so he looked the part. He stuck out his hand as he made his way toward me in the mid-sized office. I was thankful and apprehensive at the same time. Thankful that he was only trying to shake my hand, apprehensive because his hand was the size of an Easter ham. And the grip on my hand crushed like a vice.

"Deni, this is Eric Stubbs. He is an investigator at my law firm," JG said.

Eric had the softest voice I have ever heard. "Nice to meet you. I've heard quite a lot about you. It will be an honor to work with you."

"Excuse me? Work with me?" *What the fuck just happened?*

Eric obviously read the shock on my face, because he immediately removed his hand and looked to JG for guidance.

"Ah, yes. We were just getting to that, weren't we Deni? Have a seat gents." We both did.

How Eric fit in his chair is still a mystery.

"Deni, Mr. Stubbs here is licensed in the State of South Carolina and has formed relationships with many people in Charleston. He is down here what you are to New England. Eric is from Charleston and almost played professional football, which makes him a celebrity. He will be able to — "

" — OK, well then. You don't need me." I stood to leave but that big ham was back, this time on my shoulder strongly encouraging me to remain seated. Apparently this ride had not yet come to a complete stop.

"I'm sure you don't like to work with other people. I don't like partners much myself. But from what I have heard, I could learn a lot from you. I can help you with the locals," Eric said. I could not get over his voice. It was soft and tranquil. This guy had the look of an enormous polar bear, but sounded less than a teddy bear. Winnie-the-Pooh has a more grisly voice. I wonder what it took to make him mad. I would eventually find out.

"Listen Eric — "

" — call me Stubbs."

"Really? You *want* to be called Stubbs?" *Is this guy for real?*

"Deni," JG said, "it takes a minimum of thirty days for you to get your PSI license down here. You have to take an oath with the Attorney General or SLED. But you can be made a temporary employee of someone who is licensed without having to be registered. That would also get you your Conceal and Carry permit. It normally takes ten days but I greased the wheels and can have one for you tomorrow, once they determine that you have no outstanding warrants. They have a much more tolerant approach to guns down here."

"So I would work for Eri .... I mean Stubbs? Technically."

"Correct. Technically."

"But why go through all of this trouble? I am telling you Detective Fischer was as serious as a heart attack when she told me to back off. Not that I am a big stickler for rules but you seem to have a capable investigator, why pay me, uh, what you're paying me when I am not really going to be able to do shit?" I was not sure what Stubbs was being paid, but I would bet it was less than me.

"Because I need a result. And more importantly, Sierra needs that result. I need you on this, Deni. You have not failed in the past, at least not with me. No offense, Eric, because I need you on this also, but you aren't Deni. Not yet anyway."

"None taken," he whispered. If he was offended in any way, he didn't show it.

"All right. With that settled, lets move forward with the real meeting."

He didn't wait for me to orally agree to the new terms of the arrangement. But he didn't really have to, I suppose. He knew what he needed to say to get me to stay, and he said it. Like I said, sometimes a friend in need is a pest.

Stubbs unzipped his shoulder bag, which I didn't even realize he was carrying until that point. He retrieved a shoulder harness with a handgun holstered in it.

"I wasn't sure if you had a preference in your pistols, but I like the stopping power of a .45 calibre. You?"

"You are speakin' my language big-boy. What have we got?"

"Taurus *PT1911 stainless*. The key lock has been taken off the hammer but other than that it is out of the box."

The gun was beautiful. And loaded. Eight in the magazine and one in the chamber. I liked the guy's style.

"Just make sure you keep a low profile with it until your Carry Permit comes tomorrow. My gift to you as a way of saying thanks for working with me. JG can handle the paperwork to make it all legit. It will be registered to you here in the State of South Carolina."

Correction. I loved the guy. Full-on man-crush.

But it was time to get down to business.

"Deni, why don't you fill us in on what you found out over at the lab," JG said.

"Not much really. I now know the process by which a drug comes on the market. Whether that is beneficial in our investigation or not, I don't know. It does mean that there are a ton of people along the way that could halt the process if they had a problem with the drug or the company."

"Right," Stubbs said. "So why not do what you can to stop that part of the process if the end goal is to eliminate the drug? No need to kill anybody."

Smart too.

"Good point. And I don't even know what drug they were making over there. Very hush-hush. It seems Sierra's HIV theory isn't what they were cookin' up over there though. Lynde may have been lying, but I don't know for sure."

"She may have been using that as an example, Deni. That was probably one example of what bioengineers do. Or maybe that was just one drug among the many that they are researching. She has a confidentiality agreement in place, so she is not likely to divulge her actual projects. Nor will Lynde. But I will see if I can find out the exact nature of what was being tested at BIOGENESIS."

"It doesn't matter anymore, I don't think. Whatever it was, the game is over. That lab is as deserted as the Sahara. I guess they had a defector or two, so that really put the kibosh on it."

"That's where I might be able to help." It was Stubb's turn. He was studying his notes which he had also removed from his bag. "The number two guy over there Enrique Estabados, excuse me *Doctor* Enrique Estabados, went over to Nahash Pharmaceuticals, which is a subsidiary of Wyatt, the number two pharmaceutical company in the world. Anybody want to venture a guess as to the number one?"

"Ooh, ooh, pick me." I raised my hand like I was in a classroom. Seemed fitting considering I was in the office of a professor at a prestigious university.

"You …. in the corner." I loved that he played along.

"Ummmmmm, would that be PROXER?"

"Give the man a prize. And we all know that BIOGENESIS works under PROXER," he continued. He was coming out of his shell. Still soft-spoken but at least he had some personality in that immense body of his.

"That scallywag. Lynde said that they had some internal turmoil over there."

JG chimed in. "So he murders and sabotages to bring down BIOGENESIS as a way of getting at PROXER because he is a mole for Wyatt. You almost need a scorecard."

"I can help. Wyatt is winning." I was a quick study.

"By killing three people? Seems a bit strong doesn't it? I could see taking all of their trade secrets and giving them to Wyatt, but murder?"

"Stubbs, I just spoke with Lynde and he told me that these umbrella companies generate a half-trillion dollars in revenue. Each. I would kill for a burger right now, just sayin'."

"Let's go talk to Estabados then. I'll fill you in on the rest and buy you a burger on the way."

Did I mention that I love that guy?

I WASN'T SURE IF THE AMG WAS going to be safe in the parking lot at SCMU, so we took it instead of Stubb's ride over to Nahash Pharmaceuticals, a division of Wyatt. We needed to have a word with Dr. Enrique Estabados. Route 52 north runs out toward the 17 and Summerville, where Nahash was situated. I offered to let Stubbs drive since he was technically my boss, but he declined because he wanted to reference his notes when he was filling me in on the other details of the case. It suited me fine, because driving that car was a blast. That is, of course, until I got my speeding ticket.

I was half-tempted to see if I could outrun the pig, the car was under two tons and had 451 horses, so my thinking was that I had a shot. But I didn't know the roads that well and you can't outrun radio. I didn't give a shit about the ticket anyway, JG would pay the fine even if he didn't know it yet. And since I was out-of-State, no points were attached to my license. My fear in not wanting the ticket was that two unfriendly interactions with the local law in the same day might get noticed. And not in a good way.

Stubbs dropped the big bomb on me after we were through with the speeding ticket, thankfully. Because if I had heard the news before being messed with by the Charleston County Sheriff, I may have been charged with murder myself.

The first death in the three serial murders was a doctoral candidate that worked under Sierra. That much I knew. But I didn't know that she died in her home, having bled to death from a snake bite. *Snake - there it was again.* She kept a pet snake, so it was originally labeled an accidental death. Only later, upon further investigation, the lovely Carina Fischer and the M.E. determined that the snake bite wasn't consistent with *her* snake. But it wasn't until after the second murder, seventeen days later, that it was officially deemed a homicide.

Stubbs enlightened me on the second victim as well. He was the lead researcher at SCMU, which again I knew from the report. He was penultimately killed at a lab on campus, again by a fucking snake. Which I didn't know. He too bled to death, but he had a nasty whack to the side of the head to go along with it. It ripped the flesh, tearing the ear off completely. Again, it was originally labeled as accidental but this time suspicions were up. They had an entire lab full of snakes, spiders and the like, but all were accounted for in their cages. Add to those facts that the shattered orbital bone and ear that they couldn't pair with any other surface or instrument in the lab, was leading to the scratching the collective heads of the investigators. Detective Carina Fischer first and foremost. It was then that the first death was coupled with the second.

Lastly, the death of the skinny lad at BIOGENESIS. It didn't take much to kill this poor prick, according to my new friend. He had his source or sources but I didn't ask him to share them with me because if the situation was reversed, I wouldn't want him asking. Anyway, this kid was a third shift lab worker. All he did was run tests for a living. He also had a massive head trauma, sending shards of cranial bone into his brain and tore the skin and hair off the back of his skull. That alone would have done the trick, but the signature snake bite marks were present. He also bled out. Only there were no snakes in the lab. No snakes in that building.

Snakes. I fucking hate snakes.

We arrived at the main gate of Nahash at 3:30 PM. The guard working the booth was unimpressed. He was not about to let two private investigators in to the facility to question anybody. But we got in.

Apparently the way to get what you want in the South isn't to be sneaky or with beatings. Which sucks because that is what I am good at. Stubbs could have choked the life out of the guy without missing a bite of his burger. His size alone would raise some pulses. But he didn't.

No rent-a-cop wants to be doing what they were doing for work. They all take on-line classes or go to Kaplan to study Criminology or some such thing. And they end up here, or places just like it. They don't show that on the commercials. They want to be investigators, they want to be cops, they want to be anything other than a babysitter to a security gate. They make $12 an hour, they could give two shits about a $12 billion patent. Which was probably the catch twenty-two of why he wasn't promoted and why he was still a security guard, but I digress.

Stubbs offered him a way out. He gave him his business card and told him if he let us in, that we wouldn't cause any trouble and he would see about a position as an Investigator with JG's firm. He also asked him politely to not call anybody inside to warn of our presence. We needed the element of surprise, he said, which is a key element of investigating, which he was sure the guard knew.

No shit, it worked.

For the second time that day, I was inside a pharmaceutical research complex, and it looked almost exactly the same as the first. I wondered if inside all of the buildings were projected drugs for illnesses that people suffered from. And if so, how many of them were redundant? There were forty-nine parent companies with who knows how many sub-companies like the two I was in that day. There had to be two separate entities working diligently on curing the same illness.

Was it a function of keeping up with the GlaxoSmithKlines, or have we invented illnesses? I also wondered if we needed to invent new drugs to counteract the side effects of the drugs that were being invented in these buildings. I still wonder that, because I never received an answer.

We had no idea which building Dr. Enrique Estabados worked in. It wasn't like the Mall of America where we could just look at a directory. I think the guard who hoped to have another job the following Monday was supposed to tell us where to go, but we never told him who we were looking for.

We eventually found the Administrative Building. It was completely by accident because we were lost and had to turn around. But we stumbled upon it and thought it a logical place to start, even if it did ruin the element of surprise.

I must have been looking incredibly 'Metro' that day. I don't know if it was the designer clothes that I was forced to buy; or that I was made of lean muscle; or my dirty-blonde hair with a touch of gray; but I was definitely the receptionist's type. The gay male receptionist's type.

He was not into steroids and rugged good looks, which was my new friend Stubb's look. That would have been my preference. Nope, he was into the heavily tattoo'd and athletic type, which was me. All of my tattoos are covered as long as I am wearing a t-shirt and shorts, that was on purpose in case I needed to look respectable. I had taken my sport jacket off because it gets hot in the South during the summer months. The super-expensive t-shirt that I had on fit smaller than any other shirt I had ever purchased. I mean, a large is a large right? Who tries on clothes in a fitting room? But again, I digress.

So some of my tattoos, or at least enough of them, were able to be seen. Enough where he liked what he saw. I know this because that is what he commented on before we had reached his desk. He cat-called me from across the lobby.

"Hello, handsome. Are those tattoos all over your body popping out to see me? I would be more than happy to see more of them. How are you delicious?"

Yep. Full-on Liberace, ballerina, pirouette, butterflies and rainbows gay. So I played the role. I am a total whore, what can I say?

"Better now."

"What can I do you for? That accent of yours is so sexy, you just made my month." Two words. I said two words and everyone in a five mile radius knew that I was a foreigner. Well, Boston. Which in the South means that I am a foreigner.

"I'm looking for someone, I was hoping you might be able to help."

"Get rid of that slab of meat and I think you found him." I am pretty sure that he was referring to Stubbs, because he was sending him looks like daggers through his eyeballs. I was sincerely hoping that I wouldn't have to promise this guy anything. I wouldn't have lived up to any promise that I made, but I was still hoping I wouldn't have to make one just the same.

"Flattering. But I was looking for, excuse me, *we* were looking for Doctor Enrique Estabados. I lost track of which building he is in."

"Oh he isn't your type, honey. He might swing from both sides of the plate, who knows, but there is something about him that I just don't like."

"Unfortunately, we have to do some business with him, so there isn't much choice. I'll keep your comment about him our little secret though. Which building did you say he was in?"

"I didn't muffin, because he isn't here. He is out of town on business. Are you sure you have an appointment with him? Maybe I should just call – "

" – no reason to get other people involved. I don't want to disturb anyone. I lost the piece of paper with his address on it, I probably got the date wrong too." And that was the comment that sent his little pink antennae up. I never recovered. He must have hit a silent alarm or something because the storm troopers walked toward us calmly from several rooms. We were surrounded by Secret Service looking dudes.

Stubbs and I had hoped to have the element of surprise, and we turned out to be the ones surprised.

Our first instinct, mine at least, was to go a couple of rounds with the security boys, just to see what was up. Stubbs looked at me for guidance as they slowly approached us. I think they were wondering what the giant was capable of just as much as I was. But it was neither the time nor the place. Dr. Estabados was our only real lead, and he was out of town. We weren't going to find out where the slippery son-of-a-bitch was hiding by causing a scene, or getting beaten up, or arrested, or any of the above.

These well-dressed security personnel weren't cops. Not even close. While they may have looked like FBI or Secret Service, they were not well-trained. They didn't cuff us, nor did they take either one of our weapons. I was happy about that, because I had just received my *PT1911* and hadn't even had the chance to test it out yet. They also put us in the same room to question us. Rank amateurs.

The guy in charge tried to play the bad-cop role, but he was the only person in the room besides us. No good-cop. And nobody was backing him up. With two guys that individually could give the guy a viscous beating, that was a stupid move. I know what I was thinking of doing to the guy, and I am nowhere near as big as Stubbs.

He kept asking us where we were from, what we wanted, what we were doing there and why we wanted to see Dr. Estabados. Neither of us said a word. It's not like we were in Guantánamo Bay and being water-boarded. This guy put on a scowl and changed his voice from soft to ear-drum shattering loud, and he would occasionally hit the table with his open palm, but he was pretty harmless. The last time he smacked the table I think he hurt his hand, because he winced and never did it again.

I didn't look anywhere but straight ahead. Not at Stubbs, and not at my watch. So I can only guess that it was about a half-hour to forty minutes of that nonsense before the guy left the room. Maybe to bandage his hand. I don't know that either because he never came back. Someone else did and led us to an elevator and then a non-numbered floor that needed an ID badge to get to.

We then went into an office. And when I say 'an office', I mean the mother of all offices. You could have played hoops in that thing if you took out all of the furniture. It was a corner office facing Northeast, two of the adjoining walls were floor-to-ceiling windows. Those windows overlooked the trees of the Francis Marion National Forest to the right and Lake Moultrie to the left. We were well above the tree-line, so I would guess that we were at least ten floors up. I don't know what a space like that costs in Summerville, South Carolina, but you cannot buy a view like that in Somerville, Massachusetts.

The office was filled with fine furniture and fine books and fine knickknacks, but was void of humans other than me and Stubbs. We tried the door but we were locked in. I could think of worse places to be locked up, but trapped is not really my thing. I made my way over to the expansive desk to play with stuff but was thwarted by the man who was coming out of his private bathroom.

He wiped his hands on a towel and tossed it onto the floor of the bathroom from whence he came.

"Good evening gentlemen. It is almost five o'clock and I was planning on leaving for the day, then you two showed up."

"I think this is called prevening. Not evening." I looked to Stubbs who was trying not to laugh, then back at the mystery man. "Do you know what hour officially starts evening? I know it's not afternoon anymore. Happy Hour.

Yeah, it's happy hour. Prevening or happy hour I believe is the preferred nomenclature. Either way, you must have a bar in this office."

"Very funny, Mr. ? — "

" - Abbott. Bud Abbott and this is my friend Lou Costello. We're a comedy team. You might have heard of us."

Stubbs looked at me and said in his sheepish voice, "But I wanna be Abbott. He was the tall one right?"

"I am not amused gentlemen. You are trespassing on a secure facility — "

" — it's really not that secure. You should really look into that. As you can see anybody can just walk right in here and meet some hot-shot in a big corner office. What are you the President of the company?" I was fishing, and the guy knew it, but he bit anyway. My guess is that he thought he had to give a little information to get a little.

"Whomever you are, this is not a laughing matter. We have a great relationship with the Charleston Sheriff's Department, and both the Summerville and Charleston Police Departments. A simple phone call can make both of your lives fairly miserable, I presume. I'm sure you don't want that, and I don't need the headache." *Yeah, I'm sure that's why you haven't already called the cops pal.* "My name is Rueben Feinstein. I am President and CEO of Nahash Pharmaceuticals."

"A subsidiary to Wyatt Pharmaceuticals," Stubbs said.

"Pharmaceuticals?" I said, "you must have something for my headache then, Rueb. Something without side effects though please. I don't want any anal leakage or anything."

"Yes, yes. Very funny. So I see that this is not an accident, you both being here. What can I do for you gentlemen?"

"You can tell us what you were stealing from BIOGENESIS, and where Dr. Estabados is. Yeah, let's start with those two things," I said.

"I think I need to know who you are before I get into denying any of your ridiculous accusations."

"My name is Warren Dennihan and this is Eric Stubbs. You can deny anything you want, but we know that Estabados was a double agent or mole or whatever. We can prove that he was on the books as an employee of BIOGENESIS, and your fabulous little friend at the front desk confirmed that he works here. I'm certainly no genius but it seems to me that something is askew. I wonder what the media would think? Whattaya think, Stubbs? Stuff like this goes very public, very quickly right?"

Stubbs didn't have a chance to answer.

"I don't believe you know half of what you think you do." He sat behind his desk and straightened out something on his pants, he was definitely picking at something while he thought about what to do or say. "I will only say that Nahash and BIOGENESIS compete rather vigorously in different areas because we are after some of the same things."

"How politically correct, Rueb. What the hell does that mean? What are you both after? And why did you have to kill three people to get it?"

What the hell? He was talking, so why not go for broke. In for a penny, in for a pound.

He was lost in thought for a few moments. Again, I can only assume that he was looking at damage control. Because what he told us was far more than what he should have.

Everyone around this case so far was talking about confidentiality — this, and trade secrets — that. This Estabados was all about stealing trade secrets and research. In terms of sound business decisions, telling two people who stormed into his offices, whom he had not vetted, was just stupid.

"Do you know what Nahash means?"

"Enlighten me. My vocab ain't what it used to be."

"It is Hebrew for serpent."

I shit you not, I looked at Stubbs and thought, *is this guy going to confess to ordering the murders of the victims*?

"A pharmaceutical company named after a snake in a religious language. No separation of Church and State for you guys, huh?"

"Did you know that snake venom is already being used as a drug for people with heart conditions?"

Stubbs and I looked at each other and we both shook our heads. He took that to mean 'no' because he continued.

"We hold the patent, and Wyatt currently has in distribution, a drug in pill form for those with high cholesterol and who are at risk of a heart attack. You may have heard of it."

"Fluxir? Flexor? Something like that right?

"Yes. We - "

" — did *you* know that all three victims of the serial killer were either bitten by, or made to look like they were bitten by, snakes?"

"I assumed. The news coverage had been extensive. The accidental death that has now been linked to all three was originally blamed on an unruly sna — "

" — so why isn't anybody beat'n down your door?"

"I'm sure it is just a matter of time before they do. But I can assure you that we have nothing to do with these victims."

"So you're saying the snake thing is just a huge coincidence?"

"We don't keep snakes here at the lab or in any of our buildings. We hired Dr. Estabados because of his expertise at the World Toxin Bank."

"Refresh my memory on what that is again." I was playing stupid, keep him talking.

"SCMU campus houses a library which holds the most complete collection of samples of natural toxins in the world. Frogs, lizards, scorpions, eels, spiders, bees, pufferfish, snails, insects, even some mammals all secret venom for a myriad of reasons."

"And snakes." The second victim died at a lab at SCMU. This guy was an idiot.

"Yes, and snakes. We are only interested in snakes. BIOGENESIS studies snake venom to create synthetic compounds, just as we do. They also have theories on other types of toxins found in nature, which is why they have sponsored the World Toxin Bank at SCMU."

"If everything is so confidential, how do you know that? Estabados?"

"The WTB is available to researchers all over the world. For a price. We have been unable to attain the access that we need. For reasons of self-incrimination, let's just say that it is my job to know what my competitors, such as BIOGENESIS, do on a daily basis and leave it at that."

"So why try to get them out of the way? If only part of what they do is what your company is focused on, why not merge or something?"

"This is cutting edge science. There is room at the table for everyone. I don't want them out of the picture. What I want is access to the World Toxin Bank and to beat them to the cure of very specific ailments. There are over 100,000 animals on this planet that have evolved to produce venom, and every few generations, they mutate. Some venom changes with either the prey's or the secreting animal's diet. So you see, there are an infinite number of combinations, and an almost unlimited amount of research that can be executed."

"Executed. That's a good word, the appropriate one. You are basically saying that you have unlimited resources for poison."

"You have no idea what you are talking about. There is an enormous difference between a toxin and poison. Venom is a toxin. If venom were a poison, the secreting animal wouldn't be able to then eat their prey after they inject it. Venom is injected, a poison is ingested — "

" — you say tomato, I say — "

" — if you would let me finish, sir. Venom contains toxic proteins and short strings of amino acids called peptides. Because of the ever-changing mutations and diets, we can only estimate that there are about 20 million venom toxins. That we know of, or can fathom. The World Toxin Bank, which my competitor has in its hip pocket, so far has only about 10 thousand samples. So you do the math, who would have easier access to a toxin?"

"Estabados. How's my math?"

He looked away from us and fixed his gaze on the bank of windows in the corner of the room. He was lost in thought again. Probably trying to help me and the silent Stubbs understand what the hell he was talking about. I was starting to get lost. All I knew is what I had known when I was marched into this room, that Estabados was in neck-deep. My only reason for finishing the conversation was to see if Rueben was involved also.

He started talking again, but didn't bother to look at us.

"Those toxic proteins and peptides that I told you that are found in venom? Each one has a very specific purpose, and that is what makes venom such a wonderful substance." He turned to face us again, to bring home his point. "They all have varying molecules with varying targets, which is what makes the science so cutting edge. Don't you see? While one venom might target the nervous system which paralyzes the messages from nerves to muscles, another might eat cells, which makes tissues collapse. Yet another might clot blood which makes it thick so blood cannot move and stops the heart, while its counterpart in yet another strain can prevent blood from clotting. Depending on what you want to target, you can use venom to cure Multiple Sclerosis, Arthritis, Diabetes, Cancer, Alzheimer's, Parkinson's, Heart Disease .... you could isolate the target to the point of curing everything from Depression to Nicotine Addiction. The possibilities are endless."

"And you wanted all of those possibilities to yourself."

"NO. NO. NO. You are not understanding what I am telling you. Compared to BIOGENESIS, we are small potatoes. All of those facilities out there, that you passed on your way into my building, are *waiting* for samples of venom so we can begin to create these miracle drugs. We have created only one so far, and the rest are on the drawing board. It will be years before any of what we do gets to a pharmacy, if the FDA lets us get there at all. Estabados is to help us with that. BIOGENESIS has access to the World Toxin Bank, we don't. BIOGENESIS is on the verge of some major breakthroughs; but as I told you, those comparatively comprise one cell, off of one fingernail, off an entire human being."

"So where is Estabados?"

"You *still* think Dr. Estabados had something to do with these deaths?"

"I think, from what you just told us, that your good doctor was number two in a huge machine. And now he gets to be number one and in on the ground floor of what could be another huge machine. I think that he had, and maybe still does have ties to the World Toxin Bank. We have three deaths and somebody wrongly accused for them. He had motive, he had access, and now part of BIOGENESIS is shut down because of it. If you would like me to get the police involved, or the media, I would be happy to do so. Otherwise, tell me where Estabados is."

I knew he didn't want the police to be involved, otherwise they would have already been there to arrest us. There was more to this than meets the eye, and the doctor was the key to it, I was sure.

He turned back to face the windows. The long, early summer day was coming to a close and sun was fading into sunset on the other side of the building. The forest trees were reflecting the reds and oranges, while the stars were trying to wake up for the night.

"Costa Rica. He is taking samples in Costa Rica."

7

THE TWO INVESTIGATORS HAD NO SOONER left the office of Rueben Feinstein and he was on his phone. While the two gentlemen could do nothing to him legally, they could still pose quite a threat to his enterprise.

The President and CEO of Nahash Pharmaceuticals had underlings still in the building that were at his beck and call. It was late, and most of the employees that worked at one or more of the buildings had gone home for the day. A cleaning crew or two may have been lingering but for the most part the entire complex was empty. Rueben, some security personnel, and Jeffery his assistant were all that were left in the Administrative Building.

"Jeffery, get me connected with Enrique on the secure satellite phone please."

"Is this with regard to the gentleman who was flirting with me earlier?"

"Jefferey, I don't have time for your nonsense. Just get Enrique on the line right now."

"Yes sir."

Rueben had always been fascinated with snakes. He had spent his first seven years in this world living with his parents in Brooklyn, New York. He grew up in a Jewish community, not devout, but they went to Temple every week. His father paid for good seats, until he was laid-off. The garment factory could not keep up with the rising costs of doing business in the City in the 1950s. What was once a thriving business that paid it's workers well, was the shell of a building being sold for the real estate value. But there were many jobs available in the South. Rueben's father had a line on a job in South Carolina, so off they went.

Generally speaking, people in the South don't like New Yorkers. That is somewhat true today, and it was definitely true in the late 50s. They didn't like Yankee accents or their sense of superiority, even if it was just a perception. Maybe it was just the remnants of the ideals that the 'South Will Rise Again!'. Or maybe it was that not many people from New York were Baptist. The Feinsteins were definitely not Baptist.

Rueben had no friends. Not people anyway. He found a pet snake within his first week in his new home. It wasn't difficult, South Carolina was rife with them. Especially in the country. Going from Brooklyn, New York to the back woods of western South Carolina was a culture shock to say the least. Nobody liked him, and he didn't like them or their 'Sweet Jesus' ways. All Rueben had were his snakes.

"Dr. Estabados is on the secure line, Sir. The signal is five by five," Jeffery said through the speaker on Rueben's desk phone.

"Thank you Jeffery. You may go home for the night now."

"Thank you sir. Should we alert the security at the main gate about our earlier visitors?"

"I'll take care of that, thank you."

Rueben picked up his Iridium *9555* satellite phone to connect to the one just like it in another time zone. The hand-held device looked like an expensive walkie talkie but had the capability of securely speaking to anyone on the planet via satellite versus a cell tower. The secure line could also send and retrieve data by connecting it to laptops and other gear.

"Enrique. How is the field?"

"I have collaborated with the locals and we have a team here. The lab is rudimentary but we can make do."

"Excellent. When do we start sampling and when can we get molecular data to our researchers here? I have ten buildings full of people with their thumbs up their asses."

"I have some more people that I need to hire in order to ease the process. These people are very touchy about their natural resources. Any time the locals, especially the Government, thinks that we are going to damage their ecosystem, they come out with guns ablaze. Literally.

"I have the skeleton of a security team which we have already used, but should have a full compliment that is fully operational by tomorrow. Two days, maybe three, and we can start analyzing samples."

"Have there been any problems with the locals so far?"

"No. We have been covert, but there is another, more urgent problem."

"What is it?"

"The other entities down here. We are not the only ones. I am working as quickly as I can to, how shall I say? …. eradicate them and relieve them of their data. But there are at least five universities down here at the behest of other companies that are sponsoring them. New Colorado State and the University of Florida have been eliminated from the competition as of today. But we still have the University of Delaware, University of Utah, and the University of Chicago that are still an issue. Not to mention the Clodomiro Picado Research Institute and the religio-"

" — what have they learned?"

"I cannot say what the others have learned, but New Colorado and Florida have made significant strides in analyzing, among others, the Bothrops Asper. I was going over all of their data and it seems that not only are the aspers excitable, unpredictable, and unbelievably dangerous, but they reproduce faster than any other in their genus. Which makes their venom mutations occur exponentially faster. Their venom is a virtual kaleidoscope of peptides with ever-changing attack sites. We just need to fix the other problem that I was about to mention before it is too late."

"More problems? Other than the Goddamned researchers? Just get rid of them and clean it up. Accidents happen. It's the rainforest for Christ sake."

"I told you, I would take care of them. It's those religious nuts again. They are very well funded and very well organized. They have taken to air-dropping toxic mice into the field. I have no idea how they get through the very tight Government controls down here, but they are doing it."

"Air-dropping toxic mice? What the hell are talking about, Enrique?"

"I inspected one of the mice today. It's rather ingenious actually. They give the mice Acetaminophen, which is harmless to them, but is poisonous to the snake. They are killing off the snakes here like genocide."

"*What*? They give the mice Tylenol and what, just give them little parachutes or something?"

"Yes. Precisely. The little parachutes get caught in the trees, which makes them easy prey and an easy meal for our precious material. Once they are dead their venom is rendered useless to us. But at least they won't have headaches."

"This is not funny! Get on it Estabados! We cannot let them do this! Do whatever it is you have to do, but make sure you take care of it. And I mean quickly."

"Yes sir."

"Oh, and I almost forgot. The reason I called. Two investigators came looking for you today. They seemed fixated on the three murders here in Charleston. One of them, the smaller one, seemed very tenacious. The other one was a monster but he was quiet. If I were a betting man, I would say that they are coming down there to pay you a visit."

"Pay *me* a visit? How do they know that I am down here, sir?"

"I'm not sure. They might be with BIOGENESIS. Be on the look out. I will forward you the pictures from the security footage. If you see them, take care of them."

"I'm not sure I am going to be able to contain all of this .... collateral damage sir."

"Just take care of it." Rueben terminated the transmission before Enrique could respond. He then turned around to look out his windows, but there was no view. Night had befallen the forested backdrop. Everything was pitch black. He needed to think things through.

You wanted to be the number one guy? Welcome to the big leagues, son.

8

AFTER THE MEETING WITH RUEBEN FEINSTEIN, we headed back into downtown Charleston. Which, oddly, they call uptown. I again drove because Stubbs said that he wanted to jot down the conversation we had just had with the President and CEO of Nahash while it was still fresh in his mind. I was beginning to think that he didn't like to drive, because he seemed to have repeated excuses for not wanting to.

When he was finished, we called JG using the bluetooth interface technology of the *AMG*. He could hear both of us and we definitely heard him in perfect Dolby Digital 5.1 surround sound that was generated from the Harman Kardon *LOGIC7* entertainment system. Man, that car is sweet.

Stubbs informed JG that the Doctor that had defected over to Nahash was a prime suspect. Like his girlfriend and client, he too had access to the three victims. He also had the means, just like accused. But he had a motive, whereas Sierra Byrne did not.

Dr. Estabados had been an undercover spy, if you will. Informing Nahash on trade secrets, stealing information, maybe even samples from the World Toxin Bank. Not only did he not want to get caught, he wanted to get rich. Getting in on the ground floor of what could be billions of dollars was good for his wallet.

Dr. Byrne had no such interest. JG, our boss and her boyfriend, was filthy rich. She was the lead consultant or whatever to BIOGENESIS, and I was sure that she made a pretty penny as a tenured professor at SCMU. What possible reason would she have to kill colleagues that were working toward modern medical breakthroughs? None that we could think of. But that didn't stop Detective Fischer now did it?

Dr. Enrique Estabados was in Costa Rica, however, which made putting his feet to the fire all but impossible.

Or was it? JG told us that he would make the jet available to us. Stubbs was virtually dusting off his passport, but mine was back in Boston. Who brings a passport to South Carolina? It is definitely another world, but it's still in the same Country.

JG, of course, had a fix for that too. He had a company that he had used in the past that could get me a replacement passport within 24 hours. He would let us know in the morning what time the flight left.

I had never been to Costa Rica before. I didn't really have a deep desire to either. And I'm not sure why.

I dropped Stubbs off at SCMU, where we left his ride in favor of the *AMG*. He really was the Southern version of me. He drove the same Escalade that I drove back in Boston. I mentioned that I had the same ride back home. I also asked him why he didn't like to drive. He did love to drive, he said, but he found that sports sedans were a bit too confining for a man his size. He preferred his truck.

After a short conversation about the day to come, we bid each other a fond adieu. I think he might have wanted to go get a drink or something but I had other designs on the evening.

The night before, I tried to seek and destroy an old acquaintance of mine in Jennifer Beaumont. Jenna. I had failed. I couldn't even find her. At the time, she was the most beautiful woman I had ever met, in person. Inside and out. But that changed the following day, that day, when I met Detective Carina Fischer.

She told me to stay away from the case, but I felt that it was the right thing to do to inform her that she had arrested the wrong suspect. The wrong would-be serial killer. I insinuated as much earlier that day, but this time I had proof. Well, kinda. Plus I wanted to see about getting into her pants.

She hated me. Which meant that I wanted her all the more. She was hot, fiery, and confident. She knew sports and was not afraid to speak her piece. I was intrigued and I wanted her in the worst way.

When men really want something, they will go to great lengths to get it. Search everywhere to find it, even the dark recesses of their brain. I am no different. She had asked me earlier if I was with the 'eighty broad'. Which meant 80 Broad Street. I was on my way to pay her a visit. I didn't care that she told me to stay away from the case. Insinuating that I should also stay away from her.

I arrived at the Crimes Against Persons building of the Charleston Police Department on 80 Broad Street at about 9:00 PM. The old guy at the reception desk paid me no mind as he was much more interested in his *National Rifle Association* periodical. Which was fine by me. I was happy about the fact that he was preoccupied, I could not have cared less what he reads.

The vestibule on the way in told me where the Homicide Division was located, so I shuffled on past the man at the front desk that probably should have been retired. There was a man in shirtsleeves and a loosened necktie in an office off the left, and at one of the sea of desks in the middle of the room was Detective Fischer. She was slumped with her back to me under a desk lamp. I walked through the long room, weaving through the desk farm, approaching her from behind. In retrospect, it is unwise to approach someone that is armed from behind them.

"Wanna get a cup of coffee or a late supper?"

Her head shot up as she saw me come around to the right side of her desk from behind her. She had an empty chair there, so I occupied it.

"You." She paused and looked behind her and around the room. "It's a little late in the day for coffee and I don't know what a *supp-ah* is. What is that, some kinda sissy drink?"

"What? No. It's a meal."

"What'er y'all doin' here? And how did you know where to find me?"

"I came to see if I could have a chat with you. Maybe a meal."

"What, like a date? I don't date possible suspects."

"Suspect? What am I suspected of?"

"Nothin' yet, darlin'. But I told you to stay out of my way and here you are. I'm bettin' you will be."

"C'mon. What harm is it in having a friendly conversation? Think of the positive reviews your Board of Tourism will have."

"How do you know I'm not married?"

"No ring. And the way you were eye-fuckin' me earlier today, I just know. Plus if you were happy, you'd be home in bed with the guy. It's after nine."

"Yer pretty cocky, ain't ch'a? Whattaya wanna talk to me about anyways?"

"You'll have to buy me a drink first. I'm not that easy."

"Yeah, I'll bet."

She took me to what she called a 'honky tonk'. I think that is what she calls a bar, because that is what it was. They had whiskey, so I was happy.

To my surprise she had one too. We settled into a relatively quiet corner where I started the conversation and made my first mistake of the evening.

"A pretty girl like you should be a model or somethin'. How are you a cop?"

"If I had a nickel for every piece a shit with a red neck and a small dick that asked me that? I'd be a rich girl."

"I didn't mean anything by it. I was just thinkin' that it might be tough to be taken seriously, looking the way you do."

"In the beauty lies the struggle."

"What is that, Shakespeare?"

"Is playin' stupid an act, or are you really not very bright?"

"I make up for it in other ways. But back to you. People probably give you a hard time. More than they give other cops. Men."

"I can handle myself, darlin'. It doesn't take-'em long to figure out that you don't have to mess with a bull to get hurt with a horn. You Yankees all think that pretty Southern girls are fragile and lookin' for a man to take care of 'em. This is gonna be a short conversation if you don't get over that notion and right quick. Now enough about my looks, and lets get on with why you wanted to talk to me."

She may have said to ignore her looks, but I just couldn't. Her hazel eyes and pouty lips were not to be ignored. She had pulled back her auburn hair which displayed her long neck. She was tall and athletic, made taller by her high-heeled boots. Victoria's Secret models could eat their collective heart out.

"Have you ever heard of Nahash Pharmaceuticals, Carina?"

"My name is Carina. Not Carin-er, or whatever you just said."

"It's my accent, I know what your name is. Your accent is pretty thick also. Do you know of them or not?"

"Yes. They are out in Summerville. How have *you* heard of 'em?"

"Listen, I know you told me to stay away from this case, but there are things that you should know. Things that I am very sure that you don't."

"My end of the case is closed. I have my suspect locked up. The DA always wants more, but you can't bleed a stone. Hell he'd love it we could get a confession out of 'em all, but life ain't perfect. Your lawyer-friend may have gone to Harvard and all, but he's puttin' the wood to the suspect. So pardon me if I don't rush on over to side of innocent just yet."

"He went to BU."

"What?"

"You said Harvard, but he didn't go to Harvard."

"In that case never mind. Let me just call the DA and see about gettin' the good doctor released. How could I have been so careless?"

"You're a ball-buster. I like it. But there is more that you don't know. And if this case is closed on your end, why were you interviewing the protestors?"

"You've got plenty a balls to bust, I'll give ya that. You come down here and think you can just muscle your way into this. That's why we don't like you Northerners, you think you're better'n us. You think you're smarter than us too. But you don't know shit about shit."

She paused to take a sip of her whiskey. By sip I mean she slung it back.

"Did you know that your doctor, Sierra Byrne, has a juvenile record. This ain't her first rodeo. People think that juvenile records are sealed, well not when you're suspected of a Class A Felony. That thing flies open even if it was expunged.

"And has she come up with an alibi yet? Cuz she didn't have one when we arrested her. She wasn't where she claimed to be. She said that she was with her attorney, your boss. But she wasn't. In fact, nobody could place Attorney Grantes where he said he was either. He has a verifiable alibi for the first two, so he gets a pass. For murder, not for bein' a bad judge of character. I'm guessin' from the expression on your face that you didn't know any of that."

I didn't. That definitely complicated getting Dr. Byrne off the hook quickly. Where had she been for all three murders? And why hadn't JG mentioned that fact?

I ordered us another round of drinks and told Carina what had transpired the rest of my day. I told her about how competitive Big Pharma is. How they all beg, borrow, and steal to get their hands into the best universities. The best researchers. The best possible data.

I told her about our visit with Rueben Feinstein and his obvious reluctance to contact the police even when his security had been breached. About Dr. Enrique Estabados, who was essentially a double agent working for Nahash, and how he had set BIOGENESIS back decades according to Jarod Lynde. That the lab was shut down.

"My heart bleeds for 'em. But what does that have to do with tha price of tea 'n China?" She slung back the rest of her second whiskey and winked at the nearby male bartender who had been eyeing her since the minute she walked in the joint. He didn't need to be told to pour another round. He probably spit in mine.

"What that has to do with China, is that Nahash needs access to the World Toxin Bank, which they don't have access to currently. They are struggling while SCMU and BIOGENESIS are getting rich. Dr. Estabados was the number two guy, so his name wasn't going on any of the research, success or fail. PROXER stock prices are already a car payment per share, so investing in them is pointless. But if he tanks BIOGENESIS and gets in on the ground floor with Nahash, which is backed by Wyatt Pharmaceuticals and could also be elevated to the number one spot. These three murders are worth millions, maybe billions. And that, girl, is a lot of tea."

"You're a little short on proof though, Warren."

"Deni. Call me Deni. And Estabados fled the Country. He is hiding in Costa Rica. Besides, you must have a serial killer psychological profiler or something in your department. Does Sierra Byrnes being a mass murderer fly?"

"You watch too much CSI. We don't make psychological profiles on every suspect, we certainly can't afford one on staff full-time. A female serial killer is rare, which is different from mass murder. Your Boston Marathon asshole was a mass murderer. He did a lot of damage at one time. A serial killer kills outta anger, the thrill, for attention, or for money."

"Exactly. Money. Sierra Banks doesn't need money, she is dating my friend. My boss. He is stupid rich."

"That was just one of the motivations. We have to study all the psychological modeling published by the FBI, its part of my job. But they all don't fall neatly into place. For every profile that fits dead on the nose, there are the outliers. Did you know the first female serial killer ever recorded was right here in Charleston?"

"No shit?"

"None. It was back in the early 1800s. Her name was Fisher, but spelled different from mine. Anyways, her and her husband owned a hotel here, poisoned their guests and snuck the bodies out through trap doors. I think there might even be a tour if your interested."

That was an interesting side note. I wasn't sure if she was getting drunk or what the point of telling me that was. She flagged the bartender with her beautiful eyes again, but the drinks were already made and on their way over to us on our server's tray. I know I was getting drunk.

"Are you drunk, or what's your point? You still haven't said why you were conducting interviews on a closed case."

"I was dottin' my eyes, sorta thang."

"And?"

"Try and keep up with me, darlin'. What I'm sayin' is that sometimes there's just a black widow. She gets messed up as a child and does shit where she gets a taste for killin'. Like your Dr. Byrne. Serial killers are always perceived to have a high IQ, but they are usually about average. Unlike the movies, most villains don't have advanced degrees. Ninety-three IQ I think is the average figure. And serial killers usually ain't female. But they don't always fit the mold. But of all female serial killers, over half of 'em use poison and are organized. That sound like anybody you know?"

Organized, used poison, and smart? Yeah. It sounded familiar.

74

I woke up the next morning with a huge hangover and a kitten had crawled into my mouth. It may have died in there. The bright light glared in from a window that I knew was not the one from my room at JG's house. It was on the wrong side of the bed for starters. I quickly realized that I was not alone in bed, either. I would recognize that head of hair anywhere.

Carina had her back to me sleeping, snoring in fact, on the other side of the bed. She slept in the fetal position, which if I hadn't been so hung-over I would have found adorable. I lifted the covers enough to realize that I was naked, and let my hands do some reconnaissance to find that she was also. But my hands were cold.

"Aaaah. Warm your hands up first." She turned to face me. How was it possible that she was just as hot the morning after a night of drinking as she was while roaming the streets?

"What happened last night?"

"You don't remember? It was a hoot'n a half."

"I'm a little hazy."

"Lightweight."

"What do you weight, like a hundred pounds? How were you not blitzed?"

"You handled yourself alright."

"Oh yeah?"

"I did most of the work, but you can make that up to me right now."

I didn't mind that job one bit.

I had managed to have sex before my morning coffee. Which was rare. This woman was not bashful or reserved, which for me was also rare. When she was through with me, she left the bed as naked as the day she was born. She didn't cover herself in a sheet or tell me to look away, she just got out of bed and let me watch her go into the bathroom. She didn't even close the door when she got into the shower.

I guess when you look like she does, you get used to people staring at you. She was by far the most beautiful and most interesting woman I had ever been with. She didn't care what people thought, which is also unlike any woman I had ever been with. Her slender and perfect body is forever burned into my brain.

My iPhone rang while Carina was showering. It was JG. He told me that because he didn't know until too late in the day yesterday that we had to go to Costa Rica, my passport wouldn't be ready today, but we would fly out at oh-dark-thirty the following morning. I told him that was good, because we needed to talk. Today. That he needed to make time for me. He told me to meet him at 1:00 PM at a cafe on campus, and that he would call Stubbs to make sure he was there also. I liked Stubbs, but if he knew about Dr. Byrne's past and didn't tell me, we were going to have problems. I don't care how big he is.

When she returned from the shower and dressed, she was all questions.

"Are you sick? Do you have Alopecia?"

"No. I was drunk but my memory is fine. Mostly."

"Alopecia not Amnesia. The not having any body-hair thang."

"Oh. That. It didn't seem to bother you too much."

"So are you trying to show off all of those tattoos or all of your scars?"

"Being hairless isn't a choice, it's a lifestyle."

"You don't have to tell me, darlin', I'm a woman. I spend half my life shavin' my legs. Between ladyscapin', sleep, and the job, my day is pretty full. I'm askin' why *you do* it."

"You have very long legs, I'm sure it takes a while."

"Are you gonna answer me or not?"

"It's not just one reason. I have many. I don't understand why all women don't like it. Who wants a mouth full of hair? Can we get off of this subject now, please? I have a headache."

"Sure. So what are y'all plannin' on doin' today? It better be nothin' to do with this case. Don't let last night and this mornin' fool ya. I will bust you for interferin' if I have to."

I thought it was oddly sexy that she was a ball-breaker, but not that early in the morning and not with a hangover.

"I'm going to talk to the boys about what you told me last night. About Byrne's past."

"The boys?"

"JG and Stubbs. Eric Stubbs."

"Oh Eric! Now he's a sweetheart."

"You know him?"

"Everybody knows him. He's like a local celebrity. He only had two minutes of fame with the Atlanta Falcons, but he will always be famous in our hearts. Big 'ol teddy bear that one. Just don't make him mad. That boy is like a bruin in body-armor you get him mad."

"So you *really* know him."

"Not like that, but yes. We went on one date. But I never called him back. Poor thang. Since we're gettin' into pasts sorta after-the-fact, you got a girl back home?"

"Not really. I have an on and off kinda *thang* with this chick who is crazy about me."

Althea was her name but I didn't get into it with Carina. She loved me right, but loved me wrong at the same time. Every once in a while I would run into Althea while on a case. Or I made sure to seek her out so that she could help me on a case. There was nobody on earth that could handle a computer better. Not that I knew personally anyway. We would always end up in the sack, which would lead us down the same old path. She is needy and I need space.

"Girl. Or woman. Not chick. We don't like to be called chicks. It comes from the word 'shiksa'. Which essentially means an outcast woman. It's not nice."

"Well, get over it. Because you are very hot chick. And that's a compliment."

"Very funny. I gotta go to work, so you gotta go. But I'll give you my number in case you wanna call me sometime."

"How about tonight?"

"Smotherin' me already? When do you go home?"

"When this case is over."

"I'll pretend that I didn't hear that."

9

I'VE HAD DRUNKEN SEX ON THE FIRST DATE BEFORE, but I really liked it this time. It wasn't just because she was super-model hot. It wasn't that she was smart and obviously had a wealth of useless knowledge. It wasn't that she was superbly confident in herself and what she wanted. Or maybe it was. But there was something about that woman that I can't put into words that drove be me bat-shit crazy. Maybe it was her foul mouth. I know my language could use some cleaning.

I had to find my car. Well, not my car but the one that I was using. The *AMG* had been left on the street overnight and I had hoped that it would be all right. The application was automatically downloaded onto my iPhone when it was synched to the *AMG*, and fortunately is was right where I had last parked it. The map appearing on my iPhone allowed me to walk directly to the car, which surprisingly didn't take long. It turns out that if you leave your car in front of a police station overnight, nobody tows it or even touches it. I was relieved.

By the time I got back to JG's house, had some coffee and freshened up, it was about time to find the cafe. I remembered that nothing on that campus was marked, so it was going to take some time to find the place where I was supposed to meet JG and Stubbs. And it did take a long time. Even the map on my phone had a difficult time. Plenty of time to get there turned into I was late.

JG and Stubbs were already out at an outdoor table on the patio of the cafe when I got there. They didn't have any drinks or food yet, so I wasn't *that* late. Or the service was terrible.

I made my way over to them, but I was made to go through the cafe first from the inside instead of just going over or through the outside gate.

"Hey guys, sorry I'm late. JG, why is nothing on this campus marked? How does anybody find anything? How do these kids make it to class?"

"We figure it out. Let's get going because I don't have a lot of time, even less now."

He was testy today. The early summer sun was bright and beautiful. Most of the other tables were utilizing their umbrellas for shade, but we were not. I could feel my Irish skin getting a sunburn. The campus and the cafe were not busy, I assumed because it was summer and fewer students were taking classes in the summer. Either way we were out of earshot and eavesdroppers.

"I found out some things last night, and we have a lot to discuss. You two have been holdin' out on me. You might need to clear your calendars," I said.

"I'm not sure I like your tone, Warren."

"And I don't like being kept in the dark, Jacob."

"Gentlemen. Why don't we calm down and chat like civil people," Stubbs said. Odd that the big brawler was the voice of reason in this trio, but he was.

"I met with Carina last night and she told me that you provided an alibi for Dr. Byrne . An alibi which proved to be false. She said that nobody can account for her whereabouts on any of the nights the victims were murdered. She said that you weren't where you said you were, but they *can prove* that you were nowhere near the murders. Which then leaves me to wonder two things. One, you aren't guilty of murder, but you are covering them up, which is a crime. And two, did you have any part or know about this Stubbs?"

"No. What's going on JG?"

"She's Carina now huh?" JG said to me.

"I think that you are fixated on the wrong point here, kid."

"Listen, it's not what you think. I didn't kill anybody. Deni, you of all people should know that I would not risk my freedom unless absolutely necessary."

"I'm listening," I said.

"I was with Jenna the night of the third murder."

"Who?" Stubbs asked.

"His ex. Girlfriend not wife. It's a long story. I'll fill you in later."

"We had to discuss logistics. She has money and assets that were left to her from my ex-mother-in-law, and money and possessions from when we lived together. Our breakup was too painful for her, so she was moving out of Charleston. To Savannah, I think. Sierra is very smart and level-headed, but spending the night with Jenna, my ex-girlfriend whom she was jealous of, would not have been good. I knew that she was incapable of the heinous murders, so I covered for her. It was impulsive."

"Why was she jealous of your ex-girlfriend, JG?" Stubbs asked.

"Jenna has the type of conventional beauty that stops traffic. While Sierra is incredibly smart and stunningly beautiful, she was not able to get past Jenna's looks. It bothers her that her jealousy isn't rational, but deep-down she knows that things are over between Jenna and I. It would have upset her to know that I met with her that night."

JG had a point. I don't care how level-headed you are, Jenna incites attention and jealousy. It wasn't her goal or intent, but when you look like she does, it just happens. Flaxen hair and jade eyes on a body like that of Sophia Vergara. She gets noticed.

Dr. Sierra Byrne was also strikingly beautiful, albeit in less of an in-your-face kind of way. I have never succumbed to the whole jealousy thing, but in my business I have seen enough about the damage it does. Unfortunately some people lie and cheat. Spending your every waking moment of everyday wondering if your partner is one of those people, may just drive them to do so.

"Well she obviously knows that you were lyin', JG. She knows you weren't with her on the nights of the murders, and you told the police that she was with you on the night of the last one. Like you said, she's smart. Your credibility is takin' a bit of a beat'n here, kid."

"Another reason that we need to prove her innocence. In order to save my reputation, and my relationship with her, we need to extricate her from her current predicament."

"Did she say where she was on all of those nights? You covered for her —
"

" — I covered for her on only *one* of the nights. My thinking was that if she had an alibi for one, she couldn't be a plausible suspect in all three. She said that she was doing research in the labs those nights. She teaches, has projects at SCMU, the World Toxin Bank, and at BIOGENESIS. She is very busy."

"Only I have looked into her schedule and calendars. All of those facilities are secure, you need one of her ID badges to get into her offices or any of the labs. They weren't used, which means unless she passed through without using an ID, she wasn't where she said that she was on any of the nights when she said that she was there," Stubbs explained.

"And what is the likelihood that she was able to access any of those facilities without an ID, Stubbs?" I already sorta knew that answer but I was driving a point home to my boss. The other one, not Stubbs.

"Nearly impossible. The murderer at BIOGENESIS used an ID badge from a former cleaning crew employee. I say former, because the person hadn't worked there in over three years. But they took out the CCTV footage. But that employee ID wouldn't be able to get into the SCMU lab or the first victim's house," he explained further.

"Lets walk through this one more time to see if we can find some holes," I said. "The widely respected Dr. Sierra Byrne is a busy woman. She teaches at SCMU, where she had undergrads and doctoral students. Where she also heads the research for biotoxins, herpetology and venomology for that university. Her school also houses the World Toxin Bank, which is the authority on live samples of toxins, including snake venom. That university and the bank therein are funded, in large part, by BIOGENESIS, which is a subsidiary of PROXER Pharmaceuticals, whom she consults with on several projects.

"The number two Big Pharma company is Wyatt, which owns Nahash. Nahash has their own doctor working covertly under Dr. Byrne, in order to steal the research. Three deaths happen, all related to SCMU. All fingers point to Sierra because she worked with these victims, is really the only person who has unique access to two of the three crime scenes and can circumnavigate those security protocols. She really has no motive, but she also has no alibi either.

"Meanwhile this prick Estabados, has left SCMU and is the number one guy over at Nahash Pharmaceuticals. He not only fled the university, but he fled to Costa Rica in order to attain their own samples to start their own library of toxins. Do I have this right, so far?"

"You missed the part where Dr. Enrique Estabados also had the same access privileges *and* he had motive," Stubbs said.

"Right. Does he have an alibi? Was he investigated and cleared?"

"I don't know. Maybe you can ask Carina."

"Funny. We also have to discuss, speaking of information that I got from Detective Fischer, the fact that Dr. Byrne has a juvenile record."

Stunned silence infected the table. I waited for the weight of my words to settle in the brains of my two bosses. The fact that the famous Dr. Byrne had a record was obviously news to both of these men.

"Not possible," JG said. "She would have never cleared the background checks necessary for either the university or BIOGENESIS. What did Detective Fischer say that she did?"

"Juvenile record probably didn't show up on a background check. So you didn't know about it?"

"No, but that doesn't mean that she is a serial killer. What did she do?"

"I don't know, but it has to be pretty bad. We are going to need to ask her."

"I will ask her, Deni. Not we," JG said.

"Fair enough. You have anything else for me? Stubbs, no? You, JG?"

JG didn't answer. He was lost in thought about hearing for the first time that his beloved had a juvenile record that was severe enough to be re-examined and inserted into this case.

"No, but I did research Costa Rica a little bit last night while you were busy with Detective Fischer," Stubbs said after another awkward silence that was palpable.

What did he mean by busy? What did he know? Those thoughts ran through my mind along with *I gotta remember to ask Carina if she is going to look into Estabados after our chat last night.* Which is why I was only half-listening to Stubbs. Which meant that nobody was fully listening to Stubbs.

" …. Costa Rica is a big Country, we can't just take a flight over there and hope to stumble into Estabados. But there is one central but large area where many universities and research projects go because of the diverse animal populations and the rainforest."

"Wait, what did you say? Are we are going into a rainforest? Like with the wildlife and shit?"

"Yes. Exactly. Where did you think we were going? The rainforest is located in the Tilaran Mountains which has an active volcano." Stubbs shuffled through some papers and read while continuing, "The Reserva Biologica Bosque Nuboso Monteverde, in the province of Puntarenas, is a tourist mecca for the wildlife and flora. But the research universities are permitted by the Government set up camps high up in the hills and rainforest, away from the tourists and modern comforts. That is where we are likely to find Estabados."

"Yeah, fuck that. Have fun. Keep me posted and let me know what I can do for you back here."

"You're not afraid are you? From what JG has told me, you're not afraid of anything."

"I don't have a passport." That was the only thing I could come up with at that moment.

JG was out of his funk and corrected me," you do in less than twenty-four hours. You leave at 9:00 AM tomorrow."

I wanted to call Carina once I was finished with the meeting at the cafe. I say meeting instead of lunch, because once I was informed of my impending trip, I was no longer hungry. I just needed to calm down first. I was nearly at the point of a panic attack.

I really don't like flying. I should clarify, I don't mind flying now that I was getting used to private jets. What I didn't like was the probability of crashing. You never hear of anybody surviving a plane crash. 'The odds are better of getting in a car crash' people say. And the way I drive it is more than likely, but I can and have survived a car crash. My thinking is that with every flight I keep pushing the probability that something will go wrong on the flight, and you cannot survive that shit.

Aside from the flying, I really don't like going to foreign countries. I don't speak the languages, I don't know the customs, and from my experience the food always sucks. I went to Ireland some time ago on a case. It's my homeland and I had been meaning to check it out anyway, so my thinking was that it would be great. But apparently I don't speak the same language they speak, the weather was horrible, and the food was worse. That shit they serve you on St. Patty's is not what they eat in Ireland. I did love the whiskey though. That was where I fell in love with Redbreast.

But the big reason I didn't want to go on this trip was the real likelihood that I would be around snakes. I cannot express into words my hatred and fear of snakes. I am afraid of an aggressive worm. People have tried to reason with me; tried to explain that not all snakes are dangerous; but when something can move faster than me without arms, legs, or wings; I scream like a girl at a Justin Bieber show. Only not because I'm over-the-moon happy. With snakes there was the very real prospect of me soiling myself. I was going to have to bring extra underwear.

"Carina. You got a minute?" I had already added her into my contacts into my iPhone. The picture that I used was not one that she would appreciate, as I took it that morning while she was walking around naked.

"For you? Maybe one."

"Can we meet?"

"Sorry sweetie, but I don't have time for that kinda meetin'."

"That's not really what I was thinking but I like where your heads at. Have you looked into Estabados?"

"I told you that this case is off my desk. Why would I look into a case that has a suspect in lock-up? And why are you looking into him? This is all fun and games but if you go harassin' good citizens we're gonna have a problem."

"I spoke with Grantes about what you said last night. While Byrne may not have an alibi, she doesn't have motive either. Nobody but you thinks she did this. She may have been doin' somethin' shady but she ain't a serial killer. Estabados had the same access and he had a motive. Does he have an alibi?"

"Your attorney-boss lied to me, he is lucky I am not charging him with obstruction. I still might, along with you for interferin' if you don't knock it off."

"Do you know if he has an alibi or not?"

"No. Once we settled on Byrne, we stopped lookin'."

"I'm asking you to look. Please. For me," I begged.

"Why don't you do it, sense you are so hell-bent on breakin' the rules."

"Since."

"What, darlin'?"

"Since, not sense. Since I like to break the rules, not sense."

"I know how to speak, you ass. It's my accent. Yours is pretty hard to understand, we've been through this."

"Good point. Are you going to look into this or not? I would do this myself but I'm flyin' to Costa Rica in the morning. Me 'n Stubbs are gonna find Estabados."

"Is that really smart? If, and I do mean if, in the unlikely even that he is your serial killer, which I'm not sayin' he is, isn't it kinda dangerous to be huntin' him down in a foreign country? Besides, even if you do find him, it's gonna take more 'n a lick and a promise to get him back here."

"I've got Stubbs. Besides I can take care of myself."

"And *I've* seen your scars."

"I'll be back in a couple of days, can you help me or not?"

"We can talk about it tonight. You are comin' over to see me tonight, correct?"

"With an invitation like that, how can I refuse?"

"Pick me up at the station around nine," she said.

"I'll wear somethin' clingy."

That night was magic. I was not drunk and able to focus on what I was doing. I couldn't keep my hands off of her. She seemed to be having the same struggle.

If our sex was compared to a boxing match, we were in a title fight. Round after sweaty round we went. And not just toe-to-toe.

We broke for food at one point. And some water. I had never felt so good in my life.

I had to get up at 3:00 AM in order to get home, change, and pack a bag for my flight. By get up I mean that I had to get up out of bed, because I was definitely already awake.

So was Carina.

"Hey Irish. Are y'all gonna come back and see me?"

"That's the plan. Are you gonna help me out? Look into Estabados?"

"You sure know how to ruin a moment."

"We've just had about fifty moments."

"Speak for yourself."

"Really? All that moanin' and grindin' and you didn't have a good time?"

"I was fakin'," she said with a shit-eating grin on her face.

"Yeah right. Ball-buster." *Sexiest ball-buster on the planet,* I thought.

"I'll see what I can do. Off the record. Just make sure you bring that dick back here. I kinda like it. My toys just ain't gonna cut it like they used to."

She was nasty and I loved every minute of it.

"I'll do my best."

10

NOBODY SHOULD EVER SEE 3:00 AM unless they are still up doing whatever debauchery that led them to that late hour. Which is what I was doing. Getting on a plane, going to a foreign place in Central America, where there are copious amounts of creepy-crawlies like snakes that want a taste of the Irish, is not my idea of a good time. I wanted alcohol. Or a drug like Prozac. I should have been relaxed. I was until I got on the plane at 8:30. I needed sleep. I needed something to help me relax, because there was no way I was going to be able to sleep. I was going to hell on earth and I was doing it sober, elevating it to the ninth circle of hell.

With the two hour time difference, the flight took four hours. We landed at Juan Santamaria International Airport in Alajuela, Costa Rica at 1:00 PM local time. Getting through Customs and acquiring transportation required a quarter of the flight time. There was no shortage of locals looking to make money on the fare from the airport to Puntarenas. The two and a half hour drive was going to make someone's week.

We climbed into the gold 1994 Toyota *Previa* that looked like it had a million miles on it. Believe it or not, it was the best looking vehicle big enough for Stubbs, me, and all of the gear we had brought. The suspension rode like there wasn't any. I looked for a seat belt on the front passenger bench, but there was only the broken receptacle. I should have counted myself lucky, Stubbs said that he had neither end of the harness on his third-row bench behind me. Every bump along Route 1, the Pan American Highway, was a struggle between hitting our heads on the ceiling or having the seats jammed so far into us it was like an experiment in proctology. I had only been in the Country for an hour and a half at that point, and I had already had my fill.

The driver was friendly enough. He fancied himself a tour-bus driver, giving us the play by play of everything we drove past. All 136 kilometers of the drive. To be honest, I really just wanted him to shut the fuck up. I was tired and cranky. Crankier than usual. But Stubbs was eating it up. He couldn't get enough of why we had to go South in order to travel Northwest.   I wished that I had taken the seats in the far back of the van since Stubbs was so interested in what the driver had to say. Stubbs kept asking him to repeat himself. I didn't want to hear it the first time, I certainly didn't need the encore.

The roads were supposed to be major highways but were narrow, long, and windy. Every vehicle traveling in the opposite direction of us was engaging us in a game of chicken, neither driver wanting to yield on the shoulder.

The next road was a major artery, Route 27, and it was no-mans land. You could have told me we were in the middle of nowhere and I would have believed you. Mountains were always surrounding us, no matter which way we turned.

It wasn't until we crossed the 721 and headed closer to Route 23, that the road resembled a normal road. It had lines on it, delineating actual lanes for traffic, and guardrails. We went through several roundabouts headed West to some degree but remained predominantly South. We were traveling further and further away from where I thought we should be headed according the map I had purchased. It wasn't until we hit the coastal waters and kept them on our left, that I began to believe we could possibly be headed in the right direction. We traveled the coast, which was beautiful, seemingly ad infinitum before we headed East again onto Route 606 and the desolation resumed. We bounced along the long and circuitous roads through hills and mountains like Tigger and Pooh, the driver practically giving the life history of every tree.

There were a few communities once we reached the 620, but we didn't stop at them. No bathroom breaks, no food, and worse yet no drink. I wanted to have my whits about me but the tedium was driving me crazy. You can only be thrown around the inside of a *Previa* for so long before you want to kill something.

Once we reached the Reserva Biologica Bosque Nuboso Monteverde, otherwise known as the Cloud Forest, we were officially in the mountains. Green, lush, tropics with a few rustic hotels and even fewer walking paths. It was getting on 4:00 PM and we needed to find a guide further into this forest. I hoped that it would get cooler under the arboreal canopy, it was 80 degrees and humid as it had rained earlier that morning. It was said to rain again later that day, as it did every day in the 'green' or rain season. We were there in the beginning of it. I was ecstatic.

We hung out in the makeshift parking area, where the talkative driver had dropped us off, for about forty minutes when we spied a man with a hiking pack and gear. He was headed toward one of the dilapidated vehicles in the area that constituted the small park and ride. I approached him because Stubbs said his size might scare off the Latino.

"Excuse me. Do you speak English?"

"sí. Yes, but my Spanish es better. ¿Usted no habla español?"

I understood the word español but not the language. I certainly didn't speak it. In Boston we have an influx of Brazilians, which means Portugese. They both might be Latin-based, but they are not the same. You take your life into your own hands if you insinuate anything different back home. I made that mistake only once. I have dealt with a few Brazilians, so I can maybe sorta pick out a few words of Portugese, but not fluent in any Latin language. I was also brought up Catholic, as you can imagine. The Catholic schools that I attended as a kid required that we learn Latin. It would help us with other languages they had said. They were full of shit. I wonder how many 'Our Fathers' you have to say when you lie your ass off to dozens of little kids?

"Uh, no Spanish para mí." OK, I knew that much, but that was it.

"How I help?"

"We need a guide to bring us deep into the rainforest. We need to find our scientist friends."

I thought he was giving me a puzzled look, but I soon realized that Stubbs had come up behind me. Unbelievably, Stubbs spoke fluent Spanish. This guy was full of surprises. He spoke gibberish which I later found out was a bullsh story about us being from one of the universities and had to relay some sensitive information about a research project.

The guy nodded and said that he was finished working and had the next few days off.

"Tengo los próximos días apagado del trabajo a pasar con mi familia. Usted puede encontrar algún otro para dirigirle."

Stubbs was mumbling the translation to me while he spoke. I nodded my head because I knew the language that everyone spoke.

"What is your name?" I was digging into my wallet. I had plenty of cash. US dollars. I made sure he saw every bill.

"Hector." He said four or five other names after that, I think. All I understood was Hector.

I took out five $100 bills and handed them to him. What I didn't realize was that the exchange rate was about five hundred to one. I had given Hector ₡249,250 which was more than he made in a month at his regular tour job. He was listening.

I told Stubbs to tell him that he would get the other half when we got to where we were going, and I would double the amount if he would ensure that we got back here safely. We would have to revise the story we told him. There was going to be one more coming back. I hoped Estabados wasn't charming.

The prospect of almost a million Costa Rican Colones was too much for him to pass up. And my thinking was that two grand was short money if we would get outta there alive.

He told Stubbs that he was going to need to stock up on a few supplies for the three of us to make the journey, which would only take about a day, one way. Especially if we used the vast number of canopy lines along way. I gave him more money to attain said supplies.

At 6:00 PM we were backpacking our way into the rainforest. Stubbs had gathered and purchased gear for us after he had left the cafe on the SCMU campus the day before. He had gone to an REI store or something. He liked to hunt, fish, hike, camp and the like. I did not. I especially didn't like it in a place almost a continent away. And the new hiking boots were already giving me blisters. I had packed a small bag also. It contained mostly underwear. That bag was shoved into my large pack that I was lugging into the jungle.

The only thing about this little adventure that made me feel even somewhat safe was that I had Stubbs there. He knew the language and his size would make someone think twice about fucking with us. And we were able to sneak our guns into the Country. Again, that was all thanks to Stubbs. He was a clever monkey.

"If anyone sees a snake, you have my permission to shoot it. Consider it carte blanche, actually. If anything pokes out at us, feel free." I was last in the line, behind Stubbs who was behind Hector.

Hector took umbrage to my remark. "Nuestra fauna es muy preciosa a nosotros. usted no tirará nada."

"What did he say?" I asked Stubbs.

"He says 'nobody is shooting anything.'." It seemed like he used a lot more words than the four words that were translated to me, but I didn't argue.

It began to rain again by the time we reached the second canopy line. The harnesses and clips were complicated to figure out at first, but once you get the hang of it they're not that bad. I still had Hector double-check mine on the second, third, and fourth canopies because we weren't using helmets and a fall would likely kill me. The lines were long and strung up between towers that took us over these large ravines and rock formations. We were literally at or above the tree line of the rainforest. The only thing above us were the peaks of the Tilaran Mountains and sky.

It was slow going for the first few hours. We were having to deal with the tourists who were out in the forest finishing for the day after their own tour groups looking at the colorful butterflies, lizards, toucans, and other wildlife. Stubbs and I were on a mission, Hector had seen them a countless times before and just as anxious to complete this adventure so he could collect his money.

We broke at well after nightfall. Technically we were never in the light because of the forest. Our packs were set up with small, battery-powered LED lights so we could see one another without casting too much light for predators.

We eventually did stop for the night, setting up the perimeter lanterns, set up camp and ate our meals from a pouch. The MREs were better than the kind the military get, Hector said. Or at least that is what I understood him to say. He and Stubbs got on really well. I became the third wheel.

Since Hector brought it up, I asked him about the Costa Rican Military over our fire and sack of supper. He said that Costa Rica didn't have a military per se. The military was disbanded around 1950. What used to be a Government Militia was now a security for hire. Meaning townships usually hire would-be soldiers to protect their own. *Great,* I thought, *a Country full of mercenaries.*

I didn't sleep a wink that night. I was exhausted, especially since I hadn't slept the night before, but sleep would not come. I was surrounded by the loudest quiet I had ever heard. Birds and Howler Monkeys are up all night looking for food. Hell only knows what the other sounds were.

While the raised, one-man tent kept the moisture and man-eating ants off of the floor of the tent and me, the brush that we cleared to do so dug into my back. I would definitely prefer the brush in my back over the ants. Most venom-producing ants use theirs to protect the nest, I was told. Costa Rican ants use theirs to subdue and eat their prey. *Awesome.* I didn't think that bugs liked the cold, but they liked it out there that night, cold be damned. The bugs were everywhere.

The morning light started to cut through the canopy, but I was already awake. It was almost 6:00 AM and I decided to get up and see about a breakfast MRE. I was famished. Those Meals might be Ready to Eat, but they aren't very big. I'm not a big guy, I was unsure how Stubbs had been satiated. Breakfast in a sack was sounding pretty good. I was mindful to be quiet, letting the others sleep until a more respectable hour. Careful with every movement, unzipping my one-man tent. Walking about the small area with stealth.

I was successful in my efforts until I saw my first snake in Costa Rica on a nearby limb. The sound that emanated from my mouth was issued from the depths of my very frightened soul. Loud? You could say that. A more accurate description would have been that I raised the dead.

I definitely raised the slumbered. Stubbs came out of his tent with his gun ready and Hector was yelling in Spanish. Stubbs would never tell me exactly what he said. My guess is that as bad as my language can get, he said things that were worse and were directed toward me. At first I felt bad. But after some thought I decided fuck them. Stubbs got me into this mess by not coming alone, and Hector was getting paid. And the snake was a deadly one.

Over breakfast, and while we picked up camp, I would learn that there are all sorts of things that are worse than snakes. And they all lived right there in that forest. Costa Rica is home to more than 500,000 species. 300,000 are insects. Of the 200,000 species that aren't insects, more than half of them I should be afraid of.

In Costa Rica, all spiders are venomous. The question is if the jaw is big enough to penetrate human skin, and if so is the venom virulent enough to do serious damage. The ones with thick webs give you a fighting chance because they can't see very well. They use their webs to snag their prey. The large ones can see or sense you with their furry motion receptors. They can and will leap at a moving target. The Brazilian Wandering spider is the deadliest. I wished that they had just stayed in Brazil.

It is the same story with the scorpions. Only there aren't any questions with scorpions. If you were to get stung that far out in the jungle, you are dead.

Then there are the Poison Dart Frogs, the Golden Toads, some 70 species of lizards. Hector didn't elaborate on which snakes would kill me. They all would in one way or another. If it didn't eat me, it would give me a heart attack from fear. Either way I was a dead man.

We began the day and the hike earlier than scheduled, and were making good time according to Hector. We were beyond tourists and covering a lot of ground. We were all drenched from the humidity that you could almost cut with a knife. And sweat. I can't speak for the other lads, but I was drenched to the point where my skin was wrinkling. Added to the fact that my blisters on my feet had popped and you get the idea of how uncomfortable I was.

We only stopped once in mid-morning because Stubbs was admiring the congregation of Scarlet Macaws. The large and very colorful bird has a parrot-like appearance with cobalt blue wing tips; bright yellow wing radius and scapula; and fire engine red skull, vertebrae, and furcula. Who knew that the enormous football player, outdoorsman was also a Spanish-speaking birdwatcher? Upon further review, he was nothing like me. The guy could get along with anyone.

Hector and Stubbs were chatting away in Spanish, and again I was left off to the side. They watched and pointed while I was on the look-out for anything that was interested in Irish-flavored meat. We restarted our trek after a bit where we reassembled in our assigned spots in the line. Stubbs told me over his shoulder what Hector was explaining to him about the birds, like I gave a shit.

But it seems that the Scarlet Macaw is a very popular bird for a pet, people paying over $1000 each for them. Their population is threatened primarily from this but also because of their mating rituals. They form a monogamous breeding pair and share the responsibility for raising their young, which takes about two years. They cannot keep up with their demand. I was having entrepreneurial designs of my own with these birds. So it turns out that maybe I did give a shit.

About two hours after the bird watching, we stopped for water and a granola bar. This tree-hugger hiking, nature, and granola bar shit was wearing on me. I don't even like Kashi commercials. But I was hungry, so I ate it. The two guys with the International man-crush were chatting away when I heard noises and voices that were not from our party. I whistled to them to shut up, and they did.

We moved as quietly as possible toward the voices, off the path and deep into the brush. Approximately seventy yards in we spotted a clearing where an elaborate camp had been constructed of indigenous raw materials. They were a young lot, many of which were sharing the same name on their t-shirts. The time for secrecy was over.

I popped up from my crouched position and made my way into the clearing to meet the students of the University of Chicago.

The change of clothes, especially the change of socks did wonders for my comfort and attitude. I had returned back to my usual level of surliness. They had better food than our MREs and treated us to an early supper. We sat around a set of rudimentary picnic tables. The mystery meat with rice and beans was delicious. The students were going native, they said, wanting to eat the same traditional cuisine as the people of the Country they occupied. I was informed that this meal was different from gallo pinto, the breakfast dish, because the rice and beans weren't mixed. I hoped for their sakes that they slept in their own tents because beans for every meal could create quite a stink.

They originally thought that we were tourists who had ventured deeper into the rainforest in the desire to gain a more authentic cultural experience. We didn't alter their perception until we were finished with the meal. Hector remained silent, per my request, for virtually the entire time we were in the camp.

"So how long have you been out here, uh, camping?" I knew they were researchers, it didn't take a rocket scientist to understand that these kids were scientists.

They gave each other looks, all eleven of them, as if to ascertain how much or how little to share. They were under confidentiality agreements also, I was sure.

"We have been out here for three months and have several more to go. We are biologists on a research grant," the Asian girl said. I never did get her name. It was Naomi or Nanami …. something like that.

"It must be quite a grant."

"We, like, can complete our thesis and earn our doctorate degrees when we have finished and compiled our work," another student said.

"I would ask you what you are studying, but I probably wouldn't understand it anyway. Biologists, you say?"

"Uh, well, yeah. Sorta. It's complicated and we don't want to bore you," the Asian girl said.

"Thanks. And you have been so kind to feed us. We are deep into the jungle here. We are very grateful, aren't we guys?"

Stubbs nodded and Hector missed his queue. Whatever. It was time to come clean anyway. This ruse was getting us nowhere. They were running out of lies for their clandestine operation, and I was tired of pretending to be people that they were already beginning to suspect were not genuine.

"We are not out this far by accident, as you might have guessed from us having a guide."

"It's really none of our business," the Asian girl said again. She must have been the group's spokesperson.

"I would say from the looks of your camp, that it is exactly the same business. Do you know a Dr. Enrique Estabados? Or know of him?"

They all looked at each other with shock and amazement. The Asian student returned her eye contact with me, unsure of how to proceed.

"You're joking right? *Everyone* knows who he is. He has been crucial in the advancement of the World Toxin Bank. He is one of the top three or four people in the world doing …. uh …. the work that he does."

"And you are all out here doing the same type of thing, right?"

Again the looks.

"Who are you exactly?"

"We work for colleagues of Dr. Estabados, we need to find him."

"There must be some mistake. I don't think he is out here in the rainforest. He wouldn't need to be out here with his work at the WTB. And he can offer grants to students to collect samples for him."

"But just for the sake of argument, if he was out here, do you know where he would be?"

"There are all sorts of researchers out here. We are spread out all over the rainforest. This is one of the most biodiverse places on the planet. *If* he is out here, he could be anywhere. But I don't think he is, with all of the groups out here, we run into each other sooner or later. Florida, Arizona, California, NCS …. sometimes it is by accident and other times they come looking specifically to see how far the competition's research has come."

"Does it ever get dangerous?"

"Supposedly. They all have hired security to make sure their research is secure, but we can't afford it with the money we were granted. I think we are the only team without security. Anyway, we think that we are in more danger from the wildlife than the other universities. We are researchers for crying out loud, not warriors."

"So if you guys run into trouble, what is the protocol?"

"We have a supply of antivenoms, but outside of that we have a satellite phone and flares. There are dozens of tour groups that are only a half a day or so away. If we were in trouble they would see the flare above the canopy and send help. Not that we have needed to yet. Are you saying that we are in trouble?"

"No, of course not. I was just wondering."

I hoped I wasn't lying to the kids.

11

AGAINST HER BETTER JUDGEMENT, DETECTIVE CARINA FISCHER began to investigate the background and alibis of one Dr. Enrique Estabados. She was sure it was a waste of time. Time that she had a shortage of. Her case load was full to the point of being overwhelmed. Why she was revisiting a case that was for all intents and purposes closed was beyond her. But it was her decision, nobody else's. This Yankee had asked her to look into Estabados and Nahash, but nobody was forcing her.

Carina had never been involved with people she encountered through her work. She would occasionally date guys she met at her gym. Randomly if a guy said a certain thing or looked a certain way at a bar, but that never worked out. She was still single in her mid thirties because she was busy with work and because she was choosy. All women have needs, so she would allow a man into her life every so often to fulfill them, then send him on his merry way. She had broken many hearts, and that was her burden to carry. There were all too many men willing to fulfill that need. So she was desperate to figure out why was she hung up on Deni.

And why was she doing his bidding? There was absolutely no reason to reopen this case. She wouldn't. Not officially. But she had to be sure. She was an incredibly good cop that wasn't taken seriously because of the way she looked. Sending the wrong serial killer to prison while the real threat remained at large would not look good on her resume. That is why she was looking into this Estabados, she convinced herself. Not Warren Dennihan.

She decided to start out with a trip over to Nahash Pharmaceuticals. If what Deni had said was true, there was an infiltration into BIOGENESIS and possibly more by Estabados at the behest of Rueben Feinstein. The juxtapositioning of the two adversarial companies was not likely to be ethically justifiable, probably not legal. Had they gone so far as to commit murder over trade secrets? Carina found it far-fetched but remotely possible. The feeling was more visceral than rational.

The detective was pleasantly surprised to see that she would not have to fight through a mob of media teams, picketers, or protesters as she had at BIOGENESIS. Her only opposition to driving right onto the expansive property was the security guard manning the gate from the sanctity of his booth. She drove up to it, rolled down her window, and flashed her badge.

"Do you have an appointment, officer?"

"Its detective and no. But I'm investigatin' multiple homicides so I don't need one."

The guard had been given the riot act about letting other recent unwelcome visitors into the complex. He was almost fired for it. The guard was not about to let anybody beyond the outer gate without an appointment.

"This facility does sensitive research, ma'am. Without an appointment I cannot grant you access. Unless you have a warrant."

"Let me walk you through what's gonna happen if I have to get a warrant. I will make a few phone calls, and nobody will get in or out until a judge signs a warrant and an officer brings it here along with a whole mess of other cops. Then this place will be shut down for days until we go over every single inch, of every building, located on this property. The media will somehow be alerted and then it will go public that there is a major investigation here, which is all tied up with Wyatt Pharmaceuticals. That drops the stock price and some eager little go-getter is going to do an exposé on Big Pharma, maybe even dig up some dirt on you in the process. All because you won't let a decorated detective speak informally to your boss, Rueben Feinstein. We makin' any headway on gettin' me that appointment?"

"Let me make a phone call." He picked up the phone inside the booth and spent the better part of two minutes speaking to someone who was going to ease his culpability in this mess. When he was finished, he hung up the phone and said that she had an appointment in two hours, at 11:30 AM. She was told that she could come back at that time.

"Yeah, that's not what I had in mind, sugar. I'll wait for my appointment. Right here. Nobody in or out."

"Then I'm afraid that I will have to have your vehicle towed in order to clear the gate."

Now she was really pissed.

"Anybody touches this car but me and I will shoot'em. I'll call it self defense. Then I'll have you arrested for somethin' I haven't quite thought up yet, maybe reckless endangerment or obstruction, I'm not sure. Us cops are real good at makin' *somethin'* stick. Who's gonna hire a security guard with a felony record?"

"I'm just trying to do my job, ma'am. He said two hours, so that is what I'm going to do. I'm in enough trouble already."

"My advice is to open that gate and find a new job, sweetie."

You could visibly see the gears grinding in the guard's head trying to figure out what he was going to do. The thirty seconds it did take felt like an hour.

"The Admin building is the last building up on the end of this main road. Please tell him something about arresting me so I don't get fired."

Outside of Rueben Feinstein's office, Carina found herself a seat in a large anteroom. She was alone after being told by the very effeminate male receptionist in the lobby where to go. Her posterior had not yet warmed her seat when the bamboo door opened to reveal a man with salt and peppered hair.

"Detective. My schedule cleared up suddenly so I have a brief moment now if you would like."

Carina looked at her watch and feigned a look of being impressed.

"An hour and fifty minutes early? I'll consider myself lucky. You must be Mr. Feinstein."

"Rueben, Yes. And you are?"

"Detective Fischer."

"Do you have a first name?"

"Yes. But you can call me Detective or Detective Fischer."

"I see. Please have a seat."

"I'll stand. This won't take long, unless you make me mad."

"What is this concerning?"

"The three related and recent deaths."

"I'm not sure that I understand, Detective."

"Come on now, Reuben. No need to be coy. This ain't Detroit or Miami. This is Charleston. We don't have murderin' like other places. It happens, but not three related in five weeks. Surely you've seen the news. Surely you know that these victims are from the same circles that you find yourself in."

"They don't have anything to do with my company, I assure you."

"Well that's my point. Three deaths in your rival company, all of whom had hands-on knowledge of the same research that you and your company conduct. Then the number two guy over there comes over here to work, or was working here the entire time. Now doesn't that strike you as odd?"

"Maybe I should have my lawyers present. I don't think that I like what you are insinuating, Detective."

"I ain't insinuatin' anything, sir. I'm sayin' it outright. We can certainly make this more formal if ya like, but really I just want time records and such on your Dr. Enrique Estabados. I want to see his personnel file, so I can see when exactly he started working here. I'd also like to speak with him when we are through here." She knew Estabados was in Costa Rica, she just wanted to see Rueben's reaction. And she got one.

"I'm afraid what you're asking is impossible, Detective."

"Nothin's impossible sir. I just haven't motivated you. So let me see if I can fix that. See my job is to find and arrest murderers. And the people who pay those people to do their murderin'. In this case, that's exactly what I am beginnin' to think is goin' on here. I don't give a rats ass about you bein' a thief and stealing proprietary information. That's what Civil Courts are for. I care about the murder of three innocent people who were guilty of doin' no more 'n goin' to work and doin' their job.

"You puttin' up a fight is only makin' me want to dig into you more. You can think of me like a rapist. You can kick and scream all you want to, but in the end I'm gettin' my way."

"Well that is very myopic. And very strong talk for a pretty little girl like yourself. Did you come with any back-up, Detective, or did you bring only your rapier whit with you? It wasn't very smart for you to have come here alone."

She didn't notice that the room now had more than just the two people in it, else she would have retrieved her service weapon. There were several security personnel that had entered the corner penthouse office behind her.

"Miss Fischer.   I thought bringing backup was standard procedure, axiomatic.   At a minimum you should have given it earnest consideration. Unless you are here outside the scope of an official investigation.   If that is the case, then I would surmise that nobody knows that you are here.   I believe my security team will now have to sort you out."

Rueben nodded to his staff, who surrounded Carina.

12

IT RAINED AGAIN THAT AFTERNOON in the rainforest. Rain in the rainforest, go figure. But we had just dried off and had a change of clothes. It was frustrating being wet all of the time. We were either drenched from the rain, humidity that hung in the air, sweat, or all of the above.

We left the kids from the University of Chicago and told them to be careful. Eleven twenty-somethings in the middle of an inhospitable jungle; with other researchers in the general area; whom were sponsored by Big Pharma and whom wanted their data; were not odds stacked in their favor.

We trekked for a couple of hours, our bellies were full and we were more than hydrated. We seemed to be hiking through a thick mist of water. The flora dripped down onto us as we passed under it on the narrow path below. It was so humid, maybe the trees were sweating on us.

All-of-a-sudden, Hector stopped and raised his right hand signaling for us to do the same. He didn't have to tell us to shut up, it was inferred. A few brief moments went by and then he turned to signal us to crouch down. His hand had not yet been brought down to the level of his waist when we all heard it.

It was the sound like compressed air had sprung a short-lived leak, and that leak lasted but a fraction of a second. It had come from in front of us and off to the right. I returned my look back and left toward Hector who was then not crouched on the ground, but lying in the brush off to the left of the path. He had sprung his own leak.

The red that was painted on the surrounding vegetation were not blossoms, they were splatter from Hector's neck. The rain that was coming down could not wash away the crimson that was Jackson Pollocked all over the surrounding vegetation.

Stubbs was closer, he had front row seats in viewing what a high caliber projectile could do to someone's neck once it has gone through it. I didn't think that he was alive but I wanted to go check. I was stopped by Stubbs.

"Get the fuck down you idiot or you're gonna be next!"

He grabbed me and pulled me back to the hardened ground on the path. I was next to him, to his left looking directly at Hector who was motionless. His body was contorted around his backpack which was still attached to the corpse. Bloody meat was protruding out of his neck like an ultra-crimson wattle on a turkey's neck. Ants and other insects were already beginning to crawl on him, attaining their nourishment. The circle of life rainforest-style.

"Crawl into the shrubs off the path," Stubbs said. He pointed to the right and behind us, away from Hector.

"There is no need, my friends."

A Latin man was walking down the path, towards us with at least six armed men behind him. His accent was not thick, hardly any perceptible inflections. He could have been from Costa Rica just as likely as he could have been from Idaho.

"No need for you suffer the same fate as your friend. Toss your weapons away from you and toward me. Slowly."

We complied, but I was more reluctant than Stubbs. My brand new gun. I had never fired it. Gone.

One of the men behind the Latin man was dressed in camouflage and carrying a Barrett *M82 .50 BMG* sniper rifle. I no longer questioned what had done such horrific and final damage to our tour guide.

Our weapons had no sooner hit the ground, when another hit came. The words uttered by Stubbs were like those coming from a tape being played at too slow a speed.

"Behind you" had come too late.

Everything went black.

When I awoke, the back of my head and neck felt like it had been through a dull guillotine. The hit I took drew some blood, as it was now dried where it had dripped down my shoulders and chest. The throbbing was making me want to throw up.

I looked around to find Stubbs, he was still unconscious or at least pretending to be. Moving my eyes hurt bad enough, but moving my head to determine my surrounds brought on severe vertigo.

We weren't tied up. We were locked into a large timbered room with a dirt floor. Both of us were haphazardly deposited and left on the ground. My watch was missing so I had no idea what time it was. The only thing I knew for sure was that it was daylight. I could see low levels of light between the trees that were fashioned together to form our prison walls. The warps and knots were big enough to let in a small amount of light, but not a large enough spaces between to allow any view outside those walls.

I began to dig at the earth at the bottom of one wall with my hands to see if I could dig out of the prison. I heard a knocking on the timber on the other side of where my hands were. Then many knocks. The more I dug, the more attention I was getting from something on the other side of the wall. Before I could determine what it was, or dig a big enough hole underneath, a large thud came outside the main door to the front of the room.

The thud was followed by what sounded like a large piece of wood sliding on the other side of our prison door. That door opened and the Latino man from the path entered, again he was not alone with two armed men behind him.

The two thugs were holding Heckler and Koch *MP5A3* submachine guns. I'm not sure why they needed them, we were unarmed. The men were also of Latin descent, but their weapons indicated that they were likely from Mexico. I had traced one back on a previous case some years prior to Mexico, the *MP5A3* is the weapon of choice for cartels and military-types there.

"I see that you are awake. Your friend was not subdued quite as smoothly as you, it may take him some time to regain consciousness. My name is Dr. Enrique Estabados, but you probably know that already."

"If you are a doctor, then what the hell are you doing? Isn't it part of your oath or something to do no harm?"

"Ah, yes. That would be my preference. Alas, when it comes to medical research, it seems that if you do not strike first; you end up penniless, unknown, and useless."

"I don't get it. You had a good thing going over at BIOGENESIS, why kill those people and risk it all to go to a start-up like Nahash?"

"I didn't 'go over to Nahash'. I have always worked for Nahash. BIOGENESIS funded my work at the World Toxin Bank, and they refused to allow those venom samples to be studied by other factions. Namely Nahash, despite my employer's very generous donations. Very selfish of them."

"So you killed those people to shut down the project over there?"

"What are you talking about?"

"The three murders in Charleston. Seems a bit strong, even for a guy like you."

"I didn't kill anyone in Charleston. I left BIOGENESIS after I attained the necessary data for Nahash. There was no reason to kill anyone."

"So standing there with the guys behind you holding assault rifles, you are trying to tell me that your departure just happened to coincide with the deaths of three employees over there. You didn't hit my head that hard."

The look on his face was a mixture of puzzlement and anger. It was a good act, but I didn't really want to stick around for an encore.

"You can't keep us here. People know we're here and why."

"Oh, don't worry about me. I would worry more about yourself. You see, in this very unique ecosystem, your bodies will never be found. Accidents happen in the rainforest all of the time. Two American men trying to shakedown a research team in this vast land? Anything can happen."

"We have already made contact with people out here. How long do you think it will take for someone to figure out that after them, we ran into you?"

"You mean the college kids from the University of Chicago? How do you think we found you?"

He turned to leave with his rent-a-thugs but stopped short of the door.

"One more thing. If you continue to dig under that wall you find a most inhospitable creature waiting to attack you. There is a caged moat on the other side filled with Bothrops Aspers. Not only will you be trapped in yet another cage, but you will be trapped with hundreds of creatures that are hungry and will enjoy eating you. Good Day."

I didn't know what one of those things were, but I was sure that I was alright with not finding out.

13

NIGHTFALL CAME, OR IT BECAME DARK, in the part of the rainforest that we were in. Either way it was pitch black in the large prison. What I lacked in sight I also lacked in sound. Other than rain drops on the roof that was fifteen feet above us, and the movement of the creepy-crawlies on the other side of the wall, I couldn't hear shit. Neither could Stubbs.

He woke up after the dark had already come. He grumbled and groaned which is how I knew he was alive and awake. It took me some time to convince him that he wasn't blind. To be honest, I wasn't entirely sure that he wasn't. It was so dark in that cage that he could have been. Had I not seen what the room looked like during the day, I might have thought the same thing.

I explained to him the exchange Estabados and I had; and that if we could somehow manage to get beyond the things thumping on the walls at us, we still had armed soldier-types beyond them.

115

It was so quiet in there that our whispers were like we were shouting. Who knows who was listening, and for that matter who cares? We were going to die there unless we figured something out and quick.

There was another big thud followed by the same wood latch that had occurred before. It was a first for Stubbs so I was explaining that someone was coming to chat with us, maybe feed us, when the door opened.

Neither of us could see who was at the door. Whomever it was, they didn't speak, nor were they at the door very long. They threw something toward us and re-latched the door. We both thought it was food, and we were both hungry. We blindly crawled on the ground, feeling our way toward it.

He found it first. "It's a body. It's alive but must be knocked out like we were."

"Shit," I said. I went to lie back and had a pillow. I felt around and realized that there was another body deposited into the prison with us. This one was female, for sure because in attempting to feel a heartbeat I inadvertently felt up her breast. She too was unconscious. Thankfully. "There is another one. This one is a girl."

"Mine is a boy."

We both felt around to see if there was a third or more but we didn't feel any. More mouths to feed and no food. I wondered if they were going to starve us to death.

For the third night in a row I wasn't able to sleep. I was definitely exhausted, but the thought that I would soon be in a forever kind of sleep made me not want to.

I am what you would call a recovering Catholic. I was brought up very devout. But although I was Baptized, had my First Communion, and Confirmed, I never really lived according to the way I was told. In my Irish-

Catholic neighborhood, nobody did. I stole shit and then went to church on Sunday to get my Jesus Biscuit. I still went to that same church in Southie for funerals, weddings, maybe the odd 'high holiday'. I feel like a hypocrite every time I enter the Cathedral of the Holy Cross, on Washington Street. When your Catholic, you are guilty for even thinking about a sin, never mind when you actually commit one.

But I ain't gonna kid ya, I prayed that night. I prayed like my maker was in the room. Nobody knows for one hundred percent certainty what happens after you die. But I was one hundred percent certain that I was going to find out in short order. So I begged. I would deal with the hypocrisy if I lived.

The daylight began to seep through the slats of our wood walls. Little by little I could see the inside of the room. It didn't take my eyes long to adjust, they seemed to welcome light. The bodies that were thrown into our cell were those of the kids that we had seen the day prior. The kids from the University of Chicago. But there were only two of them.

I'm not sure if Stubbs was silently praying along with me through the night, but I was sure that he was wide awake. He was from the bible belt, so my guess is that he had his own conversation.

"Mornin'," I said.

"Yeah great."

"Believe me, I was hoping to wake up to someone different on my last day alive too."

"We're not going to die today."

"Really? You've got an idea of how we are gonna to get outta here?"

"I do."

"You must be my guardian angel. I'm all ears."

"I've still got my knife in my boot. I don't have anything else in my pockets, but they didn't find the knife. You said that we can't go under the wall, so we go over it."

"I hate to be the pessimist here, Stubbs, but that has to be fifteen feet up."

"Look at it. It's just brush lashing. I'm the biggest person here so I'll be on the bottom and hoist you up. You grab the little Asian girl and send her through. Depending on how heavy the other kid is, he might be able to go up also. They go for help. If those guys come in we ambush them and take their weapons."

"If we go out, we go out with a bang …. kinda-thing."

"Right. And the kids go for help. They must have some way of communicating their data back to their labs. That's what they said yesterday right? Lets hope they can communicate that we need help in time."

"You're the boss. I like the plan. Lotta shit can go wrong with it, but I like it."

The young Asian college student was awake but pretending to sleep. "Why can't we go under the wall? Over seems much more difficult."

"Because they have some bother aspirins or creepy-crawly that eats people on the other side of the walls," I said.

"Bothrops Aspers?"

"Yeah, that's it."

"If that is the case then we have to get out of here soon. Over or whatever. Those are the most excitable and vicious type of snake in this region, arguably on the planet. They move with unbelievable quickness and their venom causes; hemoptysis, gastrointestinal bleeding, hematuria, impaired consciousness, spleen issues, and localized necrosis, which means that even if you had an antivenin at the ready, you would have to amputate the limb that they bit."

I froze.

I'm not sure where my fear of snakes was born, maybe when I was born. But it is a fear that has complete control over me.

The fear that I speak of is so pervasive, so deep, that it is all-consuming. Not a hundred mile an hour puck shot at your unprotected face kind of fear. Not that split-second before a car that is speeding toward you is about to hit you; and *if* your survive, your life as you know it is over, kind of fear. Not Freddy Krueger. The fear that I speak of is beyond rational. Beyond fight or flight. The fear stops all bodily function. I mean pant-wetting terror. There is no word or phrase to describe it. If you've never felt this level of fear, count yourself lucky.

"Oh fuck me. Snakes? This is not good. This is not good." I began to pace about the dirt floor. "I get it, they're bad-asses. Why the urgency?"

"We are studying them because their venom is so potent, attacking so many specific targets that affect so many different things, that they could be the key to curing vast numbers of varying diseases. Also their venom changes with diet, which means that their venom mutates. They reproduce exponentially faster than any other snake in this environment so mutations occur faster than we can identify them."

"Kid. Enough of the science lesson. I fuckin' hate snakes. Terrified, actually. Why the urgency?"

"If we are surrounded by them, and as fast as they reproduce, with us being the only source of food .... the only thing that *is* predictable is that they *will* find a way through these walls."

"Oh fuck me. I'm gonna lose my mind. Stubbs. What do we do?"

"Your friends are going to miss you, right? They are probably already on their way with help," Stubbs asked Naomi, Nanimi, or whatever the Asian girl's name was.

She sat up and her face was a big puffy mess. She had been slapped around and crying. "My colleagues are all dead. Samuel and I are the only two that weren't slaughtered. They were after our research and you two. Mostly you two."

"Us two? How did Estabados know we were here?" Stubbs was looking at me but asking the girl.

"Estabados? Dr. Estabados? No no. We were attacked by soldiers after you left."

"And they work for Estabados," I said.

Stubbs went over to the kid she had called Samuel and tried to wake him up. "Miss? Your friend didn't make it either. The smack to his head must have created a brain-bleed. Cerebral Hemorrhaging. He was alive when they brought you here last night, but he's dead now."

She began to cry again and convulse uncontrollably. I tried to console her but she shoved me off. "This is all your fault. Why did you have to come into our camp? We've been here for months without issue. Why do they want you? We are all going to die because of you."

"Listen kid. I'm sorry, but this isn't our fault. This guy killed people back in South Carolina, and he was going to find and kill you no matter if we were here or not. You said yourself he wanted your research. We have to get it together and get the fuck outta here before we join the rest of your friends."

She wiped her eyes and tried to compose herself. Stubbs handed her his Gerber *Air Ranger* knife and re-explained the plan.

".... and be careful because this thing is sharp. Razor sharp. Like lightsaber sharp. It is made of surgical steel and will take off one of your limbs as easily as those tree limbs above us."

She nodded like she understood. The time that it had taken Stubbs to go over the plan had given her much needed time to collect herself.

I went to the door and listened to see if I could hear anyone coming, but I couldn't hear anything. Besides, after hearing the kid tell us with wonderful detail what was on the other side of those walls, I didn't get too close.

"I can't hear shit. Let's just go."

Stubbs quickly hoisted me onto his shoulders like I was his pet hampster. He reached up and held the back of my pants while I stood on his shoulders and pulled the girl up. She helped by walking up the front of Stubbs. Once she was sitting on my shoulders she began to hack away at the brush above us. It was working rather quickly and we determined that it was already raining outside because the hole she cut was already soaking us with rainwater.

Maybe it was because everything was so quiet, but the escape attempt seemed to be making a lot of noise. Thankfully it took her less than five minutes to cut a hole just larger than she was to climb through.

"What's up there?" I asked.

"They have a camp set up like us. We are toward the back of it. I can't see the other side of the cell."

"You're really light, do you think the roof will hold you?"

"Yes, but I'm not sure about you. Definitely not the big guy."

"OK. Pull yourself up, then close the knife and drop it back down to us."

Stubbs objected. If you can get up there, you should go too. She will have a much better chance of getting out of here if she has help."

"No way pal. We're getting outta here together."

The girl wasn't going to wait while we decided, I was still talking with Stubbs when the knife hit the dirt by his feet. And just like that, she was gone.

"Well that solves that."

I came down off of his shoulders in time to hear the big thud. The prison door was about to be opened again. The second part of the plan was going into immediate effect.

We both quickly took positions behind where the door would open, as the wooden latch was being manipulated. It was time to do or die. Literally.

14

JACOB GRANTES PARKED HIS VOLVO *XC90* in the parking lot of the Leath Correctional Institution for women. As usual he tried to find a spot in the shade, under a tree perhaps, because the sun was ablaze. The early afternoons of early summer in Charleston, South Carolina are the hottest of the day. They can be the hottest of the year. But those were prime spaces long taken by mid-morning, let alone by the time he had arrived well after the noon hour.

He rode the Ford *Econoline* van from the booth in the parking lot up to the prison where he needed to check in. Regardless of visitor; family member, or attorney, there were protocols for check-in. He did so every time he came to see his client and girlfriend. He had done so when he brought Deni there just two days prior. In the ten days since Sierra Byrne had been incarcerated, there were not many that went by where he didn't visit.

"Attorney Jacob Grantes to see inmate Sierra Byrne."

It almost killed him to say it out loud. To announce, even to the guards, that the new love of his life was spending her days as he had once spent a six month span. He felt for her. He knew all-too-well what it was like inside the razor-wire. To be wrongly accused and treated like societal scum. The refuse that nobody wanted to live with or near.

He went inside a room where she was already waiting. It was unusual for her to be waiting for him, it was usually the other way around. He had called and set the appointment up in advance, which he had almost always done. The guards were either getting used to the visits or it was a slow day.

"Jay. Oh thank goodness. What's going on? Any progress?"

He sat down across from her. The beauty that was once outward, for the world to see, was now getting buried deep inside of her. He could see the toll this new life was taking on her.

"We have a lead. Deni and Stubbs are working on it."

"Who did it? Who killed those people?"

"Did you know that Dr. Enrique Estabados was working for Nahash the entire time he was working with you? While he was working for the WTB and BIOGENESIS?"

"What? Of course not. Are you sure?"

"Quite."

"That explains his frustration with the WTB not being open for some of the other research institutions that were requesting access. His ideas about intellectual property were almost Communistic. The current arrangement can get a bit political. The more invested an organization was in Toxicology, Herpetology, and Venomology as demonstrated by their research and large investments into the WTB, the more access they would get to the samples held there. With competition being what it is, not all facilities can afford to keep up with investment required to have the greatest access. Enrique believed that the cures to what ails all humans were but a few short years away if all would be allowed access to the research, regardless of contribution."

"Well that doesn't jibe with what we are seeing. His altruism seemed to end at the front door to Nahash. He is and has been the number one guy over there in Venomology. Specifically snake venom. The CEO over there — "

" — Rueben Feinstein. I know Rueben. He offered me almost double my salary to leave SCMU, BIOGENESIS and continue my research with Nahash. I told him it was pointless because my research was protected under confidentiality clauses. Also, I would no longer be able to teach, tenured or not. But he persisted and checked in on me regularly to see if I was happy with my decision. He seemed to be a snake in the grass himself."

"Right. So he was the one that ordered Estabados to, uh, appropriate the valuable research. They are also making a bid to send Wyatt to number one over PROXER Pharmaceuticals. You are smack in the middle of a huge business war in Big Pharma. We are going to continue to attain evidence against them, provide as much reasonable doubt as possible. But at the end of the day, these two organizations are worth hundreds of billions of dollars. If not a trillion. My entire firm is going to use all of our resources, but if they dig their feet in? We cannot keep up. Those poor victims may never get justice."

"Oh Jay. That's awful. Not to sound crass, but what will that mean for me?"

"That is one of the worst parts of all of this. The fact is that once we bring all of the evidence to bear, the DA may decide to settle for low hanging fruit instead of fighting Goliath without having the necessary resources. That low hanging fruit being you."

"Isn't that against the law? You can't morally prosecute someone you know didn't commit a crime because punishing the right one is inconvenient. Can you?" She began to cry.

"Morally or ethically? No. But legally? We would have to prove malicious prosecution, which means we would have to prove you were innocent at trial. You wouldn't be locked up in the first place if the jury found you innocent. Unfortunately its like I tell my students, the lady with the scales is not blind. She is peaking. The District Attorney is an elected position. He would rather have a fighting chance at putting someone away as a serial murder, than being outgunned and out matched, likely being embarrassed. He can't win reelection that way. If they lose prosecuting you, he blames the jury. If he gets embarrassed, the public can only blame him."

"This can't be happening." She was a sobbing mess. The ten days she had already spent in prison, the culmination of stress and anxiety now combined with the realization that it could continue for the rest of her life, was more than she could endure. "Will they seek the death penalty?"

"Probably. Yes. But we will fight that to the bitter end. That would be years of appeals."

"No. If I am found guilty, even though I'm not, I don't want to live like this."

"Let's not go there. We are nowhere near that yet. I was just outlining the very real possibilities. That is why I have my best man on it. Deni has never let me down. He saved me from the very situation that you face, once upon a time."

"I trust you. I trust your judgement in him."

"Good. Because we need to talk about that very thing," he said.

"Trust? I know."

"I lied to the police, which is a felony. I was not with you the night of the third murder, as you well know. I lied because I was corroborating your story that you told the police. Which was the same lie, the same felony.

"Whatever you tell me, it will not affect our relationship. But as your attorney, I need to know where you were," he continued.

"I didn't lie. I *was* with you. You just didn't know it."

"But that's impossible. I was with .... Jenna. You followed me to meet Jenna."

125

"You're ex."

"But why? It was over between us. I left her for you."

"Men don't leave a woman that looks like that. Not in my experience."

"Sierra. I love you. I was married to a beauty, she turned out be a tortured soul. I was with Jenna who was also beautiful, but we didn't truly match either. You are gorgeous inside and out. I love you, Brady loves you. You have nothing to be jealous or suspicious of."

"Yeah well .... my jealousy has come back to bite me in the ass."

"More than you know. If this goes to trial, we have to try and justify you lying to the police. Then we have to convince a jury that you are not lying to them."

Sierra shook her head and looked down at her hands that were cuffed and resting on the table between them.

"This hole just keeps getting deeper."

"You don't know the half of it. Your juvenile record. Care to enlighten me?"

"My juvenile record? How could anyone know? How do you know? Those records are supposed to be sealed. Expunged."

"Not when you are accused of being a serial killer. They look at all of that stuff."

"This can't be happening."

"It is, so you had better explain. I hate to ask, but I am going to find out sooner or later if this goes to trial. I found out from Deni, who got it from the investigating detective. The DA has it and is sitting on it. They will have to give it to me eventually, but it would be best if you tell me now. I don't want to be ambushed."

"I have worked so hard to put that all behind me. To leave it all in the closet. It was supposed to stay there. Isn't that what expunged means?"

"Yes. But as I said, those things never really go away. And it obviously ties in with your current situation, so please just tell me. No judgements, I promise."

"My mother had a live-in boyfriend after my parents divorced. He seemed so at first, but he was not a nice guy."

She looked into her hands that rested on the table between them. There was a long silence which JG let linger for some time.

"Go on."

"As I developed, he was more hands-on. Especially when my mother wasn't around. I kept trying to get away from him, spend as little time as possible alone with him. But one day it went too far."

"And?"

"And I stabbed the son-of-a-bitch. Calling 9-1-1 was the worst thing I could have done. Had he actually taken my virginity, I might have had a case. I can't tell you how many times that I look back and wish that he had died. But he didn't. And he claimed that I snapped and came at him with a knife. My own mother didn't believe me. Then it got really out of control."

"Worse than that?"

"Yes. I was really into science, still am obviously. I found biology fascinating at that time, and I was doing a lot of dissections. My biology teacher would allow me to do extra credit by getting me extra specimens. I was able to learn specialized biology on real frogs, cats, sheep brains …. whatever she could get her hands on."

"So what?"

"So they said that it was an unhealthy fascination with death and killing. That I was a disturbed kid and that is why I attacked my would-be stepfather."

"I'm so sorry Sierra. What happened then?"

"My biological father came to the rescue and saved me. My biology teacher helped as well, but the damage was done. I pled out and had to see a counselor, but that was the end of it. I had never been in any trouble, nor had I after that. I had the entire thing expunged, I didn't want it to follow me even though I was never actually convicted of anything."

"I see. You know why they want to bring that into evidence, don't you? They are going to look at your juvenile case, and use it as evidence that you had a fascination back then, carried it into the serial killing as an adult."

"How can they do that, Jay? I didn't do anything wrong then, and I didn't kill anyone now."

"They are profiling you. Serial murderers don't just get sick one day and run loose on a community. They start off young, usually killing pets. That is what they are going to use to put you away. Or worse, give you the needle."

"You believe me, don't you?"

"Of course I do."

"You will make a jury see that these are all just a series of unfortunate circumstances? That each one was unproven but all together look bad?"

"I'm going to try and make sure that it doesn't come to that. Juries are fickle. Unpredictable. If the State is allowed to use your past records, records that were supposed to be sealed? That hole that you mentioned will be too deep to come out of. That hole will be the death of you."

15

THE LATCH ON THE DOOR TO THE MAKESHIFT PRISON cell was lifted and set aside. Stubbs and I waited on the back side of the door, waiting to see who and how many would enter the room. At the last second before it opened, Stubbs unfolded his Gerber *Air Ranger* knife in preparation for battle. I was behind him, ready to reallocate any weapon I could from any or all of the men that would enter.

"Whatever happens," Stubbs whispered, "there's no way this ends but grimly."

The door opened and the first guard walked through, fixing his gaze on the corpse of Samuel, the student from Chicago. The second guard was walking through when Stubbs shoved the door, knocking Estabados onto the ground in the front corner of the cell. The two guards turned around but too late. I have never seen anyone move as quickly as Stubbs did at that moment. For someone his size, it was almost a miracle.

Stubbs threw his knife at the first guard who was turning around to see what the commotion was. The blade landed at the base of the surprised guard's neck. It lodged in the dimple where the neck meets the clavicle, above his chest. The blow rendered him incapacitated as he tried to free the knife from his trachea, but it had severed the vagus nerve. His heart was speeding up faster than the initial adrenaline shock. I was quick to relieve him of his weapon, the *MP5A3.*

Immediately after throwing his knife, Stubbs pulled the second guard towards him. He used one hand on the sentry's throat, and the other to snap his left elbow, using Stubb's right armpit as a lever to hyperextend it. The left hand was the man's gun hand, the weapon dropping to ground and behind the still slightly opened door. Weaponless, with a broken elbow and wrist, and being choked to death, the guard put up no further fight.

Estabados began to crawl from his corner toward the cracked door, hesitating presumably to decide whether or not to get the other *MP5A3* which lay at the base of Stubb's feet near the door.

His hesitation gave me enough time to go around Stubbs and put the barrel of my rifle on his left temple. All parties were subdued without a shot being fired which was our unspoken, secondary goal. We both found it unrealistic in our own minds at the time. I know I had my doubts.

"Not so fast *Doctor.* How many men are out there?"

He didn't speak.

"Deni, we gotta get outta here. Look in the corner. Snakes are about to breach." He had shoved the second guard toward that corner and was retrieving his knife.

"Take me with you. You cannot leave me in here. My work is too important."

"You are gonna pay for those deaths, that's why you're coming along."

Stubbs returned his knife to his boot, commandeered the second gun, and we shut the door behind us trapping the two guards.

Outside, the snakes were agitated. Either by us or by their exertions at getting inside the makeshift prison cell. By the time we had latched the door and raised the bridge over the moat to the cell, the second guard was screaming.

I nearly shit my pants at the sight of them. There must have been thousands of snakes surrounding the cage from whence we came. The girl had told us that they were 'excitable and quick moving'. She undersold it. Those vipers were fuckin' hideous.

How I had managed to keep it together is still a mystery. The sight of a solitary, common, garter snake makes me catatonic. That was infinitely more horrifying. But I did hold it together and move away from there fast. Coming down the hill toward the main part of the camp, I was looking around to see if I could find the girl from Chicago. I didn't see her.

"Stubbs, do you see the girl?"

"No, but we are starting to attract attention. Put your gun to the Doctor's head and stay behind him. We gotta find a way outta here."

That is when the first shots were fired. The dirt and trees around us started to spit. We were being shot at from above, as the trajectory was toward the ground. Estabados had been hit. He was wailing and bleeding as I tried to drag him out of the line of fire, but using him as a shield. Stubbs ran around me, trying to lead the way. There was no way he could use either Estabados or me as a shield. He was larger than both of us combined.

Stubbs took the lead position, dragging us both behind him. Red spit from him and onto me as I lay a blanket of cover fire toward the militia firing at us. I thought of Carina and how she described Stubbs. "Don't make him mad," she said, "he's like a bruin in body armor." She was right.

I have no idea to this day how many I hit, or if I hit any at all. When my magazine was empty, which didn't take long, Stubbs tossed me his weapon from the front of our line. We were almost out of the clearing and into the deep rainforest again. I continued to fire blindly hoping to curtail the bullets being showered upon us. I stopped firing once all three of us were safely under the cover of the natural canopy.

"Keep moving. As fast as you can go," Stubbs yelled. He continued to lead us, but we were not on a path. It was raining so I could not see then sun, could not tell in which direction we were traveling.

I checked the clip to see how many rounds I had left. Four. Including the one in the chamber. I cursed myself for not thinking to check the guards for extra ammunition before leaving them in their death chamber.

We were beginning to slow down. Stubbs's heavy breathing could be heard above the nonsense that Estabados was jabbering.

I began to wonder if Stubbs was going to make it at all. He was lumbering, obviously losing steam. I knew he was hit, but from behind him I couldn't tell how badly. He stopped for a moment, forcing us to stop behind him. I was not sure if it was to regain his breath or strength, or if he needed to recalibrate his sense of direction. The seconds of waiting seemed like minutes.

Before I could ask him, the ground from underneath us gave way. All three of us fell and landed on the soft bottom of large pit dug into the earth. We were surrounded by the fallen brush that had covered the excavation. We were all laying at the bottom of that large hole dug into the earth, when I saw another horrifying sight.

It took me a few seconds to try and regain my composure, preventing myself from screaming in both fear and anger.

"Stubbs, you ok?"

"No, I'm hit pretty bad. You?" His voice was weak and garbled.

I began to take inventory. I touched a spot on my shoulder which hurt like hell. My hand came back crimson. "I think I got nicked, but I'll live."

"I've been shot also," the doctor said.

"Who gives a fuck? Stubbs. Do you see where we are?"

He was looking around the pit, getting as misty and as emotional as I was. He was cursing and mumbling something, but I didn't quite make out what. We were lying at the bottom of a deep crater, on top of dozens of dead bodies. Corner to corner, tall dirt wall to wall, the floor of the pit was covered two and three corpses deep. The most recent was an Asian girl wearing a t-shirt from the University of Chicago.

16

JG WAS LEAVING THE LEATH CORRECTIONAL INSTITUTION for women, when he noticed the front page of the newspaper. He was waiting for his van ride back to the parking lot when he noticed the guard in the reception/ waiting area reading the Charleston Post and Courier. On the front page, above the fold, was a picture of a striking woman with the heading:

Charleston Police Searching for Missing Detective

"Excuse me. May I see the front page please? The missing detective." He pointed toward the picture on the outside of the front section. The female guard lowered the newspaper, looked at JG in his suit, and decided that it was a grantable request.

He read the article which gave him very few details. The police were seeking information from anyone who has information as to her whereabouts. She was last seen at her desk in the precinct. Her issued police sedan had a GPS tracking device which led them to her car. The sedan was found behind an abandoned church, in a rarely used graveyard, down by the Atlantic Ocean. The police vehicle had been set on fire, however no human remains were detected. Both the graveyard and the coast had been searched, though a dive team was still combing the ocean floor. There was no evidence as to her disposition in her apartment, and neither her family nor her friends have heard from her. She had been missing for three days and foul play was suspected.

"Holy shit."

"Do you know her, Sir?" the guard asked.

"Yes. Sort of. She investigated the case that I am currently defending. I know more *of* her than know her personally."

"It's a crazy world we live in."

"For sure. How long before the van gets here? I have to go down to the precinct on Broad. I just might have some information that might be useful."

"It should be pulling up any minute."

When JG arrived at the Crimes Against Persons Department of the Charleston Police on 80 Broad Street, the place was abustle. Nobody was paying him any mind because they had their hands full. Charleston, South Carolina is a small city in comparison to the Los Angeleses, New Yorks, or even the Bostons of the United States. Homicides happen. People go missing. But to have serial murders and the detective who investigated them disappear, did not happen. Not in Charleston. Bigger cities, maybe. Movies and video games certainly. This was chaos.

JG spied the directory and identified where the Homicide Division was located. He made his way there, through the thickets of people, progressing slowly but surely. The sea of people were scattered about the sea of desks. There weren't enough seats for all of the parties having business there. It was a real grab-bag of characters. Police, suspects, witnesses, homeless, and others all piled into one area. None of it making any sense as all were screaming like it was the opening bell of the New York Stock Exchange.

There was one solitary man off to the side in his office. The African-American's shirtsleeves were rolled up, the knot in his tie loosely hanging below the top two, unfastened buttons of his shirt. He looked disheveled and if stress had a picture, that was it. The closed door was labeled 'Captain Simms'.

JG continued to fight the congestion, making his way to the door. He didn't knock, he just stepped inside the tiny office.

"I don't want to hear it. Somebody outside will take your statement. You'll have to wait in line like everyone else," the Captain said.

"Captain, I am Jacob Grantes. The attorney for Doctor Sierra Byrne. I am working the case that Detective Fischer worked, which implicated my client."

"Not a good time counselor. You barge in here wanting us to do what? Drop the case because the Detective has gone missing? The DA has the case, it is off of our desk. Now get the hell out of my office. I have a decorated cop that I need to find and my patience is wearing thin."

It looked like his patience had worn thin a long time ago, but JG left it alone.

"Captain, that is why I am here. I think I might be able to help in finding her."

He now had Captain Simms's full attention. He straightened up in his chair, began to button the top buttons on his shirt and straighten his tie.

"You know where she is? Is she alive? Did your client orchestrate her disappearance? I will have no truck with allowing her to take out one of my detectives. She is going to pay — "

" - CAPTAIN! My client had nothing to do with the deaths of those people at SCMU and BIOGENESIS, nor did she have anything to do with Detective Fischer's disappearance. In investigating who may have been involved in the killings as an alternate theory for the trial, we uncovered some very troubling information. That information was disclosed to your detective and now she is missing. You don't have to be a whiz to connect the dots. Will you hear me out? Before it is too late?"

Over the course of the next hour, JG went into detail about Nahash Pharmaceuticals and Rueben Feinstein. He set aside his legal obligations about lawyer-client privilege and confidentiality clauses and gave him all of the information. Two women's lives were at stake. Sierra in terms of her freedom and Carina in the very literal sense. Both men hoped it was not too late.

He told the Captain about the underbelly of Big Pharma. He told him about Dr. Enrique Estabados and his duplicity. He told him about everything that Stubbs and Deni had come up with, but were still lacking in hard evidence. JG divulged that his two investigators were currently in Costa Rica attempting to bring back Estabados who was there either hiding, conducting research, or both. He explained that without proof there was little legally that could be done but that his investigators were getting around the red-tape. He even confessed, off-the-record, about he and Sierra's false statements to the police.

There was some volleying back and forth. Mostly because the Captain had questions or needed clarification. But overall the conversation was civil and without interruption in spite of the commotion outside his office.

".... and you think that Rueben Feinstein has abducted, and possibly done worse, to Detective Fischer because she was re-examining this case."

"I don't know for sure if she was re-opening the case. You would know that better than I, she reports to you. What I do know is that Estabados is about a football field beyond being a suspect. I know that he worked for Feinstein at Nahash and that they are trying to move their parent company, Wyatt to the number one spot over PROXER. The two companies generate hundreds of billions of dollars annually, and people have killed for much less. My investigators were nosing around, that is how they found out about Estabados being in Costa Rica. They had been in contact with your detective, the same detective who was assigned the serial murders. If she started .... digging .... her .... nose .... "

JG's voice trailed off as he started to reassess all of the moving pieces. His face became pale and panic was apparent on his face. Captain Simms was trying to determine what had just happened.

"Counselor? What is it?"

"We have to get over to Nahash. Right now. I'm coming with you, end of story. I'll explain on the way."

17

THE CONVOY OF MARKED AND UNMARKED POLICE CRUISERS raced toward Summerville, South Carolina. The lead car was a Patrol Unit with two officers clearing traffic with lights and loud sirens. The regular traffic was moving aside in panic and yet thankful that the six police vehicles loaded with officers were not interested in them. No accidents were caused because of the disruption, but there were some close calls.

The officer in the passenger seat of the front vehicle shot out of the car before it had come to a complete stop when they approached the main gate of Nahash Pharmaceuticals. He drew his weapon and restrained the guard who occupied the booth. The policeman then opened the gate to the remaining five vehicles which could now race through. Only they didn't know where they were going.

"Which building is Rueben Feinstein in?" the officer demanded.

"Man, I should have listened to that other police lady. I need a new job."

"What other police lady?"

"The one that was here the other day. She wanted to see the boss too. Admin building is all the way down at the end of this main road."

The officer removed the guard from his post and deposited him into the back of the cruiser for further questioning as they all made their way to their destination.

There were twelve people in all that barged into the lobby of the Administrative Building, including eight patrolmen, two detectives, Captain Simms, and the attorney Jacob Grantes. The Receptionist, Jeffrey, was being overdramatic and feigning a heart attack. Whether he was actually under duress or if he was stalling for time was anyone's guess. Either way it didn't work. He too was placed in custody while the remainder of the troop ascended to the office of the CEO and President.

There were many men in dark suits a-la FBI or Secret Service, but all relinquished their weapons and stood aside. Highly paid security is trumped by a police team with an arrest warrant. At least it was in this case.

In the digital age, a warrant can be signed by a judge and scanned, then sent digitally to an arresting officer. There are several cases currently on appeal where a judicial opinion is pending, so the police department has deemed not in best practice. It is still done, however, in exigent circumstances. In this case, Captain Simms had the arrest warrant on his iPad mini because time was a factor.

The arrest warrant also gives the police the right to search the property if they feel the object of the warrant is hidden inside. Captain Simms was able to convince a judge that not only was Detective Fischer likely on Nahash Property but that Rueben Feinstein was complicit in her disappearance. There wasn't much in the way of hard proof, but judges tend to air on the side of the police when one goes missing.

Rueben Feinstein was sitting as his desk on the telephone when the police burst into his office. Shock was not even the word for the look upon his face.

"…. what the!? I will have to call you back." He hung up the phone and stood. "What is the meaning of this?"

Captain Simms held up his tablet. "Rueben Feinstein, we have a warrant for your arrest for abduction and accessory to murder. Please place your hands on your head and slowly walk toward us from behind your desk. We have the right to search the entire complex for Detective Carina Fischer, but you can save us all some time and energy. Just tell us where she is."

He complied with the request, slowly coming from behind his desk with his hands on his head, but he protested the reason.

"There is a grave mistake officer."

"Captain."

"Captain, there has been a mistake. I have no idea what you are talking about. Murders? I have not abducted anyone. Your detective left here, at my insistence, two or three days ago. I am sure that my security surveillance can verify that."

"But you admit that she was here."

"Of course. I called the hotline to say as much when I saw that she was missing on the nightly news."

The Captain looked at JG and then at his officers. "Cuff him and set him down over there on the couch. We are going to get to the bottom of this."

He called the squad and had someone there listen to all of the messages that had come in on the hotline but hung up as he did not wish to wait. They would call him back.

"Do you have a place where we could look at your CCTV footage?"

"Of course, Sir. Any one of my security staff can bring it up on my computer screen or the television inside that cabinet. I would do it myself but I am a bit tied up at the moment," Rueben said.

JG was incensed. "Captain. You can't be seriously entertaining this madman. He has had three days to doctor the footage and get his story straight in case we came calling. He ordered the murders of three people, surely manipulating video footage is not beyond comprehension."

"Quiet counselor. You are here as a courtesy."

One of the suited security men was brought into the enormous corner office by one of the Charleston patrolmen. He then pushed some buttons onto the massive touch-screen hidden inside the cabinet that Rueben had pointed to. It took a few minutes but the footage of Detective Carina Fischer came up on a few of the smaller screens that were split onto the large one. The security man then pushed another button or two on the right task bar and only the smaller screens in which Carina appeared were displayed, the rest had disappeared from view.

All of them watched her as she entered the complex at the main gate, headed to the building and office in which they were all currently. She was agitated and speaking to them in body language as there was no sound. The security team assembled behind her and after some conversation she was escorted by them to her car in the parking lot. She was then seen exiting the complex in her car out of the main gate.

The entire length of the demonstration was played in real-time, the onlookers watched and were absorbed in it all. It was played again so each person could try to identify anything that might indicate tampering, but nothing was found.

"You see? She left here as she came. She was spouting off accusations and quips, just as you have. All of them unfounded," Rueben said.

Captain Simms looked around the office, paced it actually, while he thought. He looked at JG then at the floor, shaking his head.

"Mr. Feinstein, we are bringing you in for questioning as you may have knowledge of a number of unsolved felonies," he said to the room.

"I will read you your rights although you are not officially a suspect. We need to have a serious chat. The pause was palpable, then Simms continued.

"You have the right to remain silent, anything you say or do can …. "

Once all of the confusion was winding down in the penthouse office of the CEO and President of Nahash Pharmaceuticals, the officers made their way down to their respective vehicles. One by one they waited out in front of the building for the Captain and his guests. They had arrived in a convoy, they were leaving as one.

Many of them were milling about. The two who had led the team, who currently had the main-gate security guard in cuffs in the back of their patrol car, were questioning him. They took turns firing questions. They were not playing 'good cop, bad cop'. They were both aggressive.

"What did you mean earlier when you said that the detective told you to find another job?"

"That was the second time this week that someone told me to find a different job. I really want to. I hate this job," he said.

"Go on."

"These two private investigators came and told me they could get me one with them if I let them in. So I did. And got in deep shit for it. So when this detective chick came, I kinda gave her a hard time cuz I was already on a shit list. I hate the job, but I still need it."

"Yeah, Yeah. Then what?"

"So I let her in. And after I do, then these protesters start raising hell by the gate. It took me a while to try and get rid of them but they wouldn't leave until the detective came out," he continued.

"What do you mean?"

"These religious nuts said that what we were doing was an anomaly or —
"

" — an anathema?"

"Sure. Whatever. One woman in particular. Said that Nahash was an abomination, against the will of God. I knew I needed to get rid of them, maybe I could get off the shit list. But they wouldn't budge. I stopped the police lady when she came out of the complex because I thought protesters had to have a permit or something to assemble. She said it wasn't her department but all of the God-fearers left right after she came through the gate."

"You're sure it went down like that? We didn't see that on the CCTV footage when she was leaving."

"Yeah, I'm sure. I was off to the side dealing with the assholes. They weren't on camera, so when she pulled up to where I was, she must have been off camera too."

The two patrolmen looked at each other then exited the car. They ran toward the entrance to the building where their Captain was walking out toward them.

They yelled to him in unison, "Captain .... "

18

THE THREE OF US WERE STANDING at the bottom of an earthen pit with dozens of dead bodies in the middle of the Costa Rican rainforest. The situation was dire and getting more so. It was nearly impossible to think. The people on top of whom we stood had lives and families and friends. Had. Until the man between Stubbs and I had come into contact with them. The smell could have gagged a maggot. I hadn't eaten anything since the day before or I would have vomited. The last meal was the one that was generously shared with us by some of the people we were now standing on top of. These poor people were rotting and the remains of the bottom layer were being attacked by hungry insects. The brush and twigs that we had fallen through had hidden the deep grave from large predators as well. So far.

The University of Chicago was not the only school represented in that mass grave. New Colorado State and the University of Florida had t-shirts attached to human remains as well. I could not hold a thought in my head. Seeing those young academics, whose entire lives were still ahead of them. Wanting to attach their names to something that would change the world. Big dreams all snuffed. Some of them now absently stared toward the sky they dreamed to. Or they were staring at me as I stood on top of them. Those images still haunt me.

There was no time to lament. I was nicked and bleeding, but would survive as long as we escaped the deep pit before hungry predators were alerted to our presence. But Stubbs was in bad shape. He had been hit four times, once in the lung. It had collapsed and he was spitting blood. He was a tough son-of-a-bitch, I had faith that he would pull through it. How many people could be hit that many times and continue standing, let alone continue running? If it weren't for being in the pit, he would probably still be running.

Then there was the very real possibility that the people who were shooting at us, the people whom worked for Estabados, the piece-of-shit with us at the bottom of the pit, would likely be on our tail looking for him. And us. Who wanted to bet that they knew where the bodies are buried?

I tried to climb up the dirt walls, through Stubbs's gurgling protestations, but I failed. Or as the college kids below us might have once said, epic fail. I could find no purchase to move up. Ten feet could have been a mile.

There had to be another way out. The girl from the University of Chicago that was imprisoned with us was on top of the pile of the hidden mass grave. She could not have been there more than twenty minutes before us. But there wasn't another way in or out. She had to have been dumped there minutes before we fell in, then the pit re-covered to hide the pile of corpses. Which was also disconcerting.

"Stubbs. Give me your knife."

He was leaning against the wall of the pit. He slowly was able to pull the Gerber *Air Ranger* out of his boot and hand it to me. He must have been hit in the leg as well because the knife and sheath were soaked in blood. Some of the crimson slime may have been from the guard he had used the knife on in our escape from the cell, but there was just too much of it. We had escaped one cell where death was moments away, only to find ourselves in another.

I began to cut the fingertips off the corpses under us, careful to do so in an organized yet expedient fashion. I wanted one from each person with no exclusion yet no redundancy.

"Jes…. What are you …. doing?" Stubbs asked trying to catch any breath. I needed to get him out of there before he drowned in his own blood.

"I have to make sure these people get accounted for. This sick fuck killed them and he is going to pay for every one."

"How can you …. victimize the victims …. twice? Let them rest. Whole."

"They're already dead Stubbs. They ain't gonna mind. We're gonna be dead too if we don't finish this and get the fuck outta here."

"I didn't kill any of these people," Estabados said. He had been shot also, but I didn't care. I wanted him to live so he could pay for his crimes. I wanted him dead also. But a relatively quick death was too easy.

"Shut the fuck up. Your lies are doin' my head in."

I put the fingertips in the cargo pocket of my pants and continued to think of a way out.

"I never killed anyone. Los Militares did. I am here for the research. The samples."

I shoved the barrel of the *MP5A3* into his mouth, breaking a few of his front teeth. "I told you to shut the fuck up."

I only had four bullets left, but if I had to I would use one to expose his brains to the light. The more he denied killing these people, the less interested I was in seeing to his survival. I wanted him to pay, yes. But he was beginning to tip the scales.

Around the barrel of the gun he continued to speak. It was difficult to understand, but he said that he had never killed anyone in his life. Apparently having someone else do the actual killing got him off the hook for ordering them dead. I had never hated someone so vehemently, nor since. How he could lie, or fool himself into believing he was innocent, while standing on top of the remains of those he had put there, was beyond me.

Stubbs had managed to gain some strength somehow, some way, and leaned a couple of the bodies against a corner of the pit. He asked for his knife back from me. Not in words, as he was breathy and bleeding. He just stuck out his hand and waved his fingers towards himself. I got the point.

Stubbs then quickly carved out some notches into the dirt wall. The grooves were deep enough where the bottom of them would not collapse under weight. He then, slowly climbed on top of the stacked bodies and found footholds in the grooves he had carved. He motioned for me to go over to him quickly. I did and with every last bit of strength he flung me up onto him, onto his back. I was able to then climb higher, high enough to hold myself on the solid ground above with my arms and armpits. I kicked and pulled myself up like I was getting out of a swimming pool until I made safe landing above them. He had the gun and knife with him below.

"Go." His footholds collapsed in that instant, sending him back down on top of the bodies. He laid there on his back for a few seconds in obvious pain. He coughed and panted as he rolled over, trying to stand.

"You can't leave me here," Estabados shouted. "I know too much. My research. I didn't kill anyone — "

He probably would have kept on going, kept on lying. But Stubbs was having none of it. He reached over and with his knife cut out the doctor's tongue. Estabados was screaming out of his blood-soaked mouth, so Stubbs knocked him out with the gun stock. He looked up at me and waved me to go. He coughed again, spraying fresh blood of his own onto the bottom of the pit and walls. Falling down on one knee, he looked up and waved me off again.

Loud voices and the trampling of brush could be heard. The noisy stampede was making it's way toward us. We both knew what that meant, but neither of us were ready to admit it. I take that back, Stubbs knew what had to happen. I was the one who refused to believe the truth. The sounds of the men were no more than seventy-five meters away. In the time it took an army-for-hire to run about ninety yards, there would be no escape.

"I'm not just going to leave you here, Stubbs."

I looked around to see if there was an ambush point. Someplace for me to hide in order to think, come up with a plan. The grave was set in the middle of a spacious clearing. In the clearing, I would be a sitting duck. In the pit, Stubbs was a fish in a barrel.

He didn't respond or even make another motion for me to leave. He looked into my eyes, and in that ten seconds, I knew what had to happen. Just before he collapsed he communicated to me everything that I wanted to say to him. My eyes began to fill, trying to convey it back, but there was no time. With those eyes he said the words that I have said back to him almost every day since.

I love you too Stubbs.

19

SOME TYPES OF CHURCHES ARE EASY TO FIND. In Boston, for example, at least one Catholic church is in every borough. In Charleston, South Carolina, if one is looking for a Baptist church, they can throw something over their shoulder and it will hit one. It is considered to be part of the bible belt, and *everybody* goes to one church or another. Methodists, Pentecostals, and a slew of others. In uptown Charleston alone there are 125 listed active and/or historical churches. On Sundays, even corporate chains like Target or Walmart don't bother opening their doors until after the noon hour. No point. They wouldn't be able to get employees to work, nor customers to sell things to.

Other types of congregations are not as easy to find, even in the South. The protesters outside of Nahash Pharmaceuticals, according to the guard watching their main gate, were Christian Scientists. In South Carolina, this religion is a minority. These organizations don't advertise and run the churches like a business. Most of the organized religions in the South are for-profit yet have the benefits of being a religion, like not having to pay taxes. These were not mega-churches like the Born-Agains or the Later-Day Saints build. These were small, private congregations that didn't evangelize. Which made them difficult to find.

JG listened to the Nahash security guard intently as he retold the story of his and Detective Fischer's interaction with the group. Grantes thought that the man would say anything to keep himself and his boss out of prison. He kept his opinion to himself, however.

Captain Simms was also listening. Of the hundreds of possible leads into the disappearance of Detective Fischer, which were only a small fraction of what was coming into the department either in person or on the hotline, Nahash was the most promising. Now that he had definitive proof that she was at the facility and had left of her own volition, the guard before him became the most promising lead.

The guard, the receptionist Jeffrey, and the CEO Rueben Feinstein were all put into the back of separate vehicles and taken to Broad for questioning. They would be put into separate rooms and would simultaneously be asked to retell their versions of the events that transpired three days prior. The interviewers would then confer to see if the stories meshed and reinterviewed. The entire time they would be watched through one-way glass and recorded.

Jacob Grantes went back to the police station with the convoy, but was no longer allowed access to the investigation. He would be called if and when it was determined that his client was wrongly accused and incarcerated. He was to go home, or back to his office, or to just plain go away. Which he did.

The attorney, however, would not simply go quietly into the good night. Not only was he a zealous advocate for his client, but that client was the woman he planned to marry. He was not going to allow Sierra to spend one moment longer in prison if he could help it. He needed some proof. Something tangible that could not be ignored. He needed his investigator. Either one of them. He wondered how they were making out.

The first round of interviews in the interrogation rooms at 80 Broad were calm and collected. The three had been split up and were asked to retell their stories. They were more statements than they were actual interviews. There were less interruptions, for sure.

Once those statements were collected, the subjects were given some caffeine to raise their already elevated heart rates while the statements were compared. Any deviation in the events would then be picked apart during the follow-ups. The real interviews.

There were always variances from story to story. No two people ever told a story the exact same way, even if they were telling the truth. It is human nature to incorporate perception and experiences into a story. Some embellish, some have an agenda even if inadvertent. The police use those small variances to pick away at the pill in the proverbial sweater until there was nothing left but a ball of yarn. That was how you sweat someone. Interrogation 101.

But these three told the exact same story. Every detail.

"Mr. Feinstein," Captain Simms said. He was going to handle the CEO personally. He walked back into the interrogation room and sat across from the head of Nahash. "We have a problem, Sir. Your statement does not match the ones we have collected from your subordinates. Would you care to go through the statement again?"

"That is impossible."

"Why is it impossible? Were the statements rehearsed?"

"Of course not. Don't be ridiculous. Facts are facts."

"Yes. But as I just said, yours doesn't match. Some of the parts of these statements can't be 'facts', as you say, because they wouldn't know what happened if they weren't present. You for example. Part of your statement discusses things that supposedly happened when Detective Fischer was entering and leaving the Complex. How could you know what happened at the main gate? You said that you were cozy in your office. Was that true?"

"When it was made public that she was missing, I knew that because she came to see me that I would be questioned. So I sought out the information from my staff. What is this really about, Captain?"

"Why was Detective Fischer at your facility questioning you in the first place?"

"It's already in my statement. She believed that I was somehow involved in the recent deaths related to SCMU and BIOGENESIS. I told her, as I've told you, that her allegations were preposterous."

"It does seem a little coincidental, doesn't it? And I don't believe in coincidence. Three people are murdered by a poison that you conduct experiments on. Those three people conduct the same or similar research for a rival pharmaceutical company. One of the main people associated with the school and that company has left that company and now works for you. The police woman who was investigating those 'coincidences' is now missing, and has been for three days following a visit to you. Either you stepped into a perfect storm of shit, or you at a minimum have information that you have not shared about these events."

"I'd like to call my attorneys now."

"You're not a suspect, you don't need an attorney. This is just a conversation. I think you have more information than you have shared with us so far."

"You've read me my rights, which means that any statement I make or have made up to this point is admissible. You are now saying that you doubt the veracity of those statements. I would like to call my legal team."

He was correct.

GAME OVER.

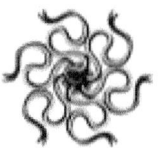

While the interrogations were taking place, two young patrolmen from the convoy broke off and went back to the scene of the burned police car. They were told to quietly look into the religious protester angle, and to start with the area down by the water where Carina's car had been torched.

The car had long since been gone-over by the forensics team. They had examined the vehicle, running tests on anything and everything that had been found. Which was not much. The car had been incinerated. They had come up empty. Time was running out, and everyone knew it. Three days and no trace of their decorated detective was meaning that the likelihood of her being alive, if and when they found her, was increasingly slim.

They walked down to the water and spoke with the man in charge of the dive team. He told them that his team had found all sorts of detritus in the waters on an abandoned shore behind an abandoned church. None of it relevant. The divers were working in shifts, combing the water in a grid pattern. They had even found a gun in the water, but it was so old and the wood stock so rotten that there was no way the weapon had been fired recently.

They asked what type of church the abandoned building was up on the hill, just inland of the abandoned shore. The Dive Commander told them that he thought he heard someone say that it was once a Christian Science Congregation, but not to quote him.

The two gave each other a knowing look. That was the second time that day that they had heard the name of that organization. First at the Nahash Administrative Building, where the guard from the main entrance had said the protesters were from. And for the second time then. This was either connected or an elaborate frame-job. Neither of the two patrolmen were detectives, but then you really didn't need to be.

One of the two young policeman asked, "Has anyone been inside that building to see if there are any clues?"

"What do you think, that none of us have ever investigated a crime scene before? You two flat-foots come out here to save the day? Of course. A team went in there as soon as we found her car. It's boarded up tighter than a drum. Nothing inside but cobwebs."

20

I DIDN'T WANT TO LEAVE STUBBS. I didn't want to leave Estabados in that pit either, but not for the reason you might think. I was officially beyond pissed off and I wanted him dead. With the armed mercenaries that were now arriving at that hole in the earth full of corpses, they would pull their boss out to safety. Dr. Enrique Estabados would live another day, he wouldn't be able to tell any more lies, however. Nor fess up to the truth.

I hoped that Stubbs would hide behind Estabados, maybe play dead. Find a way to survive. I am from Boston, there is always hope. Where I am from, the remarkable happens at the last second. I wanted my friend to pull off that miracle.

I had found the path we had come into the deep jungle upon, and I was following it back. I was not stupid enough to be on the path itself, because there might be others following me or lying in wait. I was running as fast as I could through the very thick brush off to the right side of it.

I was not running long before I heard the shots. It was like a muffled bag of popcorn in the microwave. A burst of suppressed air that were not kernels. Those pops were gunfire. The same type of sound that I had heard when our guide Hector was shot. Only this time there were many more. Instead of a Barrett *M82* or some other sniper rifle, these shots were from the *MP5s*. I had left Stubbs with only four rounds, no way to defend himself in the pit. I hoped he saved one for Estabados.

It was difficult to see where I was going. Partly because no matter how much I tried to man-up, I knew that my new friend was dead. I had left him there to die. The other reason was that under the canopy and off the path, there was even less light. And yet another reason was that the cobwebs were many and mammoth. The silky webs were strong, as if made of nylon nautical rope. I could only imagine the size of the spiders that occupied such webs. In one such web that I was able to avoid, I spotted a small bird struggling to free itself.

I don't know if I had read it someplace; or if the driver or Hector told me, but I wasn't as concerned about the spiders in the webs. They catch in webs because they can't see. It was the large furry ones that use their fur to sense their prey. They can jump onto a moving target. I wasn't afraid, not like I am of snakes. But concerned. All spiders are venomous, it is a question of if the jaw is strong enough to puncture skin and if the venom is deadly enough. Every female I have ever met is afraid of the things, and for good reason.

I was still in the same jungle, with the same number of creepy-crawlies that could kill me. But I was now alone. I was left to my own devices to get out of that hell. I am not much of a naturalist, but I am a survivor. Scorpions, lizards, Brazilian wandering spiders, among others, were all concerning.

My major fear was the snakes. If snakes had a sense of smell, I was a dead man walking. I was sweating like a pregnant nun and hadn't showered since Charleston. I saw what those fuckers could do in the enclosed moat outside the cell walls. 'Pit Viper', my ass. Bothrops Aspers were the product of hell. If one of those things got ahold of me, it was all over but the crying.

I came upon the makeshift lab of the University of Chicago, a bit further down the path and to the left. I was somewhat familiar with the layout as we had spent some time there eating lunch and changing. The place was a mess. Walls caved in, equipment destroyed. I stopped and reconnoitered the area to see if the camp was being watched. It didn't appear to be. Yet.

I wanted to see if they had a phone of some sort. Stubbs had made a good point. They had to be able to communicate their results and findings somehow. I needed to communicate with anyone who could help and as quickly as possible.

They had a satellite phone in one of the tents, but it had been destroyed. Estabados's men were smart, unfortunately.

In my search I found some dehydrated beef. I think it was beef. I didn't really taste it, I was starving. I didn't hydrate it even. I used the bottled water to hydrate myself. I ate it like it was jerky, tearing at it like a Viking.

I continued to search the camp for anything that I might need for the rest of my journey. I didn't want to spend too much time there, anybody with a brain knew I would go back the way I came in an effort to make my way home. I found their flare gun and a first aid kit. The nick in my shoulder turned out to be a bit more than a nick. I cleaned that up with antiseptic, bandaged it, and kept searching.

I finally found a trunk that was under one of the kids' bunks. He or she had backup parts for some of the equipment. Those kids knew that things could go bump in the night, especially in the rainforest, and packed backups. In the haste of destroying everything, the mercenaries had missed one trunk. I am the least tech-savvy person anywhere on the planet. It's not like I opened a trunk and it was like a hardware store or a Radio Shack. The labels were technical and there weren't any instructions. I just found parts that looked like the ones damaged and dangling from the satellite phone and I got the hell out of there.

There was a small backpack thankfully, so I filled it with water, some more dehydrated stuff of various types, some dry socks, the flare gun, a knife, a lantern, the broken satellite phone, the spare parts, and the solar charger for the sat-phone. I wasn't entirely sure if the charger was for the phone, if the charger would work with the thin sunlight coming through the canopy, or even if the damn thing worked. But I took it anyway. Time was up, I had to get outta there.

I ran like a bat out of hell, sprinting down the main path because I needed to make up for lost time. My thinking was that if the gunmen were tracking me and had not yet made it to the Chicago lab, then they wouldn't be further down the path. I was betting the lot, because if I ran into any resistance I was a goner.

Well after nightfall, I made my way off the path toward a spot to rest. I hadn't slept in days and I was exhausted, but I knew that there would be no sleep. Only a short rest. I had never watched *Survivor* or Bear Gryll's *Man vs. Wild* but vowed to if I could get out of there alive. The only things I knew about the outdoors were the things I learned from Hector and Stubbs. Which wasn't much. I really should have paid more attention. I really should learn to speak Spanish.

I used the knife from the Chicago camp to cut a little clearing, using some of the brush to make myself a place to sit but the majority to set up a small perimeter. If someone came upon me in the night, I would hear them as they snapped the twigs as they crossed the brush.

Using a couple of huge green leaves, each one could have covered my body, I was able to make a clean spot. The lamp was plenty of light to make sure that while I was taking limbs off of trees, I didn't cut anything that something gnarly was living on.

I covered the brush for my seat with one leaf, and used the other for my lap to work on rebuilding the satellite phone. I hoped it was going to be as simple as square peg, square hole, round peg, round hole. I didn't have many tools, just the bits that folded out of the knife.

The next order of business was to change my socks. Nothing dampens your spirits like damp feet. I wished I hadn't seen them. The parts of the feet that weren't blistered were damp, wrinkled sheets of skin that could peel off. The under sides of my toes were raw meat. Tender doesn't describe how much they hurt. Dry socks made it tolerable because no first aid was fixing that mess.

Next some food. More dehydrated jerky and water, I didn't want to spend the time to soak the mystery meat. Rehydrating it may have brought back the flavor. Since I didn't know what it was, I certainly didn't want to taste it.

The ingenious people at REDARC came up with a lantern that is bright, rechargeable from solar energy, yet generates light that will generate solar energy. The REDARC solar charger worked, thankfully, and was storing energy from the light given off by the lantern. The lantern could then be recharged from the solar charger. A circle of reusable energy. I would have to remember to send them a kind email.

No matter how much light, the reassembly of the phone was slow-going. Fatigue and frustration were taking over. I've never been accused of being patient. My Irish is up anyway, even when I'm supposedly calm. But that was just about the worst day ever, so I was on def-con 5. Or 1. Whichever the really pissed-off one is. Throwing the phone against a tree rendering it unfixable was a strong possibility. Not a smart idea, but a possibility.

Eventually the phone was put back together, though some of the parts were still hanging from it, and a green light indicated that it was charging. We would see if it would actually transmit once it was charged.

Then I heard them. It was impossible to tell how long it had been, since it was dark and I was without a watch. I had dozed off for a bit as well.

Either there was a stampede of moose coming toward me, which I found unlikely in Costa Rica, or the mercenaries had found me. I doused the light and stuffed everything in the backpack as I crawled into the thick. I couldn't see what, but there were things crawling on me as I crawled deeper into their world. Screaming was not an option. The path was no longer an option. Getting back home, dead or alive, might not be an option either.

21

THE CALL CAME IN ON JACOB GRANTES'S CELL PHONE at 1:22 AM. His phone roused him from his intermittent sleep. He was worried about Sierra. He was worried about his investigators whom he had not heard from in going on four days. He had not had a sound sleep in as many days. But he was experiencing some much needed rest.

"Hello?"

"Is this Jacob Grantes, the attorney in Charleston, South Carolina?"

"Yes, it is." He sat up and threw his legs off of the side of his bed. "Who is this? And do you realize what time it is?"

"It is almost 1:30 AM, yes. It is 12:30 AM here in Chicago. I understand that it is an inconvenient hour, Sir, but I received a disturbing phone call and I was told to contact you. Now."

He was wide awake now. What was going on in Chicago that would necessitate an urgent call in the middle of the night from a stranger?

"I'm listening."

"My name is Dr. Damien Pierce. I am the Dean of Toxicology and Herpetology at the University of Chicago. I have a research team on assignment in the Monteverde region of the Costa Rican rainforest."

JG was at full attention. His heart sank, yet was racing. His mind was moving faster still.

"Go on Doctor. I have some investigators there as well, is that what this is about?"

"In part. The satellite phone that I received the call from was how my team communicated with me and sent me critical data. Your man is in possession of that device which gives credence to what he is saying."

"Yes, Doctor. Please don't take offense, but get to the point. I can vouch for him."

Jacob was unsure which of 'his men' he was vouching for, but either way he wanted the doctor to cut to the chase.

"It seems that my team, as well as other research teams have been .... " Pierce trailed off.

"Your team has been what? What has happened?"

"Annihilated."

"Did you say annihilated? As in killed? All of them?"

"The transmission was not good, and there was a very heavy accent, but it was clear enough. It seems that the respected Dr. Enrique Estabados, of the World Toxin Bank is responsible for the massacre of several research institutions down there. Not individuals, institutions. I made him repeat it for clarity.

"Your man is also in grave danger. He needs help getting out of there before he befalls the same fate. He was being pursued when he called. He also says he can prove every word of what he has said. Then the transmission was abruptly disconnected. I am beside myself."

163

"What was the name of the man that called you?"

"He said his name is Warren Dennihan. He said that I was to call you immediately."

"Very good. You did the right thing. Did he say anything else? I have two men down there."

"He did not. But he did say that failure to call you or to respond would mean, and I'm paraphrasing because his language was quite vulgar, …. it would mean certain death."

" …. I understand that it is almost 2:00 AM, but I needed to speak with you urgently," JG said into his phone.

"How did you even get this number?" Captain Simms was enraged. His wife was awake and probably his kids.

"Your guy at Broad. That's not important. What *is* important is that we have proof that Feinstein and Estabados are not only serial murderers but mass murders as well. You cannot let them go free."

"Slow down. What the hell are you talking about?"

"I just received a call from a Dean at the University of Chicago. They have, or should I say *had*, a research team down in Costa Rica. As you know, my investigators went down there to find Estabados for the three murders here. It turns out that Nahash has been killing people from all over the Country, maybe even the world, trying to steal research and wipe out any competition. My guys are in trouble down there."

"Feinstein, the guard, and the fairy are being held, but they won't be for long. Feinstein came down with the thunder as soon as we started sniffing too close. A team of lawyers. We had enough for warrants which means we can hold him for twenty-four hours, Forty-eight tops, before we have to present to a Grand Jury. You know what that means."

"It means that we have to get my boys back with proof before that hearing. Has it been scheduled yet? I am going to need help Captain."

"If what you're saying is true, this is above my pay grade. We will have to get the FBI involved. They don't play well with locals. They will box us out of the investigation. Finding Carina at that point will be an exercise in futility. They are not going to let him walk or go easy, even if it does mean finding a cop. If we don't have the ability to cut him a deal, I don't know if we will ever find her."

"Do you honestly still think she is alive, Captain?"

"She is until we know for sure. If we call in the FBI, we won't know. We might never know. She's one of mine, counselor."

"If we don't get my boys out, we have no proof and possibly more dead to add to the total."

There was silence on the phone. Both men were thinking of how best to proceed. At that hour of the morning, without coffee, it was taking a bit longer than usual. The consequences of their decisions required that they think their decisions through.

"Let me make a few phone calls and I will call you back."

"No way, Captain. Make your calls, but I want to meet you at Broad. One hour. Don't make me go around you."

"And don't you threaten me, Grantes .... Goddammit .... I'll be there, counselor."

JG was waiting in Captain Simms's office within the hour. The precinct at 80 Broad was busy for that hour of the morning, but not as busy as the last time he had visited. He was led to the office, Simms had called ahead to alert his team that the attorney would be calling. Fortified with a cup of decent coffee, unlike the cliché about bad police station coffee, while he waited. But not for long.

Simms walked in with a large gentleman in pressed jeans, Oxford shirt and sweater-vest. His saddle-tan loafers were the ones with tassels. He was introduced as only 'a contact with the FBI'.

"Counselor. This is off the record and off the books, so the less you know the better. My friend here will see through the red tape in getting your investigators out of Costa Rica."

"Thank you, Sir. What do I need to do?"

The man spoke with an even keel, almost monotoned. "I am told that you are a man of means. My suggestion would be to arrange for a flight out of there as soon as possible."

166

"Done. I have a plane already in the air and on the way. We should have no problem in terms of flight paperwork with Customs, the same plane was used to bring them into the Country."

"You would think, but that is not the case. The American Consulate has begun to put pressure on the Costa Rican Government to assist in getting your boys out of there. Once they get out of the rainforest, the next step is getting the Customs officials to stamp them out of there. No stamp will only light up some flares with our TSA and Homeland Security when they arrive here. The genie will be out of the bottle at that point, and I will disassociate myself with any of this."

"Understood. How long will all of this take?"

"From what I understand from the Consulate General, it will take longer to find your guys. The rainforest is massive and obviously well-covered."

"At the risk of sounding greedy, what are we going to do about Dr. Sierra Byrne, Rueben Feinstein, Dr. Estabados, and company?," he asked the two gentlemen. It was directed more at Simms but the FBI man answered.

"Officially? Nothing."

Captain Simms interjected. "We hold them until your boys get back. All four of them. Dr. Byrne included. Hopefully within twenty-four hours we get them back here with enough evidence to put pressure on them. Getting a confession is the goal, but short of that we need to know what they have done with Detective Fischer. With the body count as high as it is, taking the death penalty off the table is our only leverage."

"What are the chances that your investigators will have Dr. Estabados in custody?" The FBI man had an agenda, but JG was unclear as to what it was.

"I only know what I have told you. They went after him and they have uncovered atrocities, but whether they have apprehended him is uncertain. What is the end-game? Use Estabados as leverage?"

"Any deal made by the Charleston Police would not have any effect on charges brought forth by a Federal Prosecutor," Mr. FBI said.

"Ah. I see. So you are vying for jurisdiction because of the Costa Rican victims being from several US States. Whatever promises or deals are made, are null and void when the Feds take over in prosecuting the case? That sets a pretty bad precedent. And Captain Simms? You're OK with walking away from these serial murders? There are three dead in your own backyard."

"The greater good, Counselor. Mass murder trumps serial murder in this case. The Charleston victims will get justice, whomever tries their case. I want my detective back and in one piece. I'd pony up the courthouse if I had to."

"And if she's not? If she is not in one piece? You'd bet the farm for nothing."

"We're not thinking along those lines. I just can't think along those lines."

22

THE SUN HAD JUST RISEN, THE STREAMS OF LIGHT were slipping past the canopy over my head. I welcomed those rays. They created warmth from the bone-chill the night had provided. The illumination provided me with some vision, however slight. I had no idea where I was, only that I was still stuck in the middle of the Costa Rican rainforest.

No matter which direction I turned, everything looked exactly the same. The thick brush, huge trees, the cacophony of sounds emanating from creatures that surrounded me, all worked in unison to create complete disorientation. The only thing I knew for sure was that it was about 6:00 AM. I had noticed back when I had a watch what time the sun came up in the early green season of the rainforest.

And that I was alive. I knew that also. Beaten up but alive. For now.

I had climbed a tree after escaping my pursuers the night before. I used the elevation to wait out the night and make my phone call on the precariously held together satellite phone. I was just as precariously balanced on a large tree branch. It was neither comfortable nor settling in any way. It had been dark and I knew not what was in the tree I had climbed. Sometimes you just have to make the best decision that you can and hope for the best.

If I wasn't fumbling to ensure my elevated balance, I was fumbling with the satellite phone. The call needed to be made. I didn't know if I should juggle the dangling parts or to just let them hang. The connection was bad but the call went through to the last number that had been dialed before I came into possession of it.

The Dean from the University of Chicago was going to help me get out of here. I was not big on trust, when you get burned as often as I've been, you get skittish to say the least. But I had to trust someone. I hoped that help would be in time.

Climbing up into a tree was a risk. Snakes, monkeys, scorpions, spiders, lizards, and all the other things that I wanted to avoid were in the trees. I needed to make the phone call and was uncertain if height would help, I still don't know if it helped. All I know is that the call went through. I had to repeat myself constantly. I had to mumble so the mercenaries that were chasing me didn't hear me. The connection cut in and out with the terminating the call. The professor kept saying something about my accent and not understanding me as well.

Going up into the tree wasn't as much trouble as coming down from it. Coming out of it would expose me if the mercenaries came calling. I decided to wait out the night up there. Fewer things wanted a taste of me in the tree, at least thus far. I would be exposed to hungry things at or below ground level. I would be an all-you-can-eat buffet by morning.

If being alone, lost in the middle of the jungle wasn't bad enough, you can add severe exhaustion to the list. I hadn't slept in days other than a brief doze.

It's not like Vegas where you can go for days partying and gambling without rest. I didn't have Red Bull and purified oxygen pumped at me to keep me awake. I had run and sweat and hidden for days without slumber. I had more running to do if I was going to get out of there alive.

I waited until the sun gave me more than just a few rays before I began to move from my perch. I wanted to see if either predators or pursuers were waiting me out, I spied none. Left, right, front, back, I had no idea where the path was positioned in relation to me. I needed to find it. Not to walk on, that was too risky. I needed it to gain orientation. The way out was that path, but it could also lead to my death.

Blindly, I picked a direction. I knew that the tree that I had climbed was in front of me when I crawled into it the night before, which meant that there were three of the four possible directions to choose from. I made sure to stay in that direction, keeping the sun to my left. South was the best I could guess. I really should have listened more to the driver in the Toyota *Previa.*

The usual morning rain began. The heavy raindrops hitting the leaves was loud, drowning the plants and animals as well as all other sound. The team that was following me chose that moment to attack. I didn't hear any shots fired, but I saw the tree bark and heavy brush around me spit into the air.

I ran.

Without precision, I zig-zagged back and forth but kept the same general direction, expending every ounce of energy I had left in the tank. Looking back, I must have looked like Forrest Gump running out of the jungle in Vietnam. Only without a weapon. I ran with knees to my chest and heels to my butt, pumping away.

They were moving in on me. As fast as I could go, they had the great equalizer. Automatic weapons.

Miraculously, I came to the path. It was both a blessing and a curse. A blessing because I could make much better time running from my pursuers. I no longer had to hurdle over bushes, fallen trees, rocks, and other obstacles. A curse because the path was only a little wider than a single person. A little wider than me. No zigging. No zagging. I was lined up for the kill.

When I heard the helicopter, I knew I was doomed. The canopy would provide great cover, but I was on the path. Eventually I would come to the gorges and ravines. The only way to cross was on the zip-lines. I would literally be a dangling target for whomever was in that helicopter. If I could even make it that far.

My lungs burned as I continued to run as fast as I could, trying relentlessly to get as far ahead of the team that chased me. I was in excellent shape. I worked out five or six days a week, sparring and training in Brazilian Jiu-Jitsu. But that wasn't running with a pack on my back. It wasn't days without sleep and undernourishment. I was spent.

The first of the rivers came quicker than I had thought. I was closer to the parking lot where Stubbs and I had met Hector than I had expected. Behind me, They were closing in. Above me, the chopper was thumping and circling. How they knew where I was, I didn't know at the time. If I crossed, I was dead. If I didn't, I was dead.

There was a shed near the tower where one end of the canopy line was attached. I kicked in the door and found the necessary harnesses and clips. I strapped on a body harness and clipped the carabiner to it.

I waited in the shed for the helicopter to circle toward me and pass over head before I climbed the tower. I clipped the carabiner to the trolley, gave it a hard pull to ensure I was clipped in and ran off the ledge to allow myself the momentum of a running start. I let the velocity take me as far down the line as it would take me, then hand over hand I pulled. The chopper was coming back.

The thumping of the rotors was getting louder from behind me. I was not yet even half-way across the line. That was the first of several that I remember we had crossed going into the rainforest. If I made it across this one, there were more to come. My chances of eluding them through all of the zip-lines were between slim and none. I needed to get rid of their air support.

I hung there, trying to get access to my backpack. That must have been a sight. I was able to finagle one arm out of the pack, giving myself just enough of an angle to unzip the bag and retrieve the flare gun.

The thumping grew ever louder and the flow of air was swaying me as I dangled like meat on a hook. I was officially spotted as the chopper came from behind me, circling fifty yards ahead of me for the return pass.

A Sikorsky *H-34* helicopter was coming directly toward me. I timed my swaying to squeeze the trigger of the flare gun as the aircraft came at me. The pilot pulled up, seeing it with plenty of time. As it circled again, the big blunt nose moved away from me, exposing the side view of the chopper. It said US MARINES on the tail. I was being attacked by the *US fucking Marines?* Impossible. They had not fired a single shot at that point.

But I was being shot at. The team that was chasing me from the ground began to open fire. That was when the Marines came back around and laid one long round of fire toward the mercenaries. I was being *saved* by the helicopter, not pursued. I had shot a flare at the people who were trying to get me out of the rainforest.

Either the ground team had had enough at that point, or were reassessing how to retrieve me off of the zip-line. Regardless, they stopped firing shots at me.

The *H-34* opened it's big side door as it steadied above me. A rope line was dropped. It took some doing to grab the line, tie it into my harness and secure myself to safety, but it worked. I was reeled into the big bird and we circled out of the immediate area.

I was home-free. Or was I?

23

BEING QUESTIONED BY THE UNITED STATES CONSULATE GENERAL, surrounded by Marines, is not my idea of a great time. The United States Embassy is not someplace I ever care to visit again. But it sure beats the shit out of being shot at in the middle of the jungle.

I was able to call JG, to inform him that I had been extracted. I didn't get into too many details, didn't tell him that I shot a flare at my rescuers. I also didn't mention Stubbs. All I said was that there was ample evidence of murder. We had bitten off more than we could chew in going down there, Estabados had an army which was funded by Feinstein. He would not be going back with us.

The Consulate General had used his considerable influence to covertly utilize a small team of United States Marines, which were stationed in Costa Rica on a mission to stave off the drug cartels in nearby Colombia. They had utilized the GPS tracking device in the sat-phone that I had repaired to hone in on my exact location for the rescue. The mission to get me out was a success, only there wasn't an official mission. It was documented as a training exercise. I was thankful that my government footed the bill for my rescue, even if they didn't know it.

While I was being patched up, stitched up, hydrated and fed, I asked if they would go in for Stubbs. It would take a ground team, but we had to see if he was ok. They were not too keen on heading into the rainforest to fight an off-the-books war. I told them about the other research teams that the Chicago kids told me were also down there. They were also in grave danger if not already dead. Bureaucratic red tape meant that they would not go back in. At least not yet.

I was brought back to the airport in a US Diplomat car. They walked me through to Customs where I was told not to speak. For once I followed the rules and did as I was instructed. Before long, relatively speaking, I was back on JG's private plane and flying home. I am pretty sure that I am not welcome back in Costa Rica. I am very sure that I don't ever want to go back to Costa Rica.

I was very thankful to be alive, but once the plane was in the air I slept like the dead. Both of the flight attendants tried to wake me once we were cleared to land in Charleston, but I wasn't able to be risen from my coma until well after the doors opened. The *AMG* and my driver were waiting on the tarmac.

I was surprised that JG wasn't at the airport to meet me. Had he told me that he would not be there for my arrival and I had forgotten? My state of mind was groggy to say the least. In either case, I was to meet him at the precinct on 80 Broad. I tried to argue that I needed a shower but there was no arguing. The main reason I didn't want to go there immediately was that I didn't want Carina to see me that way. I was a mess. I had slept about four hours in as many days. I had not showered since the last time I was in Charleston, which meant that I reeked. The pocket full of fingers in my cargo pants didn't help the stench situation.

When I arrived at 80 Broad, I was treated more like a perp than a PI. I had sweat through the clothes I had been wearing for days and unbelievably still damp. Pile on the dirt and I didn't really blame them for giving me the stink-eye. I stunk. I looked like someone who had done something dirty. Or I was homeless. Or both.

They brought me to the Homicide Division and JG was waiting there for me with another man in shirtsleeves. More staring at me. I was beginning to feel self conscious. Thankfully I didn't see Carina there yet.

JG led me into the office of the man that I had not as yet officially met.

"Deni. I'm so glad you're home. I would give you a hug but …. well, you get it right? You look terrible. And you smell worse."

"Yeah. I'm tired and I need a shower."

"This is Captain Simms. He is personally handling this Nahash thing. As well as a more pressing matter. Where is Stubbs?"

"Thank you for your help in getting me out of that hell-hole, Captain. My name is …. "

" …. I know what your name is." He shook my hand.

JG was tired of introductions. "Deni. Where is Stubbs?"

"You had better have a seat."

"Oh my God. What happened, Deni?" He did take a seat, and so did I. Simms was the last to get off his feet behind his desk.

"I have been trying to think positively about the possibility that he might still be alive. But the more I think about it, the less likely that it makes sense that they would keep him alive. They probably would have killed us both already if we hadn't escaped. To keep him alive with all that he knows …. "

"You're rambling, Deni. What happened?"

"I don't know how much the Captain knows."

"I am up to speed. I hope that I know as much as the counselor. There have been several developments while you were surviving the wild."

"We were trying to escape the prison that they have built in their camp. Estabados and his army for hire. They have it built for the other camps that they invade. If there are prisoners, they keep them there. These kids from Chicago. One never left the cell, the other died trying to escape. And we would have too. They are well-armed these mercenaries. We fell into this giant mass-grave. Dozens of kids in there. They all went down there to advance themselves and medicine, and they wound up in a pile of corpses buried in a pit …. "

The words were pouring out of me in rant. Emotion was pouring out with those words. I don't know how much of it made sense in my first telling. They asked a ton of questions that I answered as quickly but as best I could. This went on for some time, back and forth.

Finally, I emptied my cargo pants pocket on Simms's desk, much to his horror. The fingers rolled around as I pulled the pocket inside-out.

"These are the people that were in the pit. Stubbs and Estabados were in that pit when I ran away. Stubbs had been shot several times, probably collapsed his lung. There was no way he could make it out, and without medical attention …."

"So Dr. Estabados is still alive? Or is he dead also?" JG asked.

"Probably alive. His men were coming for him."

Simms was reaching for his phone that was on his desk. "I will call my contact to see about apprehending him for questioning — "

" — waste of time," I said. "He won't be answering any questions ever again. He would just deny it anyway. He denied killing any of those people, let alone the people here."

He put down the phone receiver. "Mr. Dennihan - "

" - Deni. Call me Deni."

"Deni. There have been some developments since you have been out of country. They are denying any involvement in these developments, and seem to have some evidence to back up their claims. With this latest information, however, I feel that Rueben Feinstein may be responsible for the disappearance of our Detective Carina Fischer, along with the rest of these crimes."

My heart sunk.

"What? Carina .... Detective Fischer is missing?"

"Yes. My guess is that she also had a hunch about Feinstein, went down to Nahash to question him, which led to her disappearance. Do you have any information that could help us find her?"

"No. I had no idea .... I think she might have gone down there because I asked her to look into him."

"They have CCTV footage showing that she left the complex, but they are the ones with things to hide. They are blaming a religious group, or pointing the finger in their direction anyway. We have been looking at that angle, quietly, but come up with nothing."

"No. No. No. These fucks are involved. They can point all they want, but I've literally seen where the bodies are buried."

I got up from my chair to go to Nahash Pharmaceuticals. I had no idea how I was going to get there. Logic and calmness had left the building. Stubbs and now Carina? This was personal.

Captain Simms stood from behind his desk. "Where are you going, Deni?"

"Feinstein. He and I need to have a chat. Best you not be there. It will be violent."

"He is here. Held for questioning."

"Point the way and turn off the cameras."

"As much as I would love to do that very thing, we have to handle this by-the-book or he will walk at trial.   He has three lawyers here, waiting to pounce on any violation of his rights.   Now that I have more information and these, uh, prints .... "   He looked down at his desk, at the fingers haphazardly strewn. "I will go back in there. You can watch from the one-way glass."

I hated the fact that he was right.

Captain Simms walked into Interrogation Room #2 on 80 Broad with a large evidence bag in hand. The newly acquired fingerprint evidence was quite literal and the digits would be used for shock value.

He wasn't sure how much information he was going to be able to extract from the suspect with this three lawyers sitting next to him, but this would be his last bite at the apple.

"Mr. Feinstein, I am sorry to have kept you and your attorneys waiting. We needed time to confirm your story."

"At $5000 an hour, take your time," Feinstein said.

"I told you that legal representation wasn't necessary, though your right, as you were not a suspect at that time. That has now changed. You have already signed the card with your Miranda rights on them. However if you would like, I can remind you of them?"

"That won't be necessary. I am aware of my rights."

"All right. I also need to inform you that this conversation is being recorded." Simms pointed to the microphones that were in the center of the table between them.

"Fine."

Simms then tossed the bag of fingers across the table, where it took Rueben some time to ascertain the contents.

"Those thirty-nine fingers represent the thirty-nine bodies that are currently dead and in a ditch in Central America. Costa Rica to be exact. Do you know who has built a research camp on the property where those bodies are located?"

"I have no idea."

"Nahash Pharmaceuticals."

"Impossible," he said. He shook his head but whom he was trying to convince was unclear.

"A Dr. Enrique Estabados is currently down there heading that team, is he not?"

A whispered conference occurred between the four men before one of the three attorneys spoke.

"We are advising our client not to comment on that. He can neither confirm nor deny where this Estabados is currently."

"Well advise your client this; we have proof that he works for Nahash, a company that is operated by your client, the CEO. This Estabados was working for BIOGENESIS while he was under the employ of Nahash which violates confidentiality agreements. Three people around SCMU and BIOGENESIS have been murdered, here in my city — "

" — which we understand that you have someone incarcerated for. Is that not correct, Captain?" The same attorney spoke, he was taking the lead. "Mr. Feinstein has said repeatedly that he has no knowledge of those, or any murders."

"Pardon me if I don't ooze with confidence over his word. The same person who we think is involved in those murders, at your client's behest, has fled the country and is now killing everyone in his path and piling up the bodies."

"If you had proof that our client had anything to do with those or any murders, he would be under arrest and the DA would be here."

"I am trying to determine the whereabouts of my investigating detective. I believe that your client knows where she is and might be able to improve his position by ensuring her safe return before it is too late. *Then,* I assure you, the DA will be here."

Feinstein had had enough. He was no longer listening to his attorneys.

"I have told you, ad infinitum, that I had nothing to do with those murders or the disappearance of your police woman."

"Mr. Feinstein. How much of a leap do you think it is going to take for a jury to look at thirty-nine bodies and convict you of the three here in Charleston? Add the cop who was looking into the case that has now vanished in their own backyard? The jury will eat it up. Your toast, Rueben. It is up to you for how long."

"But — "

" — oh I'm not finished. You don't need to answer that quite yet. I want you to know that this little game of yours is up. Finished. I want you to think long and hard about what is going to happen if you do not cooperate with us. The media is somehow going to get wind that the top people at Nahash are being investigated for all of these murders, abductions, and espionage and they are going to have a field day. It may have already gone viral, I can't be certain. How long do you think it is going to take before Wyatt, your parent company, to

cut ties? Your on your own, Rueben. These lawyers at $5000 and hour are gone.
You are alone. Here. With me. Care to revise your statement?"

Feinstein looked around the room, at his legal representatives who were
trying to tell him to remain quiet. The thought of him being at less than square
one was something he could not endure. His company would be gone. These
lawyers who were telling him not to explain himself, would be gone.

"Listen to me, Captain. For the last time, *I had nothing to do with those
murders at BIOGENESIS or the disappearance of your Detective Fischer.* As far as
Estabados, I will only say that we had an arrangement that when things came to
an end at his former employer, that a lucrative opportunity would be available
to him at Nahash — "

" — except that he was working for you at the same time as BIOGENESIS
and the WTB. You had to know. And you knew that this was a direct violation
of his confidentiality — "

" — which could be dealt with in the courts. That is why I pay these
men." He pointed to his attorneys.

"So why send him to Costa Rica?"

"What we do is very competitive. We have all sorts of barriers to our
research there. The Government and their natural resources. Other institutions
vying for specimens and data. Religious groups dropping poisonous mice,
wiping out our specimens. The list goes on and on. I sent him down there to
straighten it all out."

"And murder dozens of people."

"NO! I never said that. Those are your words not mine. Dr. Estabados
said that he was making the makeshift lab in the rainforest more secure against
marauders. He said nothing about killing. He said that we were the ones who
were suffering losses."

"So you are trying to tell me that all of this is just your bad luck? That you
are up to your eyeballs in felonies but that you are innocent in all of this?"

"Captain, I believe my client — "

" — be quiet," Rueben said to his attorney. "I'll answer. Captain, what I am saying is that we are always one step away from either being a hero or a villain. I never ordered anyone to be harmed in any way."

"'Show me a hero and I'll write you a tragedy.'   That is F. Scott Fitzgerald."

"My point, despite your literary insertions, is that if what you are saying is true, that Dr. Estabado is involved in all of this, then he is doing it on his own."

"To what end?"

"I don't know. I find it hard to believe. If you are asking me if I wanted research and data from others, to be the first at finding miracle cures and increasing human life expectancy a decade or more, then I admit it. That is my mission. That is what I want. Killing and risking my entire life's work? My answer is no. So please, Captain, either arrest me or let me go do that work."

I stood there behind that glass, next to JG, listening to Feinstein. I wanted to kill him. How could he continue to lie? How could he look at the evidence bag full of forefingers, which represented the dead and heaped bodies in Costa Rica, and deny his involvement.

Estabados had done the same thing prior to him losing his ability to speak. When the walls are crumbling around you, deny, deny, deny. The prime directive from above.

Was it possible that Feinstein wasn't lying? I have conducted countless interviews as both a detective and as an investigator. He was a damned good liar, or he believed what he was saying. He had convinced himself that he was innocent.

In Costa Rica, surrounded by bodies and what could have been his final hour, Estabados denied killing anybody. He was lying. I had watched him witness shots being fired, listened to him threaten. He may not have done the actual slaying but he was guilty.

But what about the murders here in Charleston? What about Carina? Estabados was out of country when Carina went missing.

I was tired. The lies were doing my head in. I racked my brain to see what was going on in Feinstein's. What had they both said that was in common? Other than that they were innocent and victims of circumstance.

I had to take my mind off of Costa Rica. We went there to get Estabados. What we found were more bodies, mine almost added to the pile. But while that was horrific, and I wanted justice for them, my focus had to remain on the three murders there. The disappearance of Carina was tied to those murders.

My mind went back to my visit at BIOGENESIS. I thought about our struggle to get through the main gate due to the media coverage and protestors. I thought about the questions regarding who could have done those terrible things and who could have known about venom testing? The list went on and on. Hate letters, emails, and phone calls came in daily. PETA, religious nuts, unions, other institutions trying to derail progress in favor of their own.

Then my mind went to Nahash. No media, no protestors. Why? Weren't they conducting the same research? The questions about their research led to the admission that most of the buildings were empty and waiting for samples. So essentially they were stealing research rather than conducting their own.

Feinstein just admitted his guilt to that. There weren't any protestors because they weren't researching yet, nothing to protest. How did the protestors know that? No PETA, no religious nuts, no unions, no competition. Not yet.

Carina's disappearance was blamed on the Christian Scientist protestors out by the main gate. When did the protestors come calling? Why? Again with the blaming of religious zealots. That was the only common thread.

I had to investigate that angle. If nothing more than to eliminate them from the conversation. Something wasn't adding up. If Sierra Byrne didn't kill those people; and Feinstein was insisting that he, and to a lesser extent Estabados, didn't do it, then who did? Sierra didn't abduct Carina, she was locked up. Estabados didn't grab her, he was in Central America. Feinstein was the common denominator, but my gut said that there was a piece missing. He pointed toward the Christian Scientists. But he would have pointed to anyone to get him out of his current predicament.

I left the viewing room of Interrogation Room #2. JG called to me as I was walking down the hall toward the exit.

"Deni. Where are you going?"

I stopped and turned around. "This is getting us nowhere. He's pissing me off and I want to kill him. But before I do, I need to get some answers."

"That's what we all want. So what now?"

"I need to take a shower and call my priest."

24

IT ISN'T VERY OFTEN IN A CITY LIKE BOSTON, **MASSACHUSETTS** that you can call your Catholic priest and get him on the phone right away. Even with the plummeting numbers of attendees at church these days due to things like; science, pedophilia, stance against abortion, stance against gays, and the constant begging for money, they always seem to be too busy. Especially at the Cathedral of the Holy Cross in the South End.

But I was the lost sheep. And Father Sean Donnelly had been my priest my entire life. The few times I had gone to church after my confirmation, he would always try to get me to come back with more frequency. I would be there for a wedding, or more likely a funeral, and looking to get out of there as quickly as possible for the after-party. Father Donnelly would fight through the crowds, ignoring the devout to shake my hand. He would ask me how I've been, how long it had been since my last confession, invite me back to church, and speaking of which how much the church could use some of my money.

The Cathedral holds seventeen hundred people. Every time it would be the same speech, and every time I would tell him that my God is less judgmental, isn't short of cash, and certainly doesn't have time for a sinner like me.

So when I called him, he got his Catholic ass on the phone.

"Deni. How nice it is to hear from you. I was just headed to Mass General."

"Sorry to interrupt your evening, Father. I need some of your time. Can You talk?"

"I have a few minutes before I have to leave for the hospital. Is it urgent?"

"Yes, and it may take a little more than a few minutes."

"You could meet me down at the chapel in the hospital. We could talk there."

"Yeah, that'd be nice except I'm in Charleston."

"Charlestown isn't that far, I could even — "

" — no Father. Not Charlestown. Charleston. As in South Carolina."

"Oh. I see. Well, what is so urgent?"

"What do you know about Christian Scientists?"

"You're not thinking of converting are you? I have been your priest for your entire life. I Baptized you."

"No Father. I'm in a situation down here, and I need to know about them. Some wicked nasty stuff has happened and fingers are bein' pointed at these religious nuts."

"Well I take offense to the slanderous term 'religious nuts'. There are extremists in every group, religion is no exception."

"Do you know about them or not?"

"Yes, of course. While they are not Catholic, it is my job to know about all that use Christ's name to justify their beliefs. What do you wish to know?"

"What do they believe in? Would they commit murder to advance their cause?"

"I doubt it. The religion was formed here in Boston, believe it or not, in the late 1800s. Mary Baker Eddy I believe was their deviser. She was a very sickly woman her entire life, developing a belief system that stemmed from Plato."

"Plato? As in the Greek philosopher?"

"Yes, very good Deni. He believed that abstract entities were figments of the material world. This Eddy woman took that notion, saying that her illnesses, *all illness and death,* are illusions caused by mistaken beliefs. That spiritual reality is the only reality. Prayer can and will correct what medicine cannot. She named her religion Christian Science ironically. Her beliefs are neither Christ-like nor do they hold any place in science."

"So they don't believe in Jesus?"

"No, they do. They believe that mankind, like Jesus, was created in the likeness of God, which is not material but spiritual. They believe in the Holy Trinity, that people create the Holy Spirit. It is identified with the New Thought Movement. Which is to say that they use the same vocabulary as the Catholics, but they completely redefine the terms. Take Jesus's death, they believe his death was simply that he manifested his divine mind. Catholics believe that he had to undergo a physical and painful death in order to cleanse mankind of their sins and that he was the first mortal man to enter into paradise. Very different theology around the same event."

"So how do they explain traffic jams if nothing is real?"

"Funny, Deni. According to them, there is no heaven, no hell, no death. Simply another level of consciousness. In order to move beyond traffic jams, you have to manifest beyond it. The current level we are in, on earth, was created in 6 days which is definitely not the King James Version of the Bible.

The snake was the first manifestation of evil that needed to be overcome. Which is why knowledge is bad, ergo medicine is bad."

"So they don't believe in medicine?"

"Exactly. No. But their faith has adapted. Contradictions always have to adapt. When children started to die because of their refusal to take medicine, the authorities forced them to adapt."

"Adapt how?"

"They were being taken to trial as their beliefs were considered criminal. I say contradiction because the founder, this Eddy woman, sued everyone and their brother. She was cunning and manipulative, which is not exactly in line with materials being figments of our imagination. The cult had to be a religion in order to collect monies without being taxed, and the only way to do that was to allow medicine in certain situations to keep the law at bay. There are even Christian Science nursing homes now. They have reinvented themselves, but only so far as it makes them profitable."

"Sounds like another religion that I know of."

"Warren? Did you call me to insult me and the Catholic faith or consult me?"

"So they do believe in medicine now."

"Again, only so far is it keeps any criminal proceedings off of their doorsteps. They are international, but the home base is still here in Boston. The Christian Science Monitor has won Pulitzer Prizes. The die hards, those that still follow Eddy's version of Christian Science, call themselves Platists. When those that weren't mentally able to heal themselves, like children and the old or with handicaps for example, they were allowed to take medicine. Because of that realignment there was a separation. That was back when Mark Twain took on Christian Science as a crusade. His daughter became a Christian Scientist and he wrote articles and books denouncing them as heretics."

"*The* Mark Twain?"

"Yes. While we were talking I went to my bookshelf here in the rectory. I am pulling up one quote that I have bookmarked. Let's see …. ah yes, here it is. 'From end to end of the Christian Science literature, not a single (material) thing in the world is conceded to be real. Except the dollar.' There is a Mary Baker Eddy Library here in Boston as well. Again I find that odd, since knowledge is supposed to be avoided as it gets in the way of spiritual reality with wisdom of the current one."

"So these Plato people, they kick it old school? No medicine? Snakes are the prime-root of all that is evil?"

"Yes. Precisely. But I have to say that snakes being the representation of all evil is not just a Christian Science thing. Every version of the bible, King James to the Book of Mormon, use the serpent as the physical manifestation of evil. Depending on which version of the Bible, the serpent is mentioned between seventy-three and eighty-eight times. None of them are positive. Each of those roughly eighty times represents evil or chaos."

"You're kinda givin' me the runaround here Father. I just want a yes or no. Is it possible that these Plato people would kill in order to prevent a medicine from being devised from snakes?"

"You didn't mention that part. That is what this is about?"

"Yes or no, Father."

"That is difficult to say. Yes, maybe. But they are but a small faction within the Christian Science community, from what I understand. Like I said, there are always extremists in every organization or group."

"So conducting research on snake venom, which is the root of all evil, to create medicines to cure people from various diseases would blow them the fu …. would really upset them? Do I have that right, Father?"

"In theory, yes. Please answer me. Is that what is going on down there?"

"How would I find out where Platists would congregate down here?"

"You have me there. I could go over to the Christian Science Headquarters here in Boston and informally ask them."

"No but thank you father. You've been very helpful. Don't go stirring up the snake pit."

"You're not going to answer me are you? When are you coming back to Boston? I would love to see you at mass."

"Yeah, I know you would. Thanks again. I'll be in touch." Then I hung up.

25

I CALLED JG TO LET HIM KNOW WHAT I HAD FOUND OUT. He didn't see the connection at first, I had to spell it out for him. I admit that it was a stretch. It seemed like a lot of trouble to go through to stop research that was being done all over the United States. It was a race to see who could research the most types of venom the quickest, in order to get the drugs on the market the quickest. Father Donnelly said that the Platists were all over the Country. International even. That being said, were they committing the same criminal acts in other states or countries in the name of religion?

JG told me that the FBI was waiting in the wings to investigate this case. From what I had uncovered in Costa Rica, this had become a national mass murder spree that was being conducted on foreign soil. There was a Dean at the University of Chicago who was going public, getting the CPD involved in the crimes against the students there. This was a powder-keg, and I needed to stay low profile.

I secretly wanted the FBI to take over the case. There was no way that Captain Simms was going to be able to cut the necessary red tape to get Stubbs's body home and Estabados behind bars, if he was still alive. But that was out of my control. Despite my desire to get justice for my new friend, I had to get justice for those who were killed here in Charleston. I had to ensure that an innocent woman was not incarcerated for life or worse, given the needle. I also had to find Carina.

JG told me where the torched car was located, and the old abandoned church. The dive team was still out on the coastal waters near there, but they had basically lost hope. I headed out that way and was surprised to see such a desolate area right on the Atlantic Ocean. That nobody had dozed the area and developed it into hotels or luxury homes on the water was a complete shock. It was an abandoned mess with homeless squatters and meeting places for drug deals. Meanwhile, I was driving down there in a $75,000 Mercedes. In the back of my mind, as I parked the *AMG* just outside the police tape, I was wondering if JG had good car insurance.

I walked down behind the church, through the back parking lot, to the edge of the hill overlooking the shore. The car was torched all right. Carina's police sedan was incinerated. Melted plastic and tires, shattered glass. What wasn't burned was stolen. There wasn't a license plate even. You can't just put a burning rag in a gas tank to achieve this kind of damage. This thing was doused with something highly combustible and ignited from afar. The police sedan was the fuel for a large fire and explosion. Even in that neighborhood, somebody had to have noticed. The flames would have been tall.

Inside the car was more of the same. Nothing recognizable. The reason for torching a car to this degree was to ensure that there wasn't any trace evidence left for an investigation. Mission accomplished. I hadn't checked with the Charleston CSU, nor would I likely be allowed to, but I was sure that there would be no evidence available to find.

Down the hill, off the shore and into the water, the police boats and divers were combing the ocean floor. There must have been a lot of junk down there. Having to comb through what was relevant evidence and garbage was not a job I wanted. Especially since they obviously hadn't found any relevant evidence. JG would have told me if they had.

I waved to the dive team, who waved back though they probably had no idea who I was. The fact that I wasn't being sneaky inside the police perimeter hopefully allayed any suspicion that I was tampering or pilfering from the crime scene.

I headed back across the parking lot toward the abandoned building. How long it had been forsaken, was a bit of a mystery. By the look of it, the building had been neglected for some time. It had been condemned for safety reasons, but not torn down.

The church was boarded up, which would make it hard to get inside. I am a magician when it comes to picking locks. If It was a matter of just a deadbolt or two, it wouldn't have been a big deal. But the place was boarded up to keep vagrants and squatters out of it. JG said that the police had been inside, so I needed to find how they went in.

The back door, facing the parking lot appeared to have been resealed recently. The plywood looked the same but the helical ridges were new, indicating they used new sheetrock screws used to hold the board in place. I didn't have a Phillips screwdriver or a drill. I gave the plywood my best kick but the stuff was thick. I could have kept kicking it, and eventually broken in, but not without attracting a lot of the wrong kind of attention.

Making my way around the outer edge of the wood, I moved my fingers to see if there was a gap to pry it away from the frame. Luckily whomever had refastened the wide-threaded screws had stripped the holes, affording me the ability to pry the left side of the board just wide enough to slip through.

The inside of the church was as black as the burned car in the parking lot. I couldn't see anything at all until I used the flashlight app on my iPhone, and even then it wasn't bright enough. I wandered around the place like a little blind mouse, while I displaced the real mice and critters that lived inside. A week ago, that place might have freaked me out. A lot had happened since then.

The little white-footed mice were running about all over the place. The church was rife with them. Which meant that I needed to cover my nose and mouth. When you live in a populated area like South Boston, you know these things will piss and shit everywhere which creates an airborne virus that will seriously mess you up, if not kill you. There was a famous landlord who became so for the wrong reasons and because of the furry bastards. He wanted to get rid of his dead-beat residents in order to gentrify. Try as he might, he could not get them to leave. They were poor and had no other place to go. He decided to populate his building with these mice in order to scare them off. It didn't scare them off and they also couldn't get rid of them. Instead the mice piss and feces made them so sick that two of the three kids died. He freed up the building but he is currently spending his time behind bars.

With my face covered, I moved about the mid-sized church looking for clues. Nothing on or around the pews. Nothing on or around the pulpit. After forty minutes I was discouraged and about to leave when I noticed that one of the hundreds of mice was bringing detritus to a nest. The nest was made of; paper, stuffing from the knee-pads on the kneelers, tiny pieces of wood and plastic. The light green paper which was used as the base of the nest is what stood out. I scared off the critters so I could remove the paper, careful not to get the piss and shit all over me.

The light green paper was actually part of a flyer. Parts of it were chewed off or stained, but the gist of it was the notification that the congregation was moving. Calhoun Street. I took a picture of the partial flyer, as best as I could given the lighting and condition of the subject. I snapped several before I could accomplish one that was usable. The flashlight app uses the flash from my iPhone, which I needed to take the picture in the dark. Also you cannot use multiple apps at one time, even with my *5S*. So I oscillated from complete dark to the flash for the photo, which I couldn't use because I couldn't see .... wash, rinse, repeat.

The relocated church was called The Church of Christ, Scientists. It was on the 100 block of Calhoun Street, near an Episcopal Church. Nobody had messed with the *AMG* while it was parked in the desolate neighborhood of the old church, thankfully. The drive was easy, just up East Bay and over onto Calhoun. I was rocking out to the Foo Fighters song *All My Life* as I made my way over to the church.

There was plenty of traffic on the street and plenty of parking. The front of the new facility could have been anything. My accountant could have used the place as his office. The only indication that this was not an office building was the large lettering above the entrance stating that it was a Church of Christ.

The door was unlocked, the lobby and overall decor of the building was sparse. The congregation area itself had neutral, beige walls with nothing on the walls. There was just the one pulpit in the front center of the room. No altar, no cross, no gold chalice. Just to the left of the pulpit was a bouquet of flowers and on the wall above, in all caps, were two quotations:

YE SHALL KNOW THE TRUTH AND THE TRUTH SHALL SET YOU FREE
    CHRIST JESUS

DIVINE LOVE ALWAYS HAS MET AND ALWAYS WILL MEET EVERY HUMAN NEED
    MARY BAKER EDDY

"Can I help you?"

I turned to see a white haired woman in what I guessed was her mid-sixties behind me.

"Yeah. Maybe. I would like to speak with the Pastor, or Reverend, or Priest, or whatever."

"That would be me. I'm Meredith Brown. You are?"

"Warren Dennihan. You can call me Deni. Do you have someplace we can talk?"

"About?"

This could go one of two ways, I thought. *I can play this straight and see how it shakes out, or I play a part and see if I can sneak the information I need.* Stubbs and Carina had taught me that I could get more by playing it straight down here. In Boston, it wouldn't have even crossed my mind.

"About things that I don't want the world to hear. Do you have a place where the acoustics aren't so good?"

"You're accent, it is very peculiar yet familiar."

"Boston. I get that a lot."

"That explains it. Right this way."

We went back to the lobby and into an office. It was a formal office, she sat behind a desk, me in a not-so-comfortable chair in front of her.

"That accent is more harsh, but it makes sense. Our Mother Church is in Boston."

"So I've heard. I'm gonna cut to the chase here, OK?"

"By all means. But we will have to make it short. I am hosting an online service in approximately forty minutes."

"How very modern of you. Prayer through a device that is only an illusion. My mind is blown."

"Are we here to discuss theology or did you have a point? 'Cutting to the chase' you called it."

"Your group here, this cult or religion or what-not, has been doing a lot of protesting outside of pharmaceutical research facilities. Right?"

"That would be not right. Incorrect."

"I've seen pictures, been there myself. I've seen the signs and people shouting about evil and against the will of God."

"And what makes you think these people are members of our congregation?"

"Because they said that they were Christian Scientists. It's also on their signs."

"Unfortunately there are several factions calling themselves that, but not necessarily true. What is this about? If it was us, which it most certainly was not, protesting is legal with the proper permits. Are you with the police?"

"I am working with the police, yes. So you are saying that you believe in modern medicine?"

"I am saying that like all religious groups, leaders must make accommodations to certain things to keep up with laws and/or current practices. Children and the elderly may need medicine in order to survive. We feel that prayer works best, if dire medicine isn't absolutely necessary. Blood transfusions are beyond that scope and the work of evil."

"Evil. Like snakes?"

"Snakes are representative of the mind's focus away from God. What is this really about Mr. Deni?"

"Just Deni. Three people have been murdered using snake venom. The same snake venom that is being used to create synthetic drugs to cure many different diseases that kill people by the millions. Outside of these research facilities are people with your belief system. The Charleston detective that was investigating those murders is now missing. She was last seen speaking with those protesters. You see how this all ties to your group?"

"Now I understand. This has been all over the news. I don't believe I can help you, and I certainly have nothing more to say. Good day." Meredith stood. I didn't.

"If I leave now, I'm coming back here with a team of people that are going to tear this place apart. A cop is missing. The more days that pass where she remains missing, the more desperate they are getting because her chances of being dead are increasing by the minute. They aren't gonna to be polite, they are gonna trash this place looking for a clue in finding her. You can sit back down and talk to me, or do it the hard way. You seem like a semi-reasonable person, so why choose the hard way?"

She sat back down.

"We are not protesting. We support the purists in beliefs, but not in practice. Our religion is about love, not destruction. It is against every fabric of our belief system that the root of all evil, the snake, could be the very thing to create a potion that makes pain go away. Not prayer, not spirituality. Don't you see? We are back in the Garden of Good and Evil, where the serpent is in the Tree of Knowledge. Are we going to go down that road again? The snake is offering us life, but what life? This world is not a reality."

"So you know who it is? The protestors, are they Platists? Your purists?"

"Yes. But they are less organized, in the formal sense. They have many numbers, they gather but not in buildings such as this one. They tithe and are active in various causes. They go to the retreats and conventions, but they do not congregate as formally as we do. Some of them have services online, like I am about to do. This minimizes the expense of having a building in many cases. Here in Charleston? If there is a chapel, I am unaware of it."

"So how do I get in touch with them?"

"You don't."

"How do they recruit new members?"

"By meeting someone. You aren't going to be able to track these people down. I'm not hiding them, they are a completely different group. It would be like Protestants and Catholics. They have the same basic beliefs, but a very different way of going about salvation."

"Do you have a name?"

"Specifically? No."

"You said that they go to your retreats and conventions, you must know somebody. If you are hiding something — "

" — I assure you that I am not hiding anything. If they are doing what they are doing, which I am not saying that they are, then they are doing it under the guise of my religion. I may want the same things, but this is harmful all the way around."

26

THE DAY WAS A TOTAL BUST. Night had fallen and I was no closer to finding Carina than I was yesterday when I was in another country. Tomorrow morning would officially be the sixth day that she was missing. There were no ransom demands. Why keep her that long and then simply let her go? My only hope was that she was being used as leverage once the killers/kidnappers were caught. Leniency for the cop. But hope was fading.

At the current rate we would never find the bastards. That is, of course, if Feinstein was telling the truth. And that was a big if. Everything pointed toward Rueben and his beloved company Nahash Pharmaceuticals. Motive, opportunity, means. Add the massive body count in Costa Rica and you could get the needle ready, no need for a trial. But there was something about the story that wasn't adding up. Estabados denied the murders, but then he denied the murders of all of the researchers as well. Could these be separate cases?

Could Estabados have been taking matters into his own hands in Central America, while others were sabotaging the research in Charleston?

The Platists seem to also have motive. In spades. But without finding them, there was no way to determine opportunity or means. There was no need for Feinstein to create more attention for himself by abducting a Charleston Homicide Detective. Stubbs and I had already been to see him, he knew we were circling the wagons. The protestors were the last to see her. The Platists. But why kidnap a cop? There would have to be several of them. Carina would not go quietly. Maybe they didn't know she was a cop. She was driving an unmarked car.

I called it a night and headed back to JG's house. He was up and about, maybe even waiting for me to arrive, though he never said.

"You're here. What did you find out?" He had a drink and handed me one. Redbreast 12 year Irish Whiskey. My favorite.

"Nothing. Less than nothing actually." I sipped my beverage. It was heaven. "This is delicious, thanks." I took another sip. "I have more questions now than I did at the start of the day."

"We're running out of time, Deni. Carina is the one running out of time."

He had hit me between the eyes and he knew it. I think he knew what my feelings were for her. He knew that her disappearance was probably eating me up. Nobody wanted to find her more than me. He didn't need to push me, I was already very motivated.

"I know, I know. I'm doin' the best I can. Tomorrow I see about punching some holes in Feinstein and his alibi. I was thinking that maybe the Estabados thing and the murders were separate. If I can isolate Rueb out of this, then that pretty much means that they are separate and I can move forward. Estabados couldn't have kidnapped Carina, he wasn't here. If he killed those researchers down there to protect Nahash, he may or may not have done it on his own. And the more I think about it, why kill the team at SCMU and BIOGENESIS if he had access to all the research? He could steal anything he wanted. Samples from the World Toxin Bank, data from any lab he had access to. Which was all of them. The only reason to knock them down was to take them out of the game."

"Right. But according to your theory, isn't that why he was annihilating the teams in the jungle?"

"Yes, but he didn't have access to their research. He can't just walk up to their lab in the middle of the rainforest and ask nicely. It's competitive. He had to destroy them to get their data. Here, he had the data at his fingertips. He went to work every day on the campus and as far as we can tell nobody at the university nor the lab knew that he was a spy for Nahash. No need to kill anyone. In fact, that would draw more attention. He had to step up his game and get out of there once people started getting killed.   If anything, those murders did more harm for his cause than good."

"You're not suggesting that Dr. Estabados is innocent in all of this?"

"Fuck no. He needs to die. And I'm willing to arrange it. But he is gonna be the Feds' problem now."

"And Feinstein?"

"Maybe, maybe not. He is guilty of stealing research, and being a huge bag of douche, but a killer? I don't know yet. We need to see how he fits into this. Tear his life apart. Is he still in custody?"

"Yes. He has been charged on a number of lesser charges. He will be cooling his heels until he goes before the Grand Jury. Then they will make a motion for bail if there is an indictment. If not, then he goes free. You've got maybe two days before the jury convenes."

"Two days. I hope Carina can hold out that long."

"You think she is still alive?"

"I'm hoping. Jesus man. I'm hoping until there isn't any. I'm hoping that the bags of shit that have her are holding her in case they get caught. Use her to try and plead down to lesser charges in exchange for her alive. Otherwise there is no need to keep her alive and she is already dead."

"I'll go see Sierra tomorrow at the prison. I'll let her know what is going on and that we are trying to get her out."

"You go over there every day, don't you?"

"Of course. I love her, Deni."

"I get it. For the first time in my life, I get it."

"We have to get her out. This case has to be solved."

"This thing is a mess, JG. I know. I'm doin' my best. I'm sorry that I got dragged into this, but thankful at the same time. I never would have met Carina."

"I know you, Deni. You'll make it happen. For both of us."

"Stubbs. That poor prick. I knew him for only a few days and I miss him. I have never seen so many bodies in one spot, man. If this turns out to be as I think it is, ya know, separate? Then he died for nothin'."

"No Deni. He died uncovering those atrocities which may never have been discovered. And from what you have told me, he died saving you."

"Yeah. I don't need the reminder."

A silence came between us. I drained my drink, JG finished his. What he was drinking was not entirely clear to me. If it was alcohol, I knew he was enduring some shit. He didn't drink very often, he said. If he was drinking then, I didn't want to rub his nose in it.

"Do you want another one?"

"Yes, but I'm getting up early. I need to get some sleep."

"There is another bottle upstairs in your suite. If you can't sleep …. "

"My brain is fried and I'm exhausted. I'll sleep."

And I did.

27

MORNING BROKE AND I WAS UP AND REFRESHED. Feinstein. I gave myself the day to enter his life. Uncover every single skeleton, in every single closet. I was going to know if his bowel movements were regular by the end of the day.

In this day and age, most of what investigators do is on the computer. You can dig up virtually whatever you want on someone by searching the web. If the person you are looking for ran track, there was a team picture on the internet. Somewhere, it was a matter of looking hard enough. Medical records are only private when the proper resources aren't available. I'm not saying it's ethical, but for the right price any information that you want to know about somebody is yours for the taking.

Only I suck at computers. I have people in Boston that do that sort of thing for me. One woman in particular. We have an on again, off again type of relationship. At that time it was off again.

She could hack into anything, I have seen her do it. She has a moral compass, so there are times that I have to figure things out without her. Progress with her help was always exponentially faster than without. I was a thousand miles away from her, there was no way that I would be able to persuade her to help me out over the phone. I am a more face-to-face kinda guy. Which means that I wouldn't be able to talk her into helping me without sleeping with her.

I needed a plan B.

After my shower I went downstairs and found that JG was home. Which was a surprise.

"I thought you were headed over to Leath to see Sierra today."

"I am. Brady had a slow start, which means he missed carpool. I drove him to school but missed my class over at SCMU. My TA is covering for me. I will go see Sierra this afternoon. I have the morning free."

"Perfect. Do you know anybody that is good with computers?"

"Of course. Attorneys have privileged information that has to remain confidential. It's kind of a job requirement. All of my staff at the firm have at least a computer and a tablet."

"I don't mean can they fill out a spreadsheet and download an iTune or whatever. I mean I need someone who can delve into someone's life electronically."

"Deni, I am a respected attorney. If you are asking me to aid in a cybercrime then — "

" — I'm asking you to point me in the direction of someone that can help me look into Rueben Feinstein. Computers ain't my thing."

"I can have you spend time with Harold, my IT guy at the firm. He is the Director of Information Technology for the largest law firm in South Carolina, he is not going to help you commit a crime. So nothing illegal, Deni. I mean it. For my sake also. I don't have plausible deniability if a hack is traced back to my law firm."

If you were told that you were meeting someone for the first time with the name Harold, you would probably have a picture in your head of what he would look like. If you were given a little more information and told that this guy is a Director of Information Technology, a fancy name for super-smart computer guy, that might further develop that picture in your head. It did for me. I was expecting a Poindexter. Maybe a pocket protector.

I need to reevaluate my stereotypes. This kid was a complete paradigm shift. Are all the cool kids IT geniuses now? Harold was in his mid-twenties and could have been on the cover of GQ. If you pointed to this guy and said that he was a Calvin Klein underwear model or did cologne ads, *that* would have made sense. Tall, dark, and handsome has a name. And his name is Harold.

I entered the chilly, glassed-in room with computer equipment stacked like library shelves in the back half of the large space. The front half had only one desk, which belonged to the handsome kid approaching me with his hand out.

"You must be Deni." I shook his hand. Not wimpy or frail like I would have expected. The metrosexual in front of me was dressed casually in jeans and a trendy, long-sleeved shirt. I was trying to decide if I liked the hipster.

"Yeah. And you must be Harold. Do you go by Harold or Harry or — "

" — Harold. No nicknames please. JG told me to free up my day. He said that you have a project for me, and that with your reputation it might involve some things on the fringe of legalities. I am to insulate him from all of that, and make sure you get what you want. So. What do you want?"

Right down to business. I *did* like that.

"It seems that JG has told you a lot about me."

"He says that you are the best investigator he has ever worked with, but a complete dunce when it comes to computers. I can tell from your accent that you come from Boston."

"Right. Well, I've been summed up in two sentences. I am down here investigating the recent serial murders, and the abduction or worse of a local detective. I believe that they are connected. Where you come in is that I need someone to find out everything they can on a Rueben Feinstein. He is the CEO and President of Nahash Pharmaceuticals, which is a subsidiary company for Wyatt Pharmaceuticals."

"I've read about them online. What other information do you have on this guy? Social Security number? Home address? Middle name? .... "

"Nope, nope, and nope."

He sat down at his desk which had two monitors, side by side, each one was bigger than my TV at home. He kicked back in his chair, banging away on his wireless keyboard. There was a mouse up on his desk but he never seemed to use it. His fingers moved at lightning speed, jumping back and forth from window to window. If that was all that the kid did, I would have been impressed. I stood over his shoulder, which he didn't like.

"This will take a while. Why don't you give me your cell number and I will call you when I have all of the data compiled."

"You don't want me to stick around? You don't really know what information I am looking for. What if you have a question?"

"Then I will call you. I will get you everything. Bank accounts, the works. I'm completely fire-walled, so there will be no worries about it coming back to the firm. My job is to protect all of our client data and to protect our computers from being exposed. I am good at my job because I can't even key into our computers without the appropriate codes. Others are not as good as me."

"Thanks Harold."

"No worries. I'm just doing my job."

I was pleasantly surprised to have my day freed up. I was going to get all of the information I wanted, hopefully, without lifting a finger. It must be nice to have a big staff. I have one other investigator in my firm and another guy that I use to help with the heavy lifting on occasion. I have contacts and people that use me for favors, and I them, but I don't have a staff at my beck and call. It was nice.

Feinstein was in lock-up. I wanted to question him, or at least be in the room with Captain Simms when he did so I could throw a couple of questions out there. But I couldn't do that without the information that pretty-boy Harry was getting me.

Nahash might be a source of information. I wondered if there still was a Nahash after recent events. I headed over there to see for myself.

Twelve minutes and no speeding ticket. I had found a station on Pandora for a band called Kings of Leon. I really did love that Mercedes. I was blasting the tune *Crawl* when I pulled up to the main gate.

The front gate was unattended, a pad lock was used to secure the gate. There were no protestors, nor any media crews. What I lack in prowess on a computer, I make up for with other skills. Say picking locks. That particular lock was not a good one. I manually opened the gate, drove through, manually closed the gate, and fake-locked it in less than three minutes. It took longer to move the car than open the lock. Anyone coming by would see the padlock. They would have to pull on the base of it to realize it was not fully latched.

I drove down to the Administration Building, which was also locked. There was a green light illuminated, indicating an alarm system to keep riffraff out. But that system is broken now.

The massive corner office of Rueben Feinstein looked like he was going to show up for work that day. Messages on his desk, computer sleeping, everything neat and tidy. That is of course until I was through with it. I didn't ransack the place, but I wasn't meticulous in my search either.

There were all kinds of files, none of it very telling. Projects that were about to be started. New-hire paperwork and resumes for top people in their respective fields. Indecipherable data from research, which may or may not have been reallocated from the parties who conducted the research. I could not find anything that linked Rueb to the three murders or to Carina.

But I did find a satellite phone. It was a different kind than the one I pieced back together in the jungle, but I knew what I was looking at. The Iridium *9555* was staring at me. Taunting me.

I was tempted to call. I had to know if the great Doctor Enrique Estabados was alive. But if I called him, he wasn't going to be able to speak with me. There was not a waking moment that went by where Stubbs and his sacrifice for me didn't enter my mind. Tipping my hand might make everything down in Costa Rica a fire-sale. They would destroy every piece of evidence, move the bodies, and vanish before justice could be done.

The phone stared back at me for an eternity. There was no upside to making that call. But I had to know.

Using the menu button on the left, and the up — down arrows in the middle, I recalled the last transmission. Before I knew it I had pressed the green button above the 1 button. Slowly, I brought the receiver to my ear.

When the transmission was connected, the voice coming through the other end was like a knife in my chest. I wasn't sure what to make of it.

"Hello. Hello."

I thought I was dreaming. How could it be?

The sound repeated in my ear. A voice I will never forget as long as I live.

It was Stubbs.

28

THE ELECTRONIC INVESTIGATION INTO RUEBEN FEINSTEIN by the IT genius, Harold Dempsey, was going rather well. Extremely well rather. He traced the CEO back to his days as a child growing up in Brooklyn, New York, in the Garment District. In theory nobody was supposed to be able to look into the past of a child. In every society, children are considered sacrosanct. Off limits. In real life however, especially in the information age, it is impossible to shield their digital footprint.

Parents these days do their best to protect their children, but in the 50s who knew what was to come. Letting your kids out of your sight was de rigueur. You didn't track your child's every movement or scrutinize every friend like parents do now. Bullying was part of growing up. It was in the 50s, just as it was in the 90's. The PTA is now more involved than ever, but still cannot protect youngsters from the dissemination of digital information. Cell phones, Facebook, Twitter, Instagram, and the like doesn't make life any easier.

Once Harold found out Rueben's full name from the public records of Wyatt Pharmaceuticals financial performance statements and prospectus, he was then able to view Feinstein's birth certificate. From there, he was able to retrieve his parent's information. Then he was able to access his parent's application for a social security number, which afforded Harold the ability to get that number from the secure Social Security Administration web files, which was called the Department of Health, Education & Welfare at the time of issuance.

Fortified with Rueben's social security number, the floodgates opened and he could access everything down to his shoe size.

At the age of seven, young Rueben was uprooted and his family moved to South Carolina. He apparently had little or no friends because Harold was able to see his library and zoo membership cards, which were used virtually ever day. Why someone had taken the time to put the information onto microfiche and then scanned into the digital world was anyone's guess, but there they were in plain sight. Rueben was always in the public library or at the Magnolia Reptile Zoo.

He graduated high school at sixteen, achieving his Bachelor's degree by nineteen from Clemson University. By the astounding age of twenty-seven, he had earned two Doctorate degrees in Ophiology and Herpetology. He was strait-laced, not even a parking ticket had been issued to him in that time.

Rueben was a financial supporter of his Jewish Temple, but there was no way to determine his attendance. He had never married. There were internal emails at Wyatt that speculated that he was gay. The people that reported to him during that time spent all kinds of company time and resources bashing their boss digitally. Apparently he didn't have any friends as an adult either.

Moving up through the ranks at Wyatt, Rueben was able to see first-hand how a pharmaceutical company should run. Shuffling through several documents, Harold was able to discern that the Board of Directors was allowing their star to branch out with his own subsidiary, his own pet project. Over the course of his almost thirty-five years with Wyatt, he had proven himself. Both he and the oligopic corporation had made millions, or more accurately, hundreds of millions.

Feinstein's millions were tied up in Nahash. He had been funding Enrique Estabados out of his personal finances for the past two years, wiring money directly into his minion's accounts.

Harold looked into Estabados's finances by dialing into his accounts. He was a shady character, this Estabados, funding all sorts of other shady characters from those accounts. If he was trying to hide it, he was doing a terrible job. The Doctor even converted some of his payments into CRC, Costa Rican money, prior to the transfer to ensure he was getting the best currency rates. Stingy and stupid.

Large payments were made by Estabados to a private security team, the Clodomiro Picado Research Institute who is the top global venom exporter, and various Costa Rican officials. All of the money being siphoned from Wyatt, who paid Rueben, who then paid Estabados, who then paid off whomever he had to with shadowy deals. Quite the operation. Most money-laundering passed around that many times would go undetected. It had. But it didn't take a forensic accountant to follow the cash. Millions of US dollars.

He then began to search into Wyatt, which was more difficult due to the encryption protocols. Harold searched through emails and what was thought to be secure documents trying to link knowledge of the money-laundering to someone high up the food chain at the conglomerate. He came up empty.

Prying into Nahash emails garnered no more insight. The monies were wired to Estabados as both salary payments and an operating budget. Enrique's salary was coming from Nahash Payroll, while his operating budget was coming directly from Feinstein.

While the movement of operating money was regular, there was nothing in terms of correspondence which would indicate that it was earmarked for specific expenditures. Rueben funded an operation to spy on and to reallocate data from BIOGENESIS. He asked unrealistically few questions about the money. It seemed as though Estabados had a blank check without any accountability. Either his lawyers told him not to ask in order to stay removed from any culpability, or he didn't want to know because he suspected.

The salary payments to Estabados from Nahash confirmed that he was working for both pharmaceutical companies simultaneously and had been for some time. There was no denying that, whether Feinstein was or not, Harold didn't know.

Other than a DUI, Rueben had kept his life clean of legal entanglements. Technically his record was spotless, because the inebriated driving was thrown out of court caused by a lack of evidence. The lack of evidence suspiciously coincided with a large donation to the arresting officer's child's football booster's club. Funny how paperwork can be conveniently lost, but the electronic trail never fully disappears.

Feinstein's social life consisted of trysts with expensive male escorts at a local five-star hotel, once per week. The orders were conducted online through a website. The same male escort was ordered every time. Rueben must be smitten. Harold wondered how Rueben would make this information disappear if it ever came to see the light of day.

Harold had seen enough. He picked up his phone and dialed. The call went to voicemail.

"Deni. Harold here. I picked and poked but it looks like other than a few relatively insignificant personal secrets, Rueben has made a conscious effort to look clean.

Nahash paid the doctor's salary, and Feinstein wrote a blank personal check for operating expenses. There is no denying that Estabados was a mole and they committed industrial espionage together. That is fact.

Feinstein was funding Estabados's operating expenses out of pocket, like I said. I'm no lawyer but it would seem that he did so because he knew that something nefarious was taking place. Why else keep it off the corporate books? I think that it will be very difficult for him to claim that he is completely innocent in this, whether he actually knew the day-to-day or not. I cannot find anything that indicates that he knew, in fact it seems clear he was diligent in not-knowing.

Beyond that, Estabados is a scumbag though. This message is probably going to get cut off so I'll fill you in fully and print you out a formal report if you would like when you come back. See you soon."

29

THE SATELLITE PHONE RESTED IN MY SWEATY HAND while I listened to Eric Stubbs call out through the tiny speaker on the satellite phone. My mind was racing as I tried to fathom all of the elements of how this had come to pass. The only way to describe the situation was to use a word that is overused, and misused, by today's youth. Surreal. I hate that word, but it is the only way to describe my shock.

I'm happy that he is alive, but how is he still alive? Where is he being held? How can I get him out? How does he have Estabados's satellite phone? Estabados was trying to proclaim his innocence, though he was lying, Stubbs cut out his tongue. Was that because Stubbs was involved? How many secrets did Stubbs have? Was he working for Feinstein the whole time? For Estabados?

All of these thoughts were running through my head. I felt like such an asshole. I believed that he was my friend, yet he had betrayed me. JG would probably be just as devastated. I don't have many friends. Even though I had only known him a few days, I had trusted him. He saved my life. Or did he? *What was his end-game?*

"Hello? Is anybody there? I can't hear you." Stubbs voice was undeniable.

"Stubbs? What the fuck? What's going on? Where are you?"

"Deni? Thank God. You made it out of here. You have no idea how much I hoped you would be ok."

His voice was weak. If it was weak before he knew it was me on the phone, I didn't hear it. But it was weak then . I wondered if he was playing me again. Or still.

"So how long have you been working for Feinstein, Stubbs?"

"What? I don't have long, Deni so don't mess around. They kept me alive long enough to torture me, looking for you. I escaped again, but they are trailing me."

"What am I a fuckin' idiot Stubbs? What's the coverup? Whats your deal, guy?"

"My 'deal, guy' is that I'm gonna die very soon. Doesn't get much more of a final deal than that."

"Then how do you have Estabados's satellite phone?"

"I stole it when I escaped. Who memorizes phone numbers anymore? This is the last number that was logged into this phone. I've been trying to call this number but there hasn't been an answer. There are international codes, so I can't just dial 9-1-1. How do you have Feinstein's?"

"I'm in his office looking for evidence. Where are you?"

"I'm in the Caribbean on a beach, having a drink with a little umbrella in it. Where do you think I am? If I don't die from my wounds, they will kill me this time for sure."

He sounded weak and fading. He was coughing, just as he was the last time I had seen him. It sounded like all of the fight he had left in him was being directed toward me. It was either an Oscar-worthy performance or he was in trouble. He was one tough bastard to have survived up to this point. If, in fact, he was really in any trouble at all.

"Why did you cut out his tongue? What was he going to say, Stubbs? He denied killing all of those people."

"He is a scumbag liar, and he is still alive."

"Convince me, Stubbs."

"I don't have the time or strength, Deni. I should have killed him. This is going to be the last time we ever talk, you want to fight? You want to think of me as a liar? Don't get me and Estabados confused."

A few moments of silence elapsed. I was collecting my thoughts, Stubbs was collecting the last of his strength.

"I'll see about getting you some help as quick as I can. You hold on." I can't honestly tell you at that point if I believed him one hundred percent or if I was just playing along. I wanted to believe him.

"Forget that, Deni. I'm a dead man. Just use the coordinates on the phone's GPS tracker to find me. I'll hide in the jungle with the phone on me. Find my body. And I got back your gun, too. The *1911* I gave you? I'm dying, Deni. Don't let me rot here. You want your gun, you come get my body and bury me proper. Promise me."

I felt like a piece of shit. The guy saved my life and I doubted him. I still doubted him then if truth be told, but I have no concrete reason why. Maybe that is why I don't have many friends. My chest was aching again, listening to him die all over again, and knowing that just like the last time there was nothing I could do about it.

"Deni? You promise me. Believe me or not, don't let me rot here. Promise."

"I promise, Stubbs. I'll make sure you don't stay there."

"They're coming. Make these assholes pay. For me. Don't make this all be for nothing."

"Stubbs, I - " But he was gone.

Again.

I listened to my message from Harold on my iPhone as I left the Nahash complex. Feinstein was clean. Ish. It sounded like Estabados was running his own show on the side, only Rueben was paying the bills. Whether that made him guilty in the eyes of the law was for people like JG to figure out. Stubbs was dying or dead. One more added to the dozens down there already. Legally or not, in my view Estabados and Feinstein were responsible for it. Whether Stubbs was dirty or not, he didn't deserve to rot down there. Not like that.

Harold wanted to tell me in person what he had found, but it sounded like he hadn't found much of anything according to the message. Forensic accounting was not going to make sure that justice was done. He could tell me that over the phone.

"Harold. Thanks for getting back to me so soon. You work fast."

"You're welcome. Are you headed back this way?"

"No. I was headed over to have a chat with Feinstein in holding. Did you find anything that would help me with that?"

"Yes and no. He is mostly clean. He made sure of it. Estabados is running his own game, but I can't find one single piece of correspondence that would suggest that Rueben officially knows about it. It is all his money though."

"So where is the 'yes' part?"

"I have a report that I have created for you that I can email — "

" — why don't you just tell me. I'm not much good with technology."

"It's very simple. You have an iPhone, it can handle emails."

"I know it can handle emails, but the writing is so small. Just tell me."

"I'll still send it to you. Have someone at the precinct show you how to open it in an app so you can print it. Even a homeless person over there will be able to help you print an email. How are you so incompetent with — "

" — just get to the point, Harold. I need your shit like I need a full-body rash."

"Bottom line? Rueben is gay."

"So what? Who cares?"

"Well, he does. He doesn't want anyone to know otherwise he would be out in the open about it. Instead, he is paying just shy of $2000 a night for a suite at the Wentworth, then another $3000 per night for his male companion. I'm sure the room-service isn't the only tip. He shells it out every week."

"Great. So what? He doesn't want some random dude knowing him or where he lives."

"Yeah but he gets the same not-so-random dude every week."

"I see. So I use that information as leverage to see what other secrets he has been keeping? Do you have the man-whore's name?"

"It is in the report I just sent you. I dove into his life, Deni. Everything is on computers now. There are no secrets. He was worth, personally, before starting up Nahash, about half a billion dollars. His personal portfolio and monies have taken a beating since then. He keeps shelling out money but nothing is coming in. He is only showing a fraction of the money going out to his handlers at Wyatt. If the Board of Directors at Wyatt knew what was going on they would have cut ties long ago. Now that he is being investigated, I'm guessing they are looking to get as far away from him as possible."

"Has that gone public yet?"

"It's starting to get some attention, from what I'm seeing. But it hasn't gone viral yet."

"OK Harold. Nice work. I'll let JG know what a help you were."

"Thanks, but he knows. Good luck over there. I don't like this Estabados guy."

"Me neither."

The precinct at 80 Broad was abuzz as usual. The late afternoon or prevening was when the place was usually busy. Cops went out all day and corralled their prey, taking them back to the police station for questioning and/or processing. This day was no different.

I was in no mood for small-talk. It had been a long day and I had made no progress on the Charleston murders, nor on locating Carina. The only thing that was discovered for certain was that Stubbs was dead. Again.

Feinstein was the purse strings behind his and the other deaths, whether he knew it or not. He was going to pay one way or another. He would help bring down Estabados and sort out who the Charleston serial killer was or he would pay the hard way. In either case, he was going to be ruined both financially and professionally.

Captain Simms was in his office, which I was beginning to suspect was usual. I didn't knock, I opened his door and entered which was also a custom he hated.

"No need to knock. Just walk right in."

"I did. Thanks."

"What are you doing here?"

"I want to have a sit-down with Feinstein."

"I'm sure you would. This is a police station. You know …. for police. Last I checked you aren't one anymore, and never were down here. Even on the off-chance that he admits anything to you, you're not a cop."

"Exactly. I don't have to read him his rights because he's not speaking with the police. No lawyer necessary. You guys can have the tape rolling and watch from the other side of the glass."

"I don't think that is legal."

"It is if I tell him that he is being recorded. He is in a police station, and he is being recorded. No reasonable presumption of privacy. It will be legal. Any deals will have to come from you or your DA though."

"He's not going to get a pass. If we cut him a deal on the three murders here, the Federal Prosecutors are going to want him for the mass graves in Costa Rica."

"That is for you to work out. I want to find Carina, and so do you. He admits to anything or gives us more evidence that gets Sierra Byrne out of prison, that'll be a huge bonus."

"Why would he talk to you?   We have been at him several times, he lawyers up and shuts up every time."

"I have uncovered some of his peccadilloes that he has worked very hard to keep in the closet."

"We moved him into holding. Give me fifteen minutes or so to get him up into an interview room and the machines set up."

"One more thing. Can you look at my phone and see about printing off this email?"

30

INTERVIEW ROOM #1 WAS EXACTLY LIKE EVERY POLICE INTERROGATION room that had ever been shown on TV or in movies. The mirrored wall with the equipment and observation room behind one side of the room; the one table in the middle of it; the painted and perforated sound panels that lined the remaining three walls; all clichéd but very real. The unoriginality of Hollywood came from somewhere.

I entered the room, where the haggard Rueben Feinstein was already alone, seated, and waiting. He wasn't handcuffed, nor did I want him to be. I wanted him to feel comfortable. As comfortable as possible in an interrogation room on a metal chair.

I took my seat opposite him, staring at him for a long while, and began my spiel.

"How ya doin' Rueb?"

"It's Rueben. What are you doing here? And where are my lawyers?"

"It's not that kinda interview. I'm not a cop, so you don't need your lawyers. Unless you want them. But why would you at a million dollars an hour?"

"Then I am not speaking to you."

"You don't have to if you don't want to. Your choice. I am just going to record your not speaking though, just so you know."

He nodded his head, indicating he understood but didn't care. I had a blue folder in my hand which I then placed on the table in front of me. It contained the attachments to the email that Harold had sent to my iPhone. I didn't open it just yet.

"Are you good with computers, Rueb?"

He didn't answer.

"I'm a genius when it comes to computers." So I lied. Who cares?

"They say that ethical people do the right thing even when nobody is watching. Trouble is that nowadays, everyone is always watchin', Rueb. Big Brother. CCTV cameras, computer footprints, cellphone trackers. So when you think nobody is watchin' …. turns out they are. You're not a very ethical guy, Rueb."

He was eying me but remained silent.

"You don't have to speak. I'm just lettin' you know what is going to be public information. As of this moment, most of what I am sayin' isn't known by very many people. But when your little gems, your little secrets come out? How long do you think it is going to take for Wyatt Pharmaceuticals to distance themselves from you? You are only about an inch away from going to prison for the rest of your life, at a minimum, maybe get the needle. I'm no cop, so I can't really save you from any of that shit, Rueb. But maybe you can help yourself here."

"There is nothing to save myself from. I have done nothing wrong."

"Have it your way. But we have evidence of bodies that have been buried near your research facility in Costa Rica. And you are about to have one more added to your list of murdered victims down there. My partner, Eric Stubbs, do you remember him?"

No answer.

"Well he has your satellite phone. Estabados has been doing some pretty horrible shit, Rueb."

"I have no knowledge of any of that. I am a — "

" — if it waddles and quacks, don't tell me it's a fuckin' hippo, Rueb."

"If he is working on his own agenda — "

" — you think you are going to separate yourself from him? You funded him. The money came out of your personal accounts. Legally, it looks like hired hits. Sponsored genocide."

After opening the folder, I took out the email attachments Harold sent me tracking Rueben's funds into Estabados's account. I showed the document to Feinstein, then went on.

"How much of a stretch is it going to be for a jury to connect the mass murders to the serial murders here in Charleston? Are you really going to stay hitched to Estabados's wagon? You are already in financial ruin, you're hemorrhaging money with nothing coming in. You have a large number of expenses, like most rich people I would imagine. But unlike most rich people you are paying for an expensive male prostitute every week, which adds up. Wyatt is about to cut you off like an amputated limb, so professionally you're just as fucked."

Feinstein's face was white. Whiter than usual. Cold sweat was beading on his forehead.

"Now, added to the all of the bodies you and your subordinate have racked up, you now have a missing detective. The same homicide detective that was investigating the serial murders here in Charleston. The serial murders that a jury is going to connect to you based on the mass murders that we can prove you funded in Costa Rica. Are you startin' to feel the weight on this? You're in some serious shit, guy."

"And you think that you can make it all go away?"

"You're not listening, Rueb. *I* can't make it disappear. But if you want the DA and the Feds to start seein' your side of things, you better start sharin' some information. Where is she?"

"I wish I knew. I have absolutely nothing to do with her disappearance."

"That is not bein' very helpful, chief."

"Listen to me.   I funded Dr. Estabados for a result.   Did I have my suspicions about how he was getting his results? I have no comment on that. But there is no way that he had anything to do with the murders here. I have been racking my brain thinking about this, he was otherwise engaged doing business for me at the times that the three people were killed here in Charleston. He was in Costa Rica, as you well know, when the detective was taken. All I wanted was to advance my research on medical solutions by synthesizing venom.   I wanted to have the first to patent those solutions, ahead of the competition. I didn't want any of this to happen. I did not order it, nor did I want anyone in my employ to kill people or draw attention to us by abducting Detective Carina Fischer."

"Then who did, Rueb?   It's in your best interest to start bein' more proactive here."

"Do you realize how many people are after this same research?   How many people don't want this research to exist?"

"I'm gettin' that vibe, yeah."

"Do you remember all of the hand-wringing that occurred when cloning research was first introduced?"

"Yes. But you're not researching making human parts or a new human."

"No. But everywhere in history, snakes are bad. From Adam and Eve to Medusa to that stupid movie *Anaconda*. It takes a lot of undoing to assure the public that snakes will save the planet from the illnesses that plague them. That venom is the solution to a longer life."

"But it's not just snake venom that is being researched, guy. Scorpions, bees, spiders — "

" — but *we* are only after snake venom. Nahash. We get threats every day. And not just strongly worded emails. We have religious groups that drop poisonous mice onto snake populations to stave off our research. Do you know how damaging that is? These people are well funded and well organized. That was what I was counter-funding. In part. That is what I thought. And that is just one example."

He had me at religious group.

"Do you know anything about this religious group?"

"I had them looked into, yes. They are an Orthodox Christian Science group called Platists."

"And?"

"And what? Do you think that they are responsible for mass murder and the kidnapping a police officer?"

"Lets put our cards on the table, Rueb. You and I both know that .... "

Some of the pieces to the puzzle were starting to come together. There were still several key pieces missing, pieces that needed to be sorted out. Dr. Enrique Estabados went down to Costa Rica to save the precious snakes from being poisoned and ruining Nahash's chances at developing miracle drugs. Maybe steal some other research. The guys he hired with guns were supposedly there to protect the snakes and deal with any resistance to others sharing their knowledge. The pit full of university researchers wasn't directly on the land Estabados had carved out to do research, but it was nearby. His private stash.

He hadn't questioned us to find out who we were or what group we were with, he just assumed. Or he already knew. Feinstein probably told him we were coming. Estabados vehemently denied being responsible for the deaths of those people in the pit, up to his last word. Clearly he was lying. But was he protecting Rueben, Nahash, or himself.

Estabados was afraid of the religious zealots. One of the reasons for his army. But would a religious group kill all of those people? Or the people in Charleston?

" …. You were saying?"

"Say for one brief second that I believe that *you* are innocent. Estabados is a different story. I've seen that fuck in action, and my partner is dead because of him. But let's just say that the mass murderers, the serial murderers here, and the abduction of Detective Fischer aren't you, but are Estabados and/or this religious group. Why are they picketing and protesting outside of BIOGENESIS and not outside Nahash? You are conducting the same research, only on a smaller scale, correct?"

"We are more specialized, yes. They do picket and protest from time to time. The detective spoke with them as she was leaving our facility the day that she disappeared. Also, you must remember, we are not fully operational as of yet."

"OK. Apart from that, how do they have access to BIOGENESIS, SCMU, and the World Toxin Bank?"

"I would have no idea. I just know that Enrique would have no reason to commit murder. It would draw undo attention to Nahash, and he had already taken the necessary research. Hypothetically."

"But nobody at Nahash was killed. And I saw the bodies in Costa Rica for myself. He killed there, for sure."

"Not to sound callous, but if you put all of those people in Costa Rica aside, what are you left with? If your burgeoning theory is accurate, two birds with one stone. The zealots are destroying all research in Costa Rica, while they frame my company in taking down another."

"Your Estabados had one agenda, Platists with another?"

"He is not *mine*. Dr. Estabados simply worked for me."

"Worked huh? Already distancing yourself? Nice. So that's what you're going with, Rueb? Final answer? You hired Estabados to steal data, and he was a bit too much of a go-getter? Without your knowledge? That all of these are separate yet entangled entities?"

"Without legal representation, that is what I am willing to say at this point."

"So where do I find these Platists?"

"I have absolutely no idea."

"You had never met with any of them?"

"No, of course not. These nuts would just breach us with emails, voicemails, and such. They organized the occasional picket out by the main gate but they were never were able to circumvent our security. You and your friend were the only ones to do that."

"I'm going to need to go back to your office. I need to see if I can get a physical address from those emails. Did you save the voicemails? Maybe we can trace them from the phone calls."

"No. I didn't save them, nor any emails. They were annoying but crazy, I thought. I had no need to save them."

"That doesn't help your cause, Rueb. I'm not saying that I buy your bullsh, but I am gonna need more than your word. Some sorta proof. Carina's life is at stake here. Those dead bodies need justice. All of them. I think it's pretty clear at this point that the woman who is currently incarcerated for all of this is innocent.

"And we are gonna need to get Estabados back here, Rueb."

"Anything I can do to help."

Now he wants to help, I thought.

"Better late than never, I suppose."

31

THE MEETING THAT FOLLOWED THE INTERVIEW WITH RUEBEN
Feinstein was nonproductive to say the least.   Captain Simms had been
watching the interview from the observation room on the other side of the
mirror. He was unimpressed with me. He still believed that Feinstein and his
international team were behind all of the bodies. The mass murders, the serial
murders, the abduction and possibly worse of Detective Fischer.   In truth, I
wasn't completely sold either, but the pieces fit better with Estabados working
his evil on his own in Central America; while the Platists worked their own
brand of terror, here in Charleston.

What I needed to do was find these religious zealots. Once I found them I
could ask them how they had access to BIOGENESIS, to the labs at SCMU, and
to the World Toxin Bank. Access was the key to proving the case. Access was

going to be the only piece that would get Dr. Byrne, JG's client and therefore my client, out of stir.

Nobody was going anywhere. Feinstein was still in lockup, and would be no matter how many lawyers or billable hours he had amassed. Dr. Byrne wasn't leaving the jug anytime soon either. Not without someone to take her place. Estabados was presumably still in Costa Rica, though the FBI was waiting in the wings if not already working to extradite him. And poor Carina. Heaven only knew her location. Heaven and whomever was holding her. I hoped that her situation had not changed for the worse.

I called Harold. The only lead in finding these people, to either prove or disprove my new theory, was to trace emails and the phone calls. I asked him if he could do that when they had been deleted. He said his expertise was in email, not phones, but yes he could. That an email, though deleted, could still be found.

I told him to meet me at Nahash. I gave him the address and raced the *AMG* over there. I am not sure why I sped there. There was nothing I could do besides wait for Harold. Maybe because the SiriusXM station was on Ozzy's Bone-yard and *Five Finger Death Punch* was blaring in my ears. I raced over there like my hair was on fire. My ears were.

So I waited in the parking lot for a few minutes. Harold had all the know-how. Except for the breaking-in part.

"Thanks for rushing right over here, Harold. An hour? Is that the best you could do?"

"I came as quickly as I could. I have other responsibilities you know. I also had to clear it with my boss."

"You're boss is my boss. Anyway, Rueben's office is right in here."

"Do you have any of his pass codes?"

"No. This is not really on the record, if you know what I mean. I'm not the police. I don't have a warrant."

We walked into the corner penthouse office together.

"That would be too easy. Wow, this is an amazing office. Look at the view."

Harold was taking too much time for my liking, looking out of the corner windows of the CEO's office.

"Yes, it is. Is that going to be a distraction?"

"No. Relax, will you?"

"Are forgetting that a woman is missing? A Charleston Homicide Detective? The longer she waits the less likely she has of being alive on the other end."

"Why would they kill her?"

"Because the people who have her have killed enough people where one more ain't gonna matter."

"And you think that these religious zealots would kill someone? Isn't that against their ethos?"

"Their what?"

"What they believe."

"They believe that medicine is evil. That everything in this physical world are illusions caused by a lack of religious belief."

"Yet they send emails?"

"According to what I've found out, the Platists are like the pure form of Christian Science. They kick it old school, but even in the old school they know how to play the system. They sued everyone and their brother back in the day. The lead lady, Eddy, won lots of cash in dozens of lawsuits. She outlived three husbands. Who outlives three husbands? These people are survivors."

All the while I was ranting about the Platists, Harold was typing away. He had managed to circumvent the security and privacy protocols, passwords and what-not. I'm not sure how he did it, only that he did it. He was able to recreate the emails of hate that were originally sent to Rueben Feinstein. The printer was practically smoking from all of the emails that Harold was printing off. But no matter how many he went through, he kept at it. Which meant to me that he had not found what I wanted him to find. A physical address.

Eventually Harold sat back in what was Rueben's office chair.

"They were good. They spoofed the IP address."

"In English please."

"They cloaked the address from which they sent the emails. For people who say that this world is just an illusion, they sure know how to operate in it."

"Are you trying to say that they are better than you?"

"It's not a matter of better than me. They knew how to make it so that anybody with the knowledge of how IP addresses work, wouldn't be able to trace them. It's like saying that a criminal who knew to use gloves, thereby not leaving a fingerprint, is better than the cops. They didn't leave anything for me to find. They aren't better than me, they just knew not to leave anything behind."

"So how do we find them?"

"That's just it. We can't. This is the end of the road."

"C'mon guy. Make an effort. You're givin' up?"

"Didn't you say that they picket or protest or something? Follow them to wherever they are from where they are picketing."

"They don't need to anymore. BIOGENESIS has been set back decades, they aren't researching venom right now. Not snake venom anyway. Nahash is out of business. Did you see anybody on the way in? You like this office so much, you can probably have it."

"Funny."

"What about the phones? Voicemails?"

"That is not really my area of expertise, but walk through the logic. They went through all of the trouble of making sure that nobody could track an email. They hid their whereabouts with highly randomized code, and a ton of it, which spoofed their IP address. They took the time to create a denial-of-service attack — eh, never mind. They went through a lot of trouble, essentially to inundate the recipient. So that being said, you think that they are going to be foolish enough to allow a phone number to be traced? *If* we could access Nahash phone records, and *if* we could pinpoint which phone call left which voicemail, that have all been deleted by the way, do you think that it is going to be linked to a traceable phone?"

"You're kinda a Debbie Downer aren't ya? I'm not givin' up. I'm gonna find these fucks."

"Your dedication is both admirable and blind. The police haven't found her after more than a week of searching. She is one of their own. They have come up blank. This was a very good idea, I'll give you that. I am impressed that you thought of it to be honest. Printing an email from your phone was daunting, so a physical address from an IP is rather ingenious for a guy like you. But it is over. You are not going to find them, ergo you are not going to find her. I am really very sorry. When people don't want to be found they — "

" — they don't want to be found. Right. But what if they came to me?"

"I'm afraid you've lost me."

"Why chase them? Let them come to me."

"Uh huh. And why would they do that?"

"You have to make it worth their while."

32

SKY PHILLIPS READ THE WEDNESDAY MORNING EDITION of the Charleston Post and Courier at her kitchen table. The article that caught her attention was on the second page in the front section. It was impossible to ignore, it took up the entire page above and below the fold. There were no advertisements, though she looked to see if this article might be sponsored. She had seen many phony news articles that were actually advertisements, TV shows that were actually infomercials. The article had to be an advert. But there was no logo to be seen. The big headline read:

Local Lab Discovers Miracle Cures in Venom

The article went on to discuss how this had come to be. That scientists collaborating from South Carolina Medical University, the World Toxin Bank, and BIOGENESIS Pharmaceuticals, a division of PROXER Pharmaceuticals, have uncovered the mysteries of several forms of natural toxins found in the venom of snakes, scorpions, bees, lizards, spiders, frogs, eels, snails and some fish such as pufferfish. That in their natural state, many of these toxins were severely dangerous if not deadly to humans. The article also elaborated that each of these toxins targeted very specific bodily functions and those targets were the sights of many forms of human disease. The scientists were able to synthesize smaller doses using the peptides found in these toxins creating drugs such as Tetrodotoxin (TTX) from pufferfish for example. Heart Disease, Diabetes, Cancer, HIV, Hypertension, Alzheimer's, Parkinson's, Multiple Sclerosis and many many more were all going to be cured within a few short months after the respective testing was completed. It went on to tell the reader to then tell their doctor to prescribe them these various drugs.

Sky ripped the newspaper into shreds. The remaining larger portions were crumpled up into a ball. She threw the balled paper at her television which just happened to be airing an ad for Cialis. She screamed at the top of her lungs toward the ceiling above her.

She was a large woman. Not large as in obese, large as in just shy of six feet and muscular. She had the physique of a body-builder. As she screamed her veins swelled, filling them with blood and raising them on her skin. Her biceps were engorged as her fists were curled into balls ready for a brawl.

After her tantrum, Sky gathered herself, leaning on her kitchen table. Both hands were flat, her arms straight-locked, as he dropped her chin to her non-feminine chest. She hovered over the table as she tried to compose herself.

The news was beyond belief. Drugs were everywhere, both legal and illegal. She had been accused of steroid use on many occasion but had never dreamed of juicing. Her body was a temple. Her mind had created the reality of her musculature.

The human mind has become weak, she thought. *Nobody mentally overcomes. Why conquer with the mind when you can pop a pill?*

She paced around her small apartment, through her kitchenette, the living room, and back again. Her abode was antithetical to her body. Her mass filled the tiny space. The lack of furniture, only that which was absolutely necessary, was both by design and necessity.

The news was intolerable. The article was against everything that she had felt or believed in. She began to ponder her options, realizing that doing nothing was not one of those options. Sky also realized that she had very little time to act, according to the news report. If the reporter was accurate, the drugs had already been produced and were in testing trials. It would be no-time at all before Pandora was out of the box permanently.

She went back into her kitchenette, retrieving a prepaid cellphone from the basket on her counter which also housed her car keys. She dialed a number into the smart-phone and waited for the recipient to answer. Unfortunately, there was no answer. She was forced to leave a voicemail message.

"It's me, Sky. I am not sure where you are or why you aren't answering your phone but we have a problem. Pick up today's newspaper, second page. It seems our efforts have been in vain. We need to come up with a plan and quickly. It is time to escalate things. Call me back as soon as you get this message."

She ended the call, tossed the phone back into the basket from whence it came. She continued to think. Rack her brain, in fact, trying to devise a plan.

In times of crisis, Sky Phillips did two things. She exercised and she prayed. Not at the same time of course. Her workout of choice was not Yoga. While she was certain that her spirituality enhanced her physique, her mass was from lifting weights. She wanted more than anything to sweat out her anger. She needed to exert herself to the point of exhaustion. Then and only then could her mind be clear. To think. To pray.

But there was no time. She needed an answer from her Maker. She needed to find a path. A path into a murky land that had just been revealed to her. This newspaper article was the beginning of the end. Satan was before her.

She was a knight in the war against evil. She thought herself to be a modern day Joan of Arc. She would lead her army to banish this new threat against God.

Would God speak to her?

Then it happened. She found God's answer in her own mind's eye.

Sky reviewed the top of the article, spying the correspondent's name. She had to ascertain if the information was accurate. She needed to know where the trials were being conducted, where the supplies of these various drugs were located. Where they were being produced.

Lance Grober. The story was written by Lance Grober. Sky went to her kitchenette and opened her Dell *Latitude E6430* laptop. She opened the website for the Charleston Post and Courier, then clicked on the **Index** button on the right. The window that popped up listed all of the assorted sections of the daily paper and myriad contributors and bloggers, again on the right. She clicked on the link for **Lance Grober, News.** That led her to his profile picture and generic information, along with the archived stories that he had reported in reverse chronological order.

Next she opened Facebook and searched for the news writer. There were many Lance Grobers, but fortified with the Courier photo, she was able to match it to the Facebook profile picture. She clicked on him.

His Timeline opened, then she clicked **About**. Amazingly, his information was readily available. Work and Education. Relationship Status. He was married to a woman with whom he had a young daughter. Contact Information. Why this information was not private was a question she could ask him when they met.

Which was about to happen.

240

33

LANCE GROBER HAD AN ACTIVE LIFESTYLE. He was always on the go. His wife and young child had consumed more than half of every day, of every week. He was happily married to his college sweetheart, and his four year old daughter was the light of his life. His little girl. But there were always recitals, both dance and violin. The girl in the pretty pink tutu and the tiara demanded a lot of time and attention. His wife was a stay at home mom, so when Lance was home she desperately needed an adult. Her husband. Work was supposed to be his little escape.

Except the Charleston Post and Courier was a heartbeat away from bankruptcy. The paper couldn't compete with the alternative media of the digital age. Nobody read the newspaper anymore, and certainly didn't want to pay for it. Alternative sources for news was winning. So his editor was always on his ass, driving him to do more with less. More hours, less pay. More in depth research, no budget. Fifteen hour days weren't enough to put food on the table sometimes.

Grober was able to carve out one hour for himself in his busy life. One hour where he wasn't eating, sleeping, working, reading a bedtime story, or listening to one his wife wanted to tell him. That hour was for the gym. Planet Fitness to be precise. It was open twenty-four hours a day, seven days a week. His varying schedule would always be able to fit in one hour.

The writer was not a weight-lifter by any stretch. Going to the gym five days a week clearly meant that he was in good shape, but he was not big. Lance was toned. He would start with fifteen minutes of cardio on the elliptical machine or the treadmill, then spend the rest of his time on the Nautilus machines. His muscle tone was from band resistance, not free-weights.

On Wednesday evening, while some of his colleagues were checking out the local talent at a happy-hour, Lance was taking his personal hour. There were, of course, plans for the night. His wife had already phoned him and told him so. But not until after he was able to work out some of his stress, leaving the things that weighed on him outside of his home. Away from his wife and young daughter.

Large format fitness centers, like Planet Fitness, are fodder for meeting people. People of the opposite sex, or same sex in some cases, could use the motions and sweat to jump-start their libidos. For some, that was the only reason for going to the gym. Women would put on make-up, wear their most fashionable jog bra and tightest yoga pants, while men would use any excuse to lift their shirts to show off their six-pack abs.

Lance found the entire charade ridiculous but no better or worse than picking someone up in a bar. Women would be in their jewelry and accentuate their poses, men would show their best body-building pose in the mirror. It always seemed that the meat market was open. But not for him. He would simply put in his earbuds from his iPod and sweat out the day. No conversation, no lingering looks regardless of how benign.

Occasionally Lance would get a long look from an admirer. Not often, but on occasion. Women who liked the shy type. Sometimes men would look. But on that night he was getting overt stares from one person that seemed to be a combination of both. It was definitely a woman, but she had a more muscular body than he did. She took him in, long at length. She would do a dead-lift with an insane amount of weight, then stare at him while he used the various Nautilus machines. It was not subtle. Even when she looked toward the mirror, her eyes found him in the reflection.

He found it odd that this woman was spending so much energy looking at him. If one was to guess what her type would be, one might think either another woman or a male who was at a minimum as muscular as she. But her focus was on him. He began to feel self-conscious. He looked at himself, no stains. Nothing had fallen out of his shorts. He looked in the mirror. No buggers, nothing was in his teeth.

When his hour was up, he went into the locker room, as usual. He showered, again the norm. After changing and packing his gym-bag he exited the men's lockers back through the gym, heading toward the door to leave. The woman was still on his mind, because he looked for her in the dead-lift area. She was gone.

Lance made his way out the front door, the cute college girl working the front reception saying goodbye to him as left. He half-heartedly said goodbye back and walked toward his car in the parking lot to the side of the building.

He pressed the button on his key fob to unlock the car, then another to pop the trunk of his Ford *Fusion*. He always kept his gym bag containing is sweaty work-out clothes in the trunk, else his wife would complain about the stink in the car. He threw the bag into the trunk and was about to close it when he heard a footstep from the graveled parking lot. Someone was behind him.

Lance turned to see who had followed him to his car when there was a thud on the back of his head. The lights went out.

"You're awake." Sky was sitting in a chair opposite Lance, who was attached to his chair with plastic zip-ties.

Lance was slowly coming back into coherence. He recognized the muscular women from the gym through the fog as he came-to. She was wearing different clothing and seated across from him. The room they were in was filled with snakes behind glass. Every wall was filled floor-to-ceiling with glass cases which housed various types of snakes. The fluorescent lighting in the terrariums were designed and hidden to look like their natural habitat. Each partitioned case was marked with a brass plaque which Grober couldn't read from his vantage point.

"Can you hear me Mr. Grober?"

"Where am I? Who are you?"

"Those questions can be answered in time. First I would like mine answered."

"My head is killing me." He looked down at himself as he tried to free his hands unsuccessfully. There was dried blood on his shirt.

"Yes, I'm sure it does. I wasn't sure how much of a hit to the head you could endure, so I was forced to hit you very hard. You need to move beyond the pain because I need you to answer some questions for me. Your cooperation will go a long way towards determining how this ends for you. If you lie or withhold the truth, you will pay for your sins. Your head will seem quite mild."

"Who are you?"

"That is really none of your concern."

"Don't hurt my family. What have you done with them?"

"Your family hasn't been touched. Yet. Your phone has been ringing incessantly, so I am sure that they are worried about you. I'm worried about you also. I'm worried that you are going to try and be a hero and not tell me what I want to know. That will be bad for you, Lance."

"What do you want to know?"

"I want to know about the article that was printed on page two of today's paper."

"The venom article?"

"Precisely."

"You could have just read the article in the paper, no need to hit me on the head."

"But you didn't report what I want to know in your article. Who is responsible for this atrocity?"

"Atrocity? These drugs will save millions of lives."

Sky rose from her chair and swung a punch to Lance's jaw. Blood and teeth sprayed from his mouth. He was almost knocked back into unconsciousness.

"I'm not asking for your opinion, I'm asking for information. Who is responsible for the discoveries?"

It took him some time to recover from the blow. The hit was not a slap, nor typical of a female's strike. It was not open-handed. It was not typical of a normal man's strike either. The woman was very strong. He spoke through the blood and broken teeth.

"Fuckin' bitch!"

She hit him again. The pain was excruciating.

Again he almost passed out from the pain.

"Many people. They have an entire team of people working there."

"Are they developing the drugs there? At BIOGENESIS? Or at SCMU?"

"SCMU. The data goes to BIOGEN but the trials are done at the Medical University. They have more equipment and doctors there in case there are complications or side effects."

"Do they create the medicines there?"

"Right now, no. Like I said, the data goes back to BIOGENESIS where they make the drug. The medication is then stored over at SCMU where it is administered for the trials. Until the formulae are finished being tweaked. Once the drugs go live, they will then be manufactured in bulk overseas. It was in the article. Why do you want to know all of this? You could have just called me. Or sent me an email."

"You wouldn't have taken me seriously or you would have said that your sources are confidential. Who is in charge of it all over there? Lynde?"

"Yes. He is overseeing it all. But the day to day is overseen by a team at SCMU. Look, I've answered all of your questions, can you please let me go now?"

"Unfortunately no. I can't let you leave here. Ever. This is going to be the last conversation you'll ever have, Lance."

"But I cooperated. You said — "

" — and you will have to forgive me. The spiritual reality is the only reality, this is all just a temporary illusion. There is too much at stake to let you interfere with my plans."

"I won't. Whatever your plans are, I'll stay out of it."

"I know you will."

Sky injected a syringe into Lance's neck.   The plunger slowly sunk, pushing the contents into his vein. He struggled to free himself from the plastic binds and the chair but to no avail. The more he struggled, the quicker his heart raced. The quicker his heart pumped the toxic blood throughout his body. His brain began to thicken.

"The snakes will digest you too slowly, Lance. If someone suspected you were inside them, and found you? I can't have that. You didn't leave me with much choice. I have to get rid of you. I'm thinking the best course is to cut you up and bury you. Someplace where nobody will find you. But don't worry, you won't be alone."

34

THE CAMPUS OF SOUTH CAROLINA MEDICAL UNIVERSITY is all but abandoned late at night. This was not a party school. Not at this end of the enormous campus.

Other colleges within the university had their fair share of partiers, undergrads gaining the full college experience. In those parts of the campus the occasional drunkard would stumble down the various paths toward their dorm, sorority, or fraternity. The paths along the green were always lit at night with solar lights and the blue emergency call stations every hundred yards.

But nobody stumbled home on the end of campus that housed the medical labs, the World Toxin Bank, the fellowship and professor offices. Those were serious students whom were well beyond binge drinking. Well beyond the late-night booty calls. Those were serious buildings where serious work was being done.

At 2:00 AM on Thursday morning, those paths along the medical green were dimly lit as usual. The odd security guard walked along the path but there was never anything to report. They preferred to work their respective shifts in the comfort of the air-conditioned buildings rather than walking the paths, especially in the humid summer nights, between the various structures. Even with recent events and the subsequent heightened security, there was little to report. In truth, there hadn't been anything to report on the grounds the nights the murders had taken place either.

Whomever had circumvented the security measures on those nights had been good. Nobody had seen anyone suspicious go into or out of any of the campus buildings. They were not well-marked at any rate, someone would have to know exactly where they are going in order to get around. Then once they were inside the unmarked building, they would need a magnetized ID card in order to attain access beyond the vestibule. Upon getting through the entrance, the magnetized ID would only gain them entrance into the specific areas that the particular card had security clearance for.

The police had caught the person who had passed through all of those barriers anyway. The mentality from those having to make the decisions about paying the extra manpower for security was that there should be no extra manpower. 'Heightened' security was still quite lax.

The person dressed in head-to-toe, black clothing dodged from shrub to shrub down the path toward the medical testing labs. The brick building that stood at the end of the paved walkway was as dimly lit as the path leading to it. The spot-lights that shown onto the brick and ivy growing up the walls did little more than show that a building was present in the dark of night. The windows, all five floors of them, were on energy saving mode. Only every fourth fluorescent light inside was turned on. Just enough for the cleaning crews and limited security.

The trespasser snuck up to the building and moved along the perimeter of the building through the hedges and ivy. When they came to the drainage pipe on the back side of the building that ran up to the roof, they took one last look at ground-level to ensure that they were not being observed. The six inch diameter drainage pipe was used to climb up to the roof of the brick building. Because it was the back side of the building, and the pipe rose between windows, the intruder climbed in the darkness unseen. The items in the small backpack rustled on the back of the intruder as it was being hoisted toward the roof. It was the only sound which could be heard, and only by the person wearing the pack.

Once on the roof, which didn't take long, the burglar peered over the lip of the roof to take yet another look to see if they were being observed. No one could be seen. Five stories up afforded quite the view of that end of the campus. Not a person in sight. Not a sound except the breathing of the person on the roof.

The building's HVAC system was set up to ensure that the labs had the best heating and cooling to suit the needs of the technicians being housed there. It was also set up with a filtering system that negated lint and allergens from contaminating the laboratories. This was achieved by utilizing two sets of huge fans to draw and push air, sifting off the pollutants into an enormous filtration room. Maintenance had easy access to that room to change the dozens of filters inside it from the roof.

There was a plastic box on the outside of the room which contained a large lever. That lever shut down the entire HVAC and filtering system for the building. Deactivating that system would set off all sorts of bells, whistles, and alarms. They would be silent, but personnel would come calling. Turning off the system was not an option for the intruder.

Since the system was running at full strength that night, and would continue to be, goggles and a mask were needed in order to move through the room and bypass the fans through the conduit. The intruder retrieved those items from the back pack, as well as a pry bar to open the locked door to the filtration room.

Moving beyond the filtration room was easy. One just needed to pull down the coarse 40x40 filter, exposing the large ventilation ducts. The ducts were large enough for a small child to walk through standing upright. That is to say that an average size adult could crawl through it without fear of claustrophobia. For the intruder, it was tight but manageable.

The system utilized two sets of large, rectangular piping made of durable galvanized steel which ran juxtaposed to one another. While they were partners in both position and purpose on the system, they had opposing duties. One set of ductwork would have a set of fans to pull the air out of the rooms, pushing the air up to the filtration room, which the intruder had just breached. The now-filtered air would then be reclaimed and sent back into the building using the twin set of ducts which ran along side the first. The temperature of the reclaimed air was modified to suit the needs of the labs, the second fan pushing it back into the various rooms.

The infiltrator slithered along inside the pre-filtered ventilation ducts, pulling and squirming further into the building. The air and debris that was pulled from the rooms were being moved toward the filter room, which meant that the burglar was literally moving against the grain. Moving with significant speed, considering the circumstances, looking through every inlet vent as they passed, seventy yards had been accomplished until a decision needed to be made.

There was a vertical shaft that was very much like the HVAC spine of the building. That spine was comparable to the trunk of an enormous tree, the branches coming off the trunk to service all of the rooms in the building, including the four floors below the intruder. A decision was needed to be made to either continue along the ductwork above the fifth floor, or slide down the shaft to the lower floors.

It was decided to continue along the top level, therefore it became necessary to somehow go over the top of chasm and continue along the same shaft. This required significant strength and agility. Lying prostrate, they stretched across the opening with their torso, gripping the ledge of the ductwork on the opposite side. With nothing to grab a hold of, the elbows were utilized to attain hold on the sides of the duct, letting the waist and legs drop down into the vertical shaft. Then, using both feet against the sides of the vertical duct and immense upper-body strength, the intruder pulled their body up onto the other side of the shaft and continued on.

Another forty yards had been accomplished when through an inlet vent, the burglar spied a male technician in a lab coat. He was working on one of the machines, all lights and computers were turned on in that lab. This was not a night cleaner, this was real work being done at almost 3:00 AM. The intruder backed up in the ductwork, squirming in reverse in the same direction as the air and debris to be filtered.

Once the previous inlet vent was reached, they peered through that vent to ensure that the adjoining dimly lit lab was empty. It was. A Kobalt *OS683* multi-purpose hand tool was produced from the small back pack. It was unfolded to produce pliers, then a Philips screwdriver was flipped out of it's recessed home. The four screws were removed, enabling the vent cover to be removed. Once removed, the burglar emerged from the shaft but only to the waist. The CCTV camera was spotted to the right of the ventilation duct, less than six feet away. The long pry bar that was used to enter the filtration room was then used to turn the camera over to the corner of the room. Satisfied that nothing in that room would be seen or recorded, the intruder dropped into the adjoining lab from the shaft.

35

I HAD NO IDEA WHAT THE HELL I WAS DOING IN THE LAB. I putzed with this, or fiddled with that. I didn't even know what some of the equipment did, let alone know how to operate the stuff. I looked into a microscope at nothing. I turned on an electrophoresis machine and put a spot plate on it, it seemed right. If the damn thing hadn't had a label and manufacturer on it, I wouldn't have even known that it was an electrophoresis machine. Whatever that was.

I opened a microcentrifuge and put something inside, hoping nothing would smoke or combust. I barely graduated high school, the only reason I passed chemistry was because I knew the teacher was cooking and distributing Meth. I got a B because nobody would believe that I had legitimately achieved an A.

Donning a white lab coat, I looked the part. That was the important thing. I also wanted to see about getting one with my name on it. When I found Carina we could play 'naughty doctor' or something fun with it. I hoped I would find her. If this didn't work, I was out of ideas.

Because of all of the sensitive equipment and because it was a university, I was not allowed to have gun. It was against SCMU lab rules, but more importantly it was against the law. SCMU was a State-funded school and schools of all kinds were off limits to weapons. Even with my conceal and carry permit. The fact that I didn't have a gun anymore, that Stubbs had it, didn't depreciate my desire to have one.

I continued to move around the lab as if I had a purpose, my only purpose was to play the waiting game. I was sure that the newspaper article would generate a move. Captain Simms knew a reporter from the Charleston Post and Courier who owed him a favor. He generated a falsified story that a Lance Grober would then write and push through his editor. The story was published and created more of a buzz than any of us realized.

The Associated Press picked up on it and ran with it. Bloomberg reported it. CNN. Even the Daily Show with Jon Stewart was planning on covering the story on Friday. It was already going viral.

I was on a short leash. If the ruse didn't work, a retraction was going to be made and Carina wouldn't be found. If it did work, then the headline was going to be about the serial murderer who was caught while destroying the lab in another attempt to destroy vital research. That destruction had set SCMU and BIOGENESIS back in their launch of these forthcoming drugs.

I heard the ID card access control system click behind me and the door to the lab opened. A mannish woman entered wearing her white lab coat and carrying a small back pack. She was a muscular girl.

"Good morning. I wasn't expecting anyone in the lab this early."

"Good morning. Uh, yeah. I had a few tests to run," I said. I didn't know what else to say. For obvious reasons there weren't many people privy to my presence, this lab tech was going to know I wasn't a researcher in about ten seconds.

Her ID card coiled back into the retractor that was fastened to her front belt loop. "I haven't seen you in this lab before, are you new?" She eyed me with suspicion and I didn't know what I was going to say.

"New here. I was transferred here to replace somebody that isn't here anymore." I hoped that somebody already hadn't filled that role, maybe this chick. If so, my jig was up.

"That's a great accent. Where are you from?"

"My mom. What's your name?"

"Sky. What's yours?" She went around the perimeter of the lab and found a desk with a computer on it. She squatted down and went inside her back pack.

I wasn't sure if I wanted to give her my real name. There was something about her that I didn't like. Her size for one. If she wasn't whom she was portraying to be, as I wasn't, then a physical altercation wouldn't be cut and dried. I'm not afraid of men, I've fought many that were bigger than me. But I don't hit women. Not hitting this one, however, would very likely get me hurt.

"I didn't hear you. What did you say your name was?" She stood up with a large pry-bar in one hand, a stick with some sort of fanged device on the end in the other hand. That device looked like an unhinged stapler on the end of a large rod.

"I didn't say. But it doesn't make much of a difference does it?"

"Not really, no. You should have turned down that transfer. Where is the data?" She was circling the long lab table that centered the room, the same table I was standing behind. I began circling away from her in the same counter-clockwise direction. I was slowly coming around toward the door to the lab.

"That door has been deactivated. The reader is broken, there is no escape."

"Then you aren't going anywhere either. Bad plan if you want the data, Sky."

"I'll go out the same way that I came in, through the vent." She looked up at the vent above my head, behind me."

I pointed to the camera. "Smile, your on TV."

"This is not my first time here. The camera isn't recording anything. You are completely isolated. Just tell me where the data is and I promise to make your death as quick and painless as possible."

I took off my lab coat and wrapped it around my arm. Sky was still circling, as was I.

"Where is she, Sky? Where is Detective Fischer?"

"That is the least of your concerns." The dawn broke and she began to realize that this might not be what it seems. I could tell by the look on her face. "You aren't a lab tech, are you?"

"You've got me there, fella. What gave me away."

"You aren't scared."

As I circled around, I came to where Sky had left her back pack. Without shifting my eyes for any length of time, I retrieved it and continued circling. I clutched the bag with my left hand, the same side that had the lab coat protecting my forearm. I rifled through it with my right hand trying to find a weapon. I found a blue, multipurpose hand tool which would have to work. This time I took my eyes off of Sky for too long.

She high-jumped up onto the elevated lab table and came running on top of it toward me. She was lightning-quick. You don't normally think that somebody that big would be that fast but she was. It must have been something in the water down there, because Stubbs had moved that quick in spite of his size.

256

I threw the tool at her as she swung the pry bar at me. I ducked in time for it to miss my head but it made contact with the back pack and glanced off of my slightly protected forearm. The bar was caught on the arm strap of the pack and I pulled it from her hand. She swung the stapler thing at me and missed. I was able to get a better view of the object fastened to the end of the rod as it swung past my face. It was a snake skull. The top of the skull and fangs were somehow adhered to where the bottom part of the snake's hinged jaw would normally be. It went by me too quickly for me to see anything else at that point.

The pry bar clanged off of the floor and under the table that Sky was standing on. I dove under it to retrieve it, and she jumped down off of the table toward me. She kicked my arm and the pack went flying away from me. It hurt like hell, the bitch was strong. I was able to grab the pry bar and swing it. I hit the side of her foot, but it was not with as much force as I would have liked. Although the table was tall, I was not able to get enough motion on my swing.

She didn't yell or indicate any pain, but she did back off enough for me to roll out on the other side of the table.

Sky again jumped up on top of the table and came for me. I swung the pry bar with both hands like it was an axe, landing it on her arm. It was the same arm that carried her make-shift, snake skull weapon, which was flung through the air away from the fray. That did some damage though she never cried out in pain. I heard the bone in her elbow break. Unbothered, she threw a punch with her left.

I have fought many men, both in and out of the MMA ring. When I get hit hard, I get angrier and fight back. I don't fight women. I've pissed off enough where they slap me or scratch at me, but Sky didn't slap or scratch. She hit like a dude. And it hurt like a motherfucker. I was in pain and angry. She was no longer a woman to me.

"You fuckin' bitch! I'm gonna give you such a pinch!"

257

She was weaponless as she jumped off of the table and came towards me. I took another one-handed swing with the bar to her knee and connected again. That too did damage, and she again showed no sign that it affected her. She blocked my third attempt, hit my wrist, sending my weapon, the pry bar, flying out of reach.

Sky kicked me in the upper-leg, just missing my coin purse and neutering me. I punched her in the throat. She would not go down. I swiped her now bad leg out from under her by kicking it with mine and grappled her to the ground.

I made work on her face with my elbows. Pain did not seem to bother her. Or she wasn't feeling any. She struggled to get out from under me as I pinned her legs down by interlocking them with mine. I knelt while sitting on her pelvis. Every time she would sit up with her incredible abdominal strength, I would go back to work with my elbows to her face, drawing more blood.

She wouldn't give up. I needed to take away her air. That was the only way to submit her. I pushed her back down as she raised her upper-body toward me again and used my forearm with the unraveling lab coat on it to apply pressure to her throat. Her head was pinned down against the linoleum floor as I leaned in for all I was worth trying to cut off her air supply.

"Where is Carina? Where is Detective Fischer?" I asked over and over again. How I was expecting her to answer was stupidity.

Sky, in a final gasp and attempt at freeing herself, flung me off to the side and rolled away. It was unbelievable. That chick was unstoppable.

She rolled over to the snake-head weapon and retrieved it with her good arm. I was already moving toward her, the swing of the weapon just missed me. She was unable to stand because of her broken leg, but she was attacking from the floor. I jumped down onto her with my knee on her sternum. That definitely cracked. I jumped up and repeated the downward knee to the sternum. I finally got a scream out of her as the snake head came at me again.

Those fangs coming at me, scared the living hell out of me. It was a damned good thing that it was dead and not real. I blocked her final swing, removed the weapon from her hand, and out of pure frustration and anger I dug those fangs into her lower neck. I swung that thing so hard that the fangs were stuck in the meat where the neck meets the shoulder. I couldn't pull them loose.

Blood was everywhere.

Under the snake skull was a small plastic pouch.

"What's in the pouch, Sky? Venom?"

She looked at me and nodded her blood-soaked face and head.

"What kind? Maybe they have an anti-venom here." I moved away from her toward the desk. I dialed 9-1-1 from the lab phone but left the receiver on the desk, off the hook.

" …. No …. medicine …. "

"Where is Carina?"

Sky rolled her eyes then closed them. She might have been praying, maybe just thinking, but she was definitely dying.

The blood was free-flowing from her facial wounds, the fangs that dug into her neck were somewhat blocking the gushing from the two holes there. I have fought bleeders before, but the blood was gushing out of the cuts on her face as if they were major arteries. She was going to bleed to death unless help came quickly.

I looked around the lab and spotted a big red panic button. Use of that was pointless. We had evacuated the building assuming that the assassin would come. The rent-a-cop campus security would be useless. 9-1-1 was called but they were likely to be too late.

"C'mon Sky. Don't you want your conscience to be clean when you meet your maker in a couple minutes? Where is she?"

She did nothing but lay there and gurgle.

259

I kicked her in the ribs. Final thoughts on conscience cleaning were not working. I tried a different approach.

"Where the fuck is she, bitch?"

When blood began to run like a river out of her mouth I knew all was lost. My elbows had taken out some teeth, her gums and mouth were bleeding profusely. She wasn't going to tell me anything.

Her secret died with her.

36

IT TOOK MAINTENANCE, THE POLICE, AND PARAMEDICS **ALMOST AN HOUR** to gain entrance to the lab slash death chamber. Sky wasn't kidding when she said that she had disabled the security reader. She disabled the goddamned door.

I had plenty of time to go through the remaining contents of Sky's bag and everything on her person. I scrutinized every item trying to determine where Carina might be.

She had brought the bare minimum. I wondered if she had military training. She knew not to have identification on her. She transported only the tools that she needed for her mission.

But she did have a smart-phone.

Sky's smart-phone was password protected. I called Harold, though it was not yet 5:00 AM. He was groggy to say the least. After some time he understood who was calling but not completely why.

" …. what kind of phone is it Deni?"

"It says Motorola on it."

"Great. What kind of Motorola?"

"AT&T."

"Look all over it. It will say something else besides AT&T and Motorola on it."

"Atrix. Is that right?"

"Deni, phones really aren't my thing but I think those phones have a fingerprint security feature on them. Unless it is the Atrix 2, you are going to need the person who owns the phone."

"Ya know for not believin' that this world is a reality, these guys have some of the latest toys this world had to offer, huh?"

"I don't know, Deni. It's really early in the morning and I'm half-asleep. All I know is that you need the person if the fingerprint function was activated."

"What if I have the person who owns the phone but they aren't, uh, awake?"

"I don't even want to know. I'm pretty sure those phones have multiple ways to get into them. We can only hope that the fingerprint feature was used, otherwise your done."

"So what do I do?"

"Is there a reader on the back of it, or is it just the screen on the front? I think there should be a little window at the top of phone on the back side of it."

"Yeah. There is."

"Now find the right finger. Well, the correct finger. Probably one of the index fingers. Depends on if the person was a lefty or a righty."

It took something like eight attempts on the two pointer-fingers, I lost count, but it eventually worked.

"I got it Harold. Thanks."

"Don't mention it. Really, Deni. Do not mention it."

"Hey don't go anywhere. Do you have a computer handy?"

"Gee, Deni, let's see. What do I do for a living? What are the chances that I would have a computer?"

"Don't piss me off. It's been a rough night and it's gonna be a tougher day. I'm in no mood."

"OK Mr. Sensitive. You woke me up and you expect not to get a little 'tude? What do you need?"

"I'm gonna go through this phone, and you need to let me know where the addresses are based on the phone numbers that I give you."

"So I guess I'm up for the day."

"Are you gonna help me or not? I'm trying to find a missing cop and people are either dead or not being helpful."

"OK, OK. Fire when ready."

Captain Simms was bullshit. I normally say bullsh, but his state was past the point of abbreviations, so I'll use the full word.

He was beyond pissed at me, took a run past furious, and was rounding the corner on mental. Another body and no closer to finding Detective Fischer. He had lied to the press to create this mess in an attempt to draw out yet another *suspected* serial killer. That suspect was now dead. That suspect was never questioned. There was a strong possibility that the wrong person was currently incarcerated, and would continue to be because of it. Simms had let an out-of-state private dick lead this little ploy and it had run riot. Because this had taken place on a state-funded university, the South Carolina State Bureau of Investigators were looking to take over the case and the FBI was waiting in the wings. In the words Simms used, I had created a "cluster-fuck of epic proportions".

I wanted to tell him that epic was over-used in today's vocabulary, but he was already unamused and definitely not a fan.

It took JG all he could do to keep me out of the hoosegow. I watched him promise Simms to keep me away from this case and that I was going to get out of his jurisdiction forthwith. Meaning I was to fly anywhere out of Charleston, preferably out of South Carolina. If not, I was going to jail.

Everybody involved knew that JG was lying when he promised that. I was in for a penny, in for a pound on this one. I wasn't flying anywhere. I wanted to see this through. For JG. For Sierra Byrne. For Stubbs. For Carina. Hell, for myself.

What I didn't say out loud, nor even admit to myself, was my ulterior motive for finding Carina. I thought I was in love with her. How that was possible, I'm not sure. I didn't know her that long. I don't even know for sure if it was love, but I had never felt that way about a woman before in my life. She was like a wicked-beautiful, female version of me. And I certainly love me.

I had been taken from SCMU to the police station at 80 Broad in the back of a cop car. JG had come to the police station to find out what was happening, and to ensure that I wouldn't be locked up. He was already having difficulty freeing one of his clients.

JG took me back over to SCMU to retrieve the *AMG*. I told him that I had one more card up my sleeve, thanks to Harold. If the address that he gave me turned out to be a dud, we were out of options. On the drive over, JG tried to talk me out of continuing.

"I have reasonable doubt on Sierra's case. At this point it seems clear enough, or at a minimum plausible, that this Sky Phillips was the nut-job that killed the three victims surrounding BIOGENESIS. We have the murder weapon, at least one of them. I am going to schedule a motion hearing to see about getting Sierra out of Leath. There is no way they can keep her incarcerated after what happened this morning.

"You have done your job, Deni. There is no reason to get yourself further into trouble down here. Forget the address, let the cops handle it from here," he said as a final thought.

"What about Stubbs?"

"The Feds are all over it. They are already cutting through the red-tape to see that justice is served for him. Whether that was Nahash or this other zealot, Sky, is of no concern to us anymore."

"Fuck you, pal. It matters to me. I almost died in that grown-over hell-hole and the only reason I ain't on top of the pile of bodies down there is because of Stubbs. I wanna know who tried to make me a corpse. Stubbs is dead because because we went down there. *You* sent us down to a snake-infested jungle, I'm not gonna let it be for nothin'."

"There is nothing I can do to keep you out of jail *when* you get caught in the middle of this investigation."

"So nobody finds Carina? Nobody figures out the truth?"

"Have faith in the police. I am pretty sure the SBI is taking over the South Carolina cases, including Detective Fischer. Listen, there is a line from a Denzel

Washington movie, I forget which one, but he says, 'it's not about the truth, it's what you can prove.' Or something like that. Anyway, my point is the same. We may never find out exactly what happened, all we know is that Sierra is innocent, which is why I had you come down here."

He pulled up beside the Mercedes, just to the right of it lining up my passenger door to the *AMG's* driver door. I opened my door but remained seated.

"Fine. Take me off the books. You're done payin' me. Can I borrow your car for a few days?"

"Deni. Don't do this."

"I heard you. Can I borrow it or not?"

"Yes, of course. But don't come back to the house tonight. I have Brady to think about. We can't harbor a possible felon."

I got up and slammed his car door shut.

"I wouldn't dream of it."

37

THE ADDRESS THAT HAROLD provided me with was not technically located in Charleston. It was just outside the city limits. I took the 52 out of downtown, or uptown as they call it there, to Algonquin Road. It wasn't an Indian Reservation or anything, it was in the cemetery district. Four cemeteries were set around a small pond. How many people were plotted there because of the Algonquin Indians was a question I would have liked to have answered, but I didn't have the time for a history lesson just then.

My destination was on the back side of the Magnolia Cemetery. This was the furthest out, the most desolate of the four, and it would make it that much easier to dump a body. Which made me nervous about Carina.

At the end of Algonquin Road there was a closed gate. The sign said 'Road Closed'. My choices were to take the right onto Huguenin or proceed on foot. To the left was a field with half a dozen silos behind it. The brick wall on the corner of Huguenin and the gated remainder of Algonquin barricaded the Magnolia Cemetery.

I left the *AMG* parked in front of the gate, though it stuck out like a sore thumb. I climbed over the chain-link fence and continued on foot down the closed road. The brick wall and the bone yard was to my right. The chain-link fence continued on my left separating me from the field. Further ahead down the road, to the very end, was a small building with a parking area. Beyond that building was a wooded area with the tops of more silos set behind it. I turned around to look behind me. Nobody was around. Two hundred yards I continued to the very end of the road. The sound of my foot falls were about as loud as anything that I have ever heard. Sneaking up on the building was not an option. Maybe that was the point they were trying to make. It was very loud and clear.

There was an old Ford *F-150* parked on the back side of the building. The noon sun had not come out to play for the day, clouds still lingered overhead though there was no rain. The day was warm, as they all are in the South as far as I could tell. I put my hand on the hood of the truck, I couldn't tell if the damn thing had been there ten minutes or ten years.

I squatted down beside the *F-150* and listened. I don't mean listen like you do when somebody is trying to tell you something, I mean I listened like I was blind and the only information coming in was from sound. Nothing. My breathing was louder than the light breeze. Time to go in.

There was what I assumed to be a front door that faced the parking lot, for lack of a better term. That door was locked. I moved to the right around the building toward the woods and found another entrance. That door was propped open with a door jam about five inches. Again, I was without a gun. I was in the gun-amnestied South and without a gun. Pathetic.

Peering in through the small opening, I spied a room that was dimly lit. There was a raised area to the right which I assumed was used as a pulpit. The rest of the room was used for seating. By the main entrance where the door was locked was a set of tall bookcases, filled with some type of literature. A man was in front of them with a book that he was perusing. He had a straight line of sight to me, but he was engrossed. I needed to get through the door, but the opening wasn't wide enough. I moved it open a bit in order to slip in but the hinges creaked and echoed throughout the small room.

The man was startled and turned to see whom was entering. He cared not to find out who I was, he decided to shoot first and ask questions later. My Brazilian Jiu-Jitsu was, nor is, any match for bullets. The first one ricocheted off the wood door frame near my face, shrapnel-slivers burned the right side of my face. I dove inside and under a pew, the bullets continued to fly.

It was hard to keep my right eye open. I don't know if the burning and stinging was from pieces of debris in my eye or blood. Maybe both, it was hard to tell at that point. I just knew that I was bleeding like a stuck-pig. I was getting very tired of being shot at with no way to shoot back.

There were no other rooms to hide in, my only shelter was the pews. The dark oak from the wooden benches was spraying like toothpicks at me. I crawled as fast as I could from one row to the next, trying to get closer to him. My only hope was when he went to reload his gun. I kept count as best I could, and he was at or beyond eight so I knew he didn't have a revolver. That meant that reloading was going to be exponentially quicker. I would have maybe a second to attack him while he changed clips and reloaded the chamber.

The shooter was moving toward me, waiting for me to pop up from behind one of the benches. We were both shortening the gap between us. He was about nine or ten feet away from me, on the other side of a pew, when it was my time to move. Whether he knew how close he was to me or not, I will never know. I just know that he immediately regretted following me, realizing that he did not have another clip on his person. I saw the look on his face when I popped up and dove on him. We both toppled over the back of one row of pews and onto another row. He was below me as I broke my fall with his body.

Smashing his gun-hand against the hard floor with both my hands, I simultaneously drove my knee into the side of his ribcage.

With the gun skittering across the floor under the pews toward the front of the room, I moved to a side mount. It was difficult to get perpendicular to him between benches, but with the man struggling I was able to knee him to the end of the row. I neutralized my attacker with a shoulder-hold or Kata-gatame, meaning the arm and hand that used to be holding a gun was now pinned against his neck. I needed information about Carina so I didn't choke him out with an arm triangle, I just kept working the side of his body with my knees. Royce Gracie would have been proud.

"Where is Carina? Where is Detective Fischer?"

My attacker was not yet the submissive. He continued to take a beating in silence. Whatever mind thing Sky and this guy used, it worked to repress pain. I had been in several MMA fights where the guy would tap-out after suffering less. This particular guy was pissing me off.

"Where is she asshole?"

Nothing but groaning. I finished moving him out into the aisle by pushing him with my upper body and knee-strikes. Once in the aisle, I was able to have enough room for a Kimura. I grabbed his wrist with my hand on the same side, my opposite arm was put behind his arm. I cranked his arm away from him which put immense pressure on his shoulder and elbow joints. He would tell me what I wanted to know or I would have a new arm. His.

No Jedi-mind-trick can withstand an arm-bar. The scream that came out of the man was unlike any I had heard, and I had heard plenty in my day. I may have snapped the poor prick's arm, for all I know. I was pretty pissed.

"Talk to me! Where is she?"

" …. rrrrrrrrr. Let me go!"

"Not a fuckin' chance. Tell me where she is or I rip it off and beat you with it."

" ….. aaaaaaaaa. Not here anymore!"

"Where? I'm losin' my patience here, guy."

" …. nnnnnnnnnnn. Taken. Not here …. rrrrrrrr …. "

"Last chance. WHERE?"

He said nothing. Nothing usable anyway. He continued to groan and gasp, grumble and howl. This was getting me nowhere, so I choked him out. Once he passed-out I was able to drag him back into the entrance where he was originally reading a book.

I wanted to tie him up.

I wanted to see if he had another clip.

38

JACOB GRANTES'S IPHONE RANG TWICE BEFORE HE
ANSWERED. The caller ID said that it was Warren. He was not entirely sure
that he wanted to take the call.

"Hello?"

"JG. What are you doing?"

"I'm filing a motion to get Sierra out of Leath, like I told you about two
hours ago. Dare I ask what you are doing?"

"Are attorney-client conversations over the phone privileged?"

"Yes, unless the conversation is taking place prior to or during the act of a
crime. I take it back, I definitely don't want to know."

"I know where Carina *was*. She isn't here anymore, but the guy knows
where she is. I think."

"Where are you?"

"Out behind a bone yard called Magnolia."

"I'll call Captain Simms and – "

" – no, no, no. If he shows up here right now it would not be good."

"The police can question him, Deni. They can …. they *can* question him, right? You didn't kill him?"

"He's not dead but he is takin' a nap. He had some rope in the back of his truck, so he is all tied up right now. The motherfucker shot at me."

"Are you all right?"

"I've got shit in my eye and I'm bleedin' like it's my job. But otherwise I'm fine."

"So what now? Should I prepare myself to bail you out when the phone call comes? Because I am pretty sure that bail will be denied to you at this point."

"No. My goal is to stay outta the hoosegow. Can you find out more about Sky Phillips?"

"Like what? Between the press and the information that I have compiled to provide in my motion, we know quite a lot about her."

"Where she lives, works, hangs out – stuff like that."

"The police have already cordoned off her home, Carina wasn't there but they are still searching for evidence."

"What else?"

"Her neighbors said that she was a recluse. Didn't really socialize, kept to herself. She was obviously a fitness-buff so they are looking into where she worked out."

"What about where she worked? Did she work at SCMU? She had an ID badge."

"It belonged to one of the victims, the first one. The victim that was killed in her home. It was never deactivated. Six weeks and three deaths later, they never deactivated it. Unbelievable."

"So where did she work?"

"I just had it here in front of me …. Magnolia Zoo."

"Let me guess. Reptile Park?"

"It doesn't say. Why would you guess that?"

"These assholes are full of contradictions."

"You think that they hid a decorated homicide detective in a public zoo?"

"I'll let you know."

"Are you awake yet?" I gave the man who shot at me a good whack to the head to wake him if he wasn't. He rustled a bit, realizing his situation. His situation being that he was tied to the front double-doors to the church-like building, those doors open outward toward the small parking area and the Magnolia Cemetery behind it. Anybody pulling on those doors to open them would pull the arms off of him. He was seated at the base of the doors, legs straight out towards me, arms stretched above his head.

"Do you know who I am?"

"No, and I wouldn't give a fuck if I had a pocket full. Let's get back to where we left off, you and I. Where is Carina Fischer?"

"Not here."

"Thank you Captain Obvious. I know she ain't here. I looked around this one-room palace while you took a nap. I want to know where she *is*." I picked up the tire iron which I had leaned against the bookshelf after I had removed it from the *F-150*. "The cops will be here eventually, they will collect you. In how many pieces is going to be the question."

"I don't know."

"I don't know either, that is up to you. How many things am I gonna have to break off of ya before you break and tell me where she is?"

"That's not what I meant. I don't know where she is."

"You would be smart not to mistake my calmness for patience. I've run out. Where is she?"

"I don't know what you are talking about."

"We will see, won't we?"

I swung the tire iron down on the inside of his right knee. The thud was mixed with a snapping sound. Everything after that was wailing.

"Fight it off with your mind. Isn't that what you do?" I shouted to him over his sobbing and blubbering. It lasted for what seemed like an eternity.

"I'm gettin' tired of your bullsh, here guy. She *was here,* you said so yourself. Did she leave here alive?"

"Yes. Yes, she was alive …. aaaaaaaaaaaaah! Help!"

"You want another tickle? Stop screamin'. Where is she right now?"

He replied through gritted teeth, "I don't know."

"You better start guessin'. This is about to get really fuckin' painful for you, so you better make an effort here."

"They didn't tell me. I don't know."

"Who are *they?*"

He just looked at me. Looked through me really. I was tired of playing games. Carina's life was at stake, and this guy was the only person standing between me and finding her. I may have believed him not knowing where she was until he held out who had come to get her. He liked pain, obviously. I didn't mind dispensing it.

"Have it your way tough-guy."

The tire iron came down on the other knee. I gave it all I had on his left knee. It sounded like I had cut through a head of cabbage with a dull knife. You never get used to that sound. It is both gnarly and nauseating. It was grisly work but it was necessary.

The man tried to pull himself up with his tied arms as he screamed louder than my ears could take. Tears and spit and sweat were pouring out of his ghostly white face.

"Just tell me where she is and I will go away. I haven't even used the lever-end of this thing yet. I wonder what I can pry apart on you?"

He continued to wail and cry. I had found another clip for his Sig Sauer Pro *SP2022* in his truck, when I had found the rope and tire iron. I couldn't take the noises he was making, so I retrieved his 9 mm pistol from the floor under a pew and loaded it.

"I can make all of the pain go away very quickly, guy. Tell me where she is."

"I don't — "

" — don't sit there and tell me what you don't fuckin' know. You had better start tellin' me what you do know.   Apparently you are still not motivated. You want pain? That's what you'll get."

I walked back toward him with the *SP2022* in my right hand, and the tire iron in my left. I placed the muzzle of the pistol on the inside of this hanging right wrist, pressing it between the ulna and the radius. I fired the weapon, sending a 9 mm projectile through his wrist. The screaming grew still more intense. Next, I put the Sig into my back pants pocket and switched the tire iron from my left hand to my right. Then I pushed the lever end into the hole that I had just made.

"If I send this lever through your wrist, I can't tell you how much it's gonna hurt. I can't tell you because I've never done this shit before. I'm makin' this up as I go along. Are you as curious as I am as to how much it's gonna fuckin' hurt? You might even pass out again. Tell me where she is asshole!"

"Noooooooooooo.   Stooooooooop. Please, please, please. No. No more. The snake pit. I think the snake pit."

"At the Magnolia Zoo?"

"I think. They never told me."

"Because Sky worked there?"

"Yes. And the others."

"What others?"

"The other parishioners who work there …. access to snakes and the mice they eat." It did look like he was about to pass out again.

"What do you mean access to the snakes and the mice? Stay with me."

"Specimens need …. food." Then he was gone.

And so was I.

39

THE MAGNOLIA PLANTATION WAS VAST TO SAY THE VERY LEAST. The property consists of the Gardens, the main house, the train and boat tours, the historic buildings tour retelling the events *From Slavery to Freedom,* the wedding and events wing, and we haven't even mentioned the various areas of the Zoo and Nature Center.

The Zoo and Nature Center has a bird and peacock wing, swamp garden, safari animals, reptiles, and list goes on and on. Once I was inside, I understood how immense the place was. I could have had a three-day pass and not seen the entire place. They charged me $39.50 admission for the rest of one day, Thursday. I was not interested in the price of more as I was hoping that it wouldn't be necessary.

I called JG to let him know where I was going and what I had done. He asked surprisingly few questions. He simply said that he would let Captain

Simms know about the man in the remote church building and the suspected whereabouts of Detective Carina Fischer.

The zoo was busy. Because it was summer, the children were not in school nor were the parents at work in the middle of the week. Trying to move through them and around them was a chore as I was moving at an entirely different pace than the families I was trying to heisman through.

Deer exhibit. Who gives a shit? I have seen more as road-kill than were on display. Bobcats and birds of prey, no thank you. You can keep your peacocks too, though they had every color in the rainbow.

Forty-five minutes beyond the admission gate and I had finally come upon the Reptile Park and Alligator Amphitheater. 'CLOSED FOR RENOVATIONS' the sign said. They were sorry for the inconvenience, it also said. I'll bet.

I looked around before climbing the gate and running into the turtle building to ensure that I was not spotted. Only the safety lights were illuminated, but it was enough for me to see my way out the other side. I was stealth in moving from building to building, not wanting to be stopped or even seen. I ran through the lizard kingdom, out the other side then through the spider hall.

The spiders were all in their own individual terrariums. With the lights off, they might have been sleeping. I didn't stick around to find out. I had seen enough of them in their natural habitat, I didn't need to see them behind glass. It had the feel of a spider pet-shop. I continued to move through that building and then entered a new one, which was hell on earth.

The next building was engulfed by a swamp garden, which took me back to earlier in the week in Costa Rica. That was frightful enough. I guess they wanted to make this layout as authentic as possible. Bully for you, first rate. I raced through the swampy exterior and into the concrete building, which is where I nearly soiled myself. The building was filled, wall-to-wall with snakes.

There was glass between the serpents and I, but I had my fill in Central America. I hated them before, during, then, and I still do to this day. They terrify me more now than ever. They surrounded me. I don't know if they noticed me or not, but in my mind they were all trying to break through the glass trying to have a go at me. I have nightmares to this day.

There was a chair in the middle of the large observation room, but I didn't sit in it. I was curious about it but I didn't linger. All I wanted was out. The room was just as dark as the others, energy-saver safety lighting was the only illumination. Everywhere I turned was a fanged fucker looking for a meal. I managed to find the red exit sign on a far wall. Out the other side I went, my body still shivers just thinking about it.

Once outside, I was able to catch my breath and gather myself. I also saw where the renovations were taking place. Another tall fence where it looked like a foundation was being poured.

My heart sank. I hoped that what I was thinking was wrong. *They wouldn't kill somebody and bury them in the middle of a busy zoo would they?*

Nobody was around. No construction workers, no zoo workers. If there were cameras in this area of the park, nobody was watching them. I had free-reign and I didn't belong there, imagine what could be done if you worked there? Right under their noses.

I climbed the tall fence and looked around the construction zone. The renovation company had dug into the ground, made trusses where about a quarter of them were filled with concrete. They were going to build another exhibit right there. The sign said they were 'EXPANDING OUR KINGDOM'.

There was a trailer that was toward the back of the area where a foreman had set up his temporary office for the job. It was locked but that didn't stop me from breaking out my pins and getting inside. I'm not sure what I was expecting to find, but what I did find was a desk with filing cabinets and plans. Rummaging through it all produced no evidence. Whomever the foreman was, he or she hadn't updated any of the plans or the progress journal in several weeks. *Was construction put on hold?*

As I turned to leave, I saw a rack with a few hard-hats and safety-vests hung underneath them. Which gave me an idea.

If you have never operated a backhoe before, I can tell you that it's a friggin' blast. I had never sat in one before that day, let alone moved the giant bucket that is attached to the arm. It takes some getting used to.

The stabilizers were already in place on the JCB *4CX-17 Super*, all I needed to do was swing the cab around so the back-boom was above the concrete slab. Only I was swinging it the wrong way and it may have tore a huge hole in the side of the foreman's trailer. Oops.

I then pushed the lever that looked like a shifter on a manual transmission forward instead of back toward me. The bucket on the back-boom then went through the other side of the trailer instead of away from it. I corrected it and figured out how to swing it around so it was above the concrete foundation.

With the position of the bucket over the spot I wanted to dig, I then pushed the right control stick to the right to open the bucket for scooping, then lowered the main boom to engage the concrete. Pushing the left lever to lower the boom into the hard foundation, I pulled the right lever to drag the bucket into a scooping motion, then began rolling the bucket forward by moving the right control lever to the left. It sounds like I was smooth, but I wasn't. I did some serious damage to the nearby equipment and the poured foundation didn't come up easily. It took some time.

Finally I had attracted some attention. Outside the construction fence there were six people shouting at me to stop. Pleading with me actually. I pretended not to see them, I definitely didn't hear them. I kept at it for one more pass before one of the six produced keys to open the fence.

I stopped the boom and shut the *4CX-17 Super* down. The area was quiet. The small crowd was no longer yelling at me, they were pointing at the bucket at the end of the boom, the looks on their faces were ones of horror.

There was a navy-blue Converse *All-Star* sneaker sticking out of the bucket. It was attached to a leg wearing dirty denim jeans. The leg was protruding out of a concrete chunk of foundation that was dug out of one of the trusses. It looked like a concrete lollipop stuck out of the bucket of a backhoe. The lollipop stick was a denim leg and sneaker.

The fun was over.

Sometimes I hate being right.

ALMOST THE ENTIRE CHARLESTON HOMICIDE DIVISION AND
EVERY CSU investigator arrived within a half-hour of digging a clothed leg
and foot out of the newly poured foundation.   Whatever cop wasn't at the
Platist church behind the Magnolia Cemetery was now at the Magnolia Reptile
Zoo . They had utilized a service road so as not to disturb the rest of the patrons
who had paid admission that day.   The fenced-in construction area was
cordoned off with police tape. It was as if the durable construction barrier was
an easily dismissed suggestion and the thin, plastic, yellow police tape was a
demand. It was the velvet rope syndrome in plain use.

The denim leg and hipster sneaker that was found, was a detached and
severed limb.   The   remaining concrete was broken off of the appendage,
requiring the equivalent of an archeological dig to recover the rest of the body.

The CSU did a preliminary examination of the leg, determining that it was recent and was removed from a body of a male. In other words, not Carina.

I was both relieved and discouraged. I had come to the zoo thinking that she was being held here. The reptile wing was closed for renovations making it a prime location for nefarious bidding. I didn't find Carina. Instead, part of a male corpse was discovered that was recently buried under newly poured concrete.

It was beginning to seem like I would never find her. Ideas for further investigation were absent from my brain.

The very dramatic and destructive act of using the heavy equipment to dig up the construction area was devised to attract attention. I wanted to tear down the Platist's playhouse and draw them out into the open. Let them know that it was over. I had the suspicion when I first came upon the construction site but I was hoping that there wouldn't be a body under the foundation. That is what I told myself at any rate.

JG was late in getting over to the site. He had been busy with court filings and heading over to Leath to tell Dr. Sierra Byrne the good news. The motion hearing the following day, on Friday morning, was the only formality in delaying her immediate release. She was going home an innocent woman.

When he arrived, I was already stuffed in the back of a police cruiser. Captain Simms was still extremely pissed-off. Thankful that he was going to have a murder solved, one that he didn't yet know existed, but displeased that I was still in his jurisdiction and causing so much damage was an understatement.

Had I been sitting on my handcuffs in the back of the cop car the entire time, I would have been displeased. But I had moved my hands down below my butt and looped my legs through, working my hands to the front, in my lap. While my hands were moving past my ass, I pushed my wallet out of my back pocket and onto the seat. My pins were located in there. It was much more difficult to pick the lock on the handcuffs, especially with my hands in them, but I was able to get free.

Simms and JG came to the cruiser, releasing me. I handed the Captain the police handcuffs. This didn't further ingratiate me. He was much more calm than when he had me put there, however.

"Any leads on who the leg belonged to?" I asked both men, but I had assumed that Captain Simms was in the better position to comment.

"We are still pulling parts of him out of dirt and concrete but we have a hit on the hand that we found."

"And?"

"And it is an ongoing investigation in which you are not apart of."

"So I lead you here, and you are giving me nothing back?"

"There is more than one person under there."

"Oh shit. Carina?"

Simms looked at his shoes. He said nothing but he didn't need to. I read my answer in his body language.

"Fuck …. Ah, shit. No question? Definitely her?" I could lie and say that tears weren't welling up in my eyes, that I didn't have a horrible knot in my throat, but I won't. It was the feeling that you get when you know something absolutely fucking horrible has happened; where you know the truth but nobody had proven it to you yet, so you hold hope when there really isn't any.

"It's her," Simms said. He was still looking at his shoes, probably for the same reason I was trying to hide my eyes.

"And there were others?"

"So far one other. The reporter I used to draw out Sky Phillips. Lance Grober. The leg. His wife had reported him missing but it hadn't been twenty-four hours yet, so they blew her off. How am I going to tell her that it was our scheme that got him killed?"

285

"It was my scheme. It's my fault."

"Yeah well, it doesn't really matter does it? You're not a cop and I made the phone call. We will be lucky if she doesn't sue the city."

"It worked though. I wouldn't have known for sure how to get at the Platists, known to go to the hidden church. Known to come here. He would still be missing."

"I'm sure that will be a big comfort. I'll have to remember that when I'm giving her the news that her husband was cut up into pieces."

"I'm just trying to — "

" — I know what you are trying to do. Did you know that you were almost killed by Detective Fischer's gun?"

"What? What are you talking about?"

"Those tears in your cheek and forehead were ricochets off the shots fired at you in the church, right? The statement you gave the officer on the phone said that you were fired upon."

"Yes …. "

"The weapon that you recovered from the, uh, suspect at the church? The one you gave me when I arrived? It was Carina's Sig."

"Holy shit. How were they going to explain that away? If they had killed me."

"Lord only knows. You would have been the next one buried down under the foundation I would bet. Carina would never be recovered, nor you for that matter."

"I lost track of how many times people have tried to kill me. This case alone. Speaking of which, what are we going to do about Feinstein, Estabados, and recovering Stubb's body?"

JG interjected. "That is out of Captain Simm's hands. Feds are involved. Whether they were involved in the mass murder in Costa Rica, or if it was the Platists, they're taking over."

"So we went down there for nothing?"

"No. If it weren't for you and Stubbs those bodies may have never been found. There would be no closure to any of those disappearances, no closure for the families of the victims," JG said.

"You'll have to pardon me if I don't feel like a fuckin' hero. Stubbs, Carina …. "

Simms said, "We will make sure that justice is done. For both of them."

"You're out. It's on the Feds now. Besides, there will never be enough justice."

"That's the best we can do, Deni."

"All the justice in the world won't mend a beat-up heart."

The walk back to JG's car was a long one. Not because it was far away, but because we took it slow. I was going to get a ride from him, down the service road, and over to the *AMG* in the main parking lot of Magnolia Zoo. JG wanted to talk, I really didn't.

"Are you all right?"

"I'm pretty far from OK. This entire trip, this entire case, has been a kick in tha dick."

"I know and I — "

" — no ya don't know. Stubbs, Carina .... "

I didn't finish my thought. I couldn't. I was emotional and I didn't want to talk about it. We walked for about thirty yards before JG decided he had something else to get off of his chest.

"Just listen to me. Please. You did what you were supposed to do. I've told you that. Your job was to uncover evidence that would exonerate Sierra, and you did that. Everything else that you've accomplished is over and above what was asked of you. The espionage, the mass murders in Costa Rica, the serial murders here in Charleston .... all will be solved because of you. Justice will be done because of your work. You should be proud of yourself."

"Save it, Jacob. Really. I appreciate that you are trying to cheer me up, but take a break from it. Please. Just give me a ride back to the car."

"And then what? What are you going to do from there, Deni?"

"Get drunk. I'm going to try and forget that all this shit ever happened to me and get absolutely polluted."

EPILOGUE

I STAYED IN CHARLESTON FOR A FEW MORE WEEKS. To some degree because I needed the rest. I couldn't go back to Boston and start on a new case. Not yet. I had a beat-up heart from a new friend that I had lost and a new lover that I was certain that I had loved and lost. I needed to see what was going to be done about them.

Venom was supposed to save millions of lives. The cures would prolong life, save relationships, allow new ones to form. Yet the pursuit had killed so many. Costa Rica. Charleston. Who knows where else. Those kids were so young, all they wanted was to make a difference. And they died in heap with indifference.

The serial murders surrounding BIOGENESIS, SCMU, and the World Toxin Bank were about inhibiting the discovery of new cures. How a religious group could take the lives of those who were vested in saving millions was beyond my belief system. Would the rest of the people involved ever be held accountable? JG had told me that they would, but I still had my doubts.

There was an investigation into the Platists. Captain Simms wanted to make sure that all parties involved in what had happened to the five victims, including the reporter and Detective Fischer, were made to pay for their crimes. That was going to take some time.

One fact that had come to light, was that the reason Sky Phillips knew her way around campus was because she, and her cohorts at the Magnolia Zoo, were always on the campus. She was always delivering snakes or lab mice to the various labs spread out throughout SCMU. I found it odd that they would work so closely with the very being that was supposed to be the root-sum of all evil. But that group was filled with contradictions.

Rueben Feinstein was handed over to the Feds. The US Attorney's Office was putting together a case against him. The Federal Prosecutor was a real hard-ass, which was a good thing. I had had my run in with one in my past that was anything but ethical and in my mind, Feinstein would be allowed to cut a deal. That slippery son-of-a-bitch would say or do anything to keep his ass out of jail. My guess is that he would testify against his minion, Estabados.

That same hard-ass prosecutor was instrumental in apprehending Dr. Enrique Estabados from the Costa Rican Government, which went a long way toward making feel like this prosecutor was not like the one I had dealt with in the past. The Doctor was also being housed in segregation at a Federal Prison. He probably had to put every lie he ever told henceforth in writing. Stubbs had made sure that he would never speak a lie again. I hoped that Feinstein and Estabados had adjoining cells.

The rumor was that it was going to be years before either Feinstein or Estabados were brought to justice. There would be a lengthy investigation, followed by a lengthy trial. I toasted myself that those two fuckers wouldn't be breathing free air any time soon, if ever again.

The funerals of Eric Stubbs and Detective Carina Fischer were held separately. Both were widely attended.

Carina's was first. Her body was local and less red tape surrounded her arrangements. She had the full 'gone but not forgotten' honor service. The city was at a complete standstill. All officers were in their starched uniforms and white gloves to pay their final respects. Her closed casket was topped with her peaked cap and white gloves. The procession and three-volley salute drew as many tears as there were people. After which I got fuckin' hammered.

Stubbs's took a bit more time. His funeral was held almost two weeks later, the ceremony at Saint Michael's on Broad Street. It is one of the largest churches in the Southeast and it wasn't nearly big enough. He was a local celebrity for his fifteen seconds as a professional football player. He was also loved by everyone who knew him. All of the press surrounding his death, in part to grease the wheels of his return home, had further moved him toward sainthood. Nothing happened in Charleston that day either. There had to be tens of thousands of people around the church and the cemetery. I almost killed something when we arrived at Magnolia Cemetery to bury him. The small make-shift Platist church off in the distance was mocking me. I drank myself to sleep that night also.

I was staying with JG, Sierra, and Brady for the first couple of days but the constant inebriation was too much for any of them. JG was not much of a drinker anymore. He had been once-upon-a-time, and still had a craft beer once in a blue moon, but had given it up for the most part just prior to leaving New Hampshire.

Sierra was grateful for her freedom but judgmental. Even in my state I could see her looking down her nose at me. I hardly knew her, so it was just as unfair of me to judge her.

Brady didn't like it either. That's what JG said anyway. I moved to a nice hotel, the penthouse suite, and I never had to pay the bill. I probably couldn't afford the cost of the mini-bar.

The day after Stubbs's funeral, I was summoned by Captain Simms. Meaning that police officers had come to collect me. I was again stuffed in the back of an unmarked cruiser and taxied to 80 Broad.

It was difficult to say if I was more hungover or drunk. Probably a mix of both. I was depressed. I wasn't working out, and I was hardly eating. All of my meals were liquid. The alcohol was not helping me out of it, but was pushing me further into it. I know that in retrospect, though at the time it seemed to heal what was ailing me.

The officers never told me why I was being dragged over to the police station. I was in no mood or condition to get into a confrontation, or even resist in any event. On the ride over I had convinced myself that I was being arrested for my involvement in the deaths of my friend and of Carina. If I had to do it all over again, I would have found a way to do it differently.

I was a mess, and those that witnessed the two officers helping me into the station probably thought I was a perp. For all I knew, I was. Captain Simms looked at me with pity and concern.

"Taking this kinda hard, aren't you? You didn't know either of them very well did you?"

"Stubbs is in a box instead of me. He made sure I got out of the jungle. That means something to me."

"And Detective Fischer?"

"You know damn well why I'm upset about her. I've never met a woman like her. Probably never will again."

"I have your gun. It was found on Stubbs but is registered to you here in South Carolina. Taurus *PT1911*. The Feds' ballistics team cleared it. None of the GSWs on the bodies down in Central America match this weapon."

"Stubbs gave me that gun."

"And in your current state, I will continue to keep it safe for you."

"What does that mean?"

"It means you are going to get dried out."

I was put in lock-up within the bowels of the police building, fortunately in my own cell. I slept for two days straight other than to take a piss. They offered food but I don't remember eating.

JG and Sierra had come to collect me after my rest in the jail. There was no bail to post, I wasn't being charged with anything. They had been called to come pick me up and it was hoped that they would encourage me to leave Charleston.

Captain Simms was happy to be rid of me, shook my hand, and I'm sure he hoped it would be for the last time. He had me sign for my property, including my gun. All things considered it was rather nice of him.

The ride to the hotel produced little conversation. The country song *I Will Never Forget You,* by that young girl who won on the show *The Voice*, Danielle Bradbery, was softly playing on the car radio. I was a little choked up. Don't judge me, listen to it.

While I was packing my things in the hotel room, JG sat on one of the plush chairs and spoke.

"You don't *have* to leave. Nobody is forcing you to. You could stay down here, I need a lead investigator."

"I have two homes, one in New Hampshire, one in South Boston, and a business up there. I can't just …. I can't stay here after everything that has happened, even if I wanted to."

"You have been. I'm not sure if you know how long you've been down here."

"What is this an intervention? I'm going home."

"No, it's not. And I thought you would say that. I just wanted you to know that I appreciate everything that you have done and all that you have endured. I'm sorry I got you into this mess."

Sierra came out of the bathroom or the other room of the suite.

"I'm not sure I'll ever be able to thank you enough, Warren."

"You can start by calling me Deni. And we don't ever have to bring this up again, if you ask me."

She nodded like she understood. JG gave me a 9x12 manilla envelope.

"You're pay. I think the check in there should cover you. Also the title to the Mercedes *AMG*. I'll take care of the rest of the expenses on the credit card I gave you."

"*Oh yeah.* You probably want that back."

"It had crossed my mind."

"Listen, about the car. You don't have to — "

" — it's the least I can do. Besides, it's best if you don't fly home with a pistol. I had the Mercedes detailed, pulled anything that was mine out of it. The valet has it when you check out." He tossed the valet chip at me.

"Will you say goodbye to Brady for me?"

"Sure will. He wants a pet snake, and he wants to name it Deni."

"You're shitting me."

I had a sixteen hour drive ahead of me up to Boston. I headed out that night. I'd had enough sleep to get me there without a lengthy stop, but I would if I felt like it. I was in no rush. I think JG gave me the car because he knew I wouldn't drink and drive. Drinking and flying was another story.

I got on Interstate 95 and headed North. I left Charleston, South Carolina behind me. The memory of the events that took place there, however, leaving those behind is another story.

AUTHOR'S NOTES
AND ACKNOWLEDGEMENTS

The previous work is one of fiction, any resemblance to specific and true incidents is purely coincidental. Some of the places, laws, crimes, procedures and the prison experiences are based upon real research, however. They were used to add a legitimate feel to a completely fabricated story. Without the help of the people and entities listed below, this book at worst doesn't get written, at best isn't nearly as rich and believable.

There is no such university as SCMU that I am aware of, though there are many educational and research facilities that this fictitious place emulates. There is no venom library there, obviously, but the World Toxin Bank does exist and is helmed by Zoltan Takacs. He left the University of Chicago to collect "blueprints for toxin libraries". This library holds all the liquid gold secreted from animals the world over, and is used to research and create synthetic drugs. The research is real, the cures are also very real and/or just a step or two away from being in your medicine cabinet. The creepy-crawlies that scare us out of our minds, fodder for horror movies and halloween, are the very things that will cure what ails us. Very poetic I think.

The faction of Christian Science which I named Platists in this novel, are not real per se. In every legitimate group, there are always the outliers that take themselves a bit too seriously. While these particular outliers are not named Platists, they do exist. The old adage "there is one in every crowd" came from someplace. Or places. This debatable cult or religion is no exception. The beliefs and the history of Christian Science have been tweaked a bit to suit the needs of the story, but generally hold true. It was not my intention to impugn any religion or cult, but merely use the facts to enrich a story. Many thanks to the Mary Baker Eddy Library in Boston, MA, for their hospitality despite not agreeing with one single thing that I said. I would encourage any and all to read not only the works that I cited, but others as well to form your own opinion. The Christian Science Monitor has won seven Pulitzer Prizes from 1950-2002. Many thanks to them for speaking with me, and they too are located in Boston, MA.

I would like to thank the people of Costa Rica, especially the fine folks at Clodomiro Picado Institute, the Serpentario Monteverde Costa Rica, the Corcovado National Park, The Monteverde Cloud Forest Reserve, the HUGE pharmaceutical company and research universities they sponsor (which will remain unnamed per their request) for your unbelievable hospitality. Your patience throughout all of my questions and incessant screams for safety amidst the snakes is the stuff of sainthood.

To my friends, family and acquaintances who are a part of this novel in spirit. I hope that you can see yourselves in some of the characters, as I drew upon the nuances of your characters that make you who you are, to make mine come alive. Thank you for being a part of my life and part of the fabric of this work.

Finally, but most importantly, I would like to take the time to thank those that spoke to me in "hypotheticals" or "off the record". You risked your livelihood to speak to me about your expertise and your organizations. Be it the FBI or the Big Pharma Company that shall go unnamed, I thank you with all of my being. I am just a guy trying to spin a good yarn. Without your insights into the mind of a serial killer, policies and procedures, drug procedures and legislation, and many many other topics, this is a little yarn that never gets spun. If you enjoyed this book, it is largely because of them.

Thanks for your time and I hope you enjoyed the read.

-sw-

REFERENCES

Apitherapy (http://www.cancer.org/docroot/ETO/content/ ETO_5_3XApitherapy.asp?sitearea=ETO). From American Cancer Society.

Bartol, Curt R.; Anne M. Bartol. (2004). *Introduction To Forensic Psychology: Research and Application.*

Bates, Ernest Sutherland and Dittmore, John V. *Mary Baker Eddy: The Truth and the Tradition.* A.A. Knopf, 1932.

Bellwald, A.M. *Christian Science and the Catholic Faith* (http://archive.org/ details/christianscience00belluoft). The MacMillan Company, 1922.

Bradeb, Charles S. *Spirits in Rebellion: The Rise and Development of New Thought.* Southern Methodist University Press, 1963.

British Medical Journal. "Mark Twain on Christian Science" (http:// www.ncbi.nlm.nih.gov/pmc/articles/PMC2412999/?page=7), 2(2025), October 21, 1899.

Camfield, Gragg. *The Oxford Companion to Mark Twain.* Oxford University Press, 2003.

Cather, Willa and Milmine, Georgine. *The Life of Mary Baker G. Eddy and the History of Christian Science* (http://www.unz.org/Pub/ MilmineGeorgine-1909). Doubleday 1909, latest edition University of Nebraska Press, 1993.

Censo Nacional 2011 (http://www.inec.go.cr/Web/Home/pagPrincipal.aspx)

Clodomiro Picado Institute. Costa Rica. Various Interviews.

College of Agriculture and Life Sciences. University of Arizona. Various interviews.

Commonwealth vs. David R. Twitchell (http://masscases.com/cases/sjc/ 416/416mass114.html), decision of the 1993 appeal.

Corcovado National Park. Costa Rica. Guided tour.

Eddy, Mary Baker. *Historical Sketch of Christian Science Mind-healing,* 1888.

Eddy, Mary Baker. *Miscellaneous Writings,* 1897.

Fox, James Alan; Jack Levin (2005). *Extreme Killing: Understanding Serial and Mass Murder.*

Gardner, Martin. "Mind Over Matter" (http://articles.latimes.com/1999/ aug/22/books/bk-2412), *Los Angeles Times,* August 22, 1999.

Holland, Jennifer S. "Venom", *National Geographic,* February 2013 (p. 68-83).

Kaplan, Fred. *The Singular Mark Twain: A Biography.* Anchor, 2005.

Multiple Sclerosis Society, *Bee Venom Study* (http://www.mssociety.ca/en/research/CAT980602.htm)

Organization for Tropical Studies. (http://www.ots.duke.edu/)

Quimby, Phineas Parkhurst. *The Complete Collected Works of Dr. Phineas Parkhurst Quimby.* Seed of Life Publishing, 2009, first published 1921.

Serpentario Monteverde Costa Rica. Costa Rica. Various Interviews.

South Carolina Code of Laws, Unannotated (current through end of 2013 session). *South Carolina Legislature,* Title 40, chapter 18, sections 20-372.

The Monteverde Cloud Forest Reserve. Costa Rica. Various Interviews and guided tours.

Twain, Mark. *Christian Science* (http://www.gutenberg.org/ebooks/3187), 1907

Vitello, Paul. "Christian Science Church Seeks Truce With Modern Medicine" (http://www.nytimes.com/2010/03/24/nyregion/24heal.html), *The New York Times,* March 23, 2010

ABOUT THE AUTHOR

Photo ©2013 WWPGroup

Scott Wellinger is a well-travelled editor and novelist. His writing features, among others, the fictitious private investigations of Warren Dennihan. A native of New England, he was born in Vermont and was educated in Boston, Massachusetts. He holds a Master's Degree in Applied Economics and when he is not traveling, he is on a golf course.

Also by scott wellinger:

CRASH
A Warren Dennihan Novel (first of series)

Sinn
A Warren Dennihan Prequel

A sample of **CRASH** (first edition) follows. It is available for purchase wherever books are sold.

CRASH

A Novel By Scott Wellinger

Dedicated to my family. They live by the credo *you cannot build a big enough mess which cannot be fixed with a little extra love and support.*

PROLOGUE

THE NIGHT HAD DRAWN DOWN like a blanket over the small New England town, tucked in the mountains of southern New Hampshire. A cloudless, late summer sky made the bright stars the only form of illumination, which were little more than pinholes of light off in a distant universe. The pine forest that shot up from the fertile ground gave off a rich perfume reminiscent of Christmas, which was less than half a year to come. Above the tree-line, the natural rock formation known as *The Old Man on the Mountain* was a slight, silhouetted backdrop bidding the tourists a final goodnight whilst he slept. The narrow, windy roads meandering through the hills below that watchful cliff north of Boston, Massachusetts, were fortified with guardrails and graveled pulloffs to accommodate the looky-loo tourist vehicles. The fall foliage leaf-peepers were still a month or so away, but the hiking and camping season was still in full swing. The heavy traffic from the visitors trying to get a last trip in before the arrival of colder nights, was nonexistent in the hours after dusk. The hikers, campers, and naturalists had long since ventured home for the night or abandoned their parked vehicles on one of the pulloffs on the side of the road, as they made camp somewhere in the darkened forest.

The *Old Man* was the sentry for several communities below his perch on the White Mountains; the county and township of Wayland, New Hampshire was by far the most affluent. The old and new money was drawn from the financial hub of Boston in the form of large salaries. The town flourished as the commuters preferred to spend their ample earnings in the sanctity and "tax-free" state of New Hampshire over the Metropolis of Boston which fed them to the South. Another form of income for Wayland was the tourism, but the affluent of the community was torn in that while the outsiders boosted the economy, they trampled over their turf. The people of money from Wayland did appreciate the financial relief from tourism, which was their dilemma in refraining from ousting their numerous intruders. The visitors should be felt yet not seen.

The winters were the most difficult for the citizens to avoid the onslaught of outsiders. The skiers would come from the flatlands to trample the towns and, in their opinion, the face of their great State. Throughout the rest of the year, they spent their time and income away from the flatlanders at the Wayland Country Club. Golf was just one activity taken in there, and in truth many claimed to play more often than they had a tee-time for.   The sanctuary was more for camaraderie and companionship than the activities the club promoted. A place for the wealthy to rub elbows with others of their kind in the same area.

This particular night, those with money were keen to show off just how much they had and were willing to part with. The Gala and Charity event that was taking place in the pavilion was under way, all of the who's-who in place and opening wallets for the silent auction, though whom or what charity would be receiving these sums was anybody's guess.   While the sprinklers were misting water over the lush back-nine of the manicured golf course, which could be seen out of the large windows, elegant gowns and tuxedos flattered the bodies of the occupants in the club. Live, light jazz music and the mumbled conversations of the local power couples mingling under the giant chandelier could be heard faintly in the distance, while the rest of the community went about their Saturday night.   The well-to-do's had their evening festivities, freeing their assistants and staffers to have theirs.

Arelia Diaz had made her plans weeks prior, when she learned that she would have a rare night off. She was a live-in maid for one of the rich and beautiful, though she called herself a caretaker, and was looking forward to blowing off some built-up steam with a night of dancing with her girlfriends. The initial response from her friends at her invitation for a night out on the town was a jealous decline, until they too were informed that they would have the night off. Her friends in the area were also in the employ of other event attendees and would also have the night free from; babysitting, nannying, serving, cleaning, maintaining, cooking, or the myriad other tasks their employers were too important to perform.   A night of dinner; gossiping over the comings and goings of their respective power families, and certainly dancing would be just the cure for the tedium that ailed them. Only one friend, Marina could not make it. She was told that she would have to take care of a child, though her employer didn't have any children.

Arelia was a mid-thirties Brazilian woman who had left her own family back in Recife. Other than her gaggle of female friends, she was alone in the United States. She had no spouse or children, which was the mainspring for many nights of tear-soaked cheeks and a saturated pillow. The oldest of four daughters, she saw limited opportunities in her native village and networked into an immigrant sub-community tucked into the American Northeast almost ten years prior. Alone but not alone, she was content in managing a dream household, though it was not her own.

Ms. Diaz did not consider herself to be what the Americans called a *cougar*, she was too young to be considered for the part, but she was going to be on the prowl this night. All women had needs, this was a rare opportunity, and she was going to make the most of it. She painted on a pair of the most expensive jeans she could afford, her ample bosom bursted out of the front of her new, sparkling, black-yet-shear blouse, exposing her black push-up bra, and donned a pair of high heels which lifted her four inches higher than her usual five-foot-three inch frame. With her raven hair done (in what was coincidentally called a Brazilian Blowout), and her makeup accentuating her big, beautiful brown eyes, she would be turning some heads. She still had what it took to bag any man she wanted, despite her lack of practice.

She would not be bringing anyone back to her suite at her employer's palatial home, this was not allowed, nor did she have any intention of staying with an interested gentleman. Her duties would resume bright and early in the morning. Her employers would likely be as moody as usual, as demanding as usual. Maybe they would even be a little hungover, though they would never in a million years admit that to the help.   The agenda for the night would be dinner, *Forró* dancing, and a copious amount of flirting. Unfortunately the line would have to be drawn at flirting.

She was given an older, red, Honda *Civic* to use in her daily errands, which she was using while on her way downtown to meet her girlfriends. It was a small yet able car, in spite of the age, much like Arelia believed herself to be. She had plenty of life left, this was just a means to an end. A way to go back to Brazil with enough money saved to provide for a family she would make, and their family after she was gone.

Diaz was used to the car and all of the idiosyncrasies that came along with it. She loved the limited freedom that the car provided her, but she loved the stereo system the most. In the ten years of being the caretaker, she was never allowed to listen to her music loud enough to be heard by anyone in any part of the house. Nor was she allowed to use headphones as she was always on call. Always. Failure to hear, much less respond to a call from the main house would mean an immediate end to the life she had built here. Relegated to vehicular sonic therapy, she would blast her beats as loud as the car stereo and tiny speakers could muster.

She had the windows down, feeling the night air through her already blown locks of hair. The outside sounds were competing between the crickets, the sounds of the Country Club in the distance, and Arelia belting out the Portuguese lyrics over the loud music of her favorite band *Falamansa*. She was blissfully unaware that this would be her final concert.

As she rounded a sweeping blind turn on Wayland Country Club Road, the singing and car-dancing was immediately interrupted by the harsh LED, high-beam headlamps glaring into her eyes from seemingly nowhere, yet everywhere. She knew nothing of candlepower light measurements, but the retina-burning headlamps blinding her surely could have illuminated Fenway Park. Diaz could not see anything, much less navigate the rolling left turn. She could not see the lever protruding off of the steering column to flash her own high-beams at the offensive driver coming towards her. Could not see her bearings on the road. She was desperate to see a yellow line. A white one. Anything to pinpoint if she was in a lane. There were no vibrations from the warning grating on the side of the road, because there wasn't any grating on the side of the road. No reflectors, not that she would have been able to see anything being reflected in the already blinding light. She would have welcomed the grazing of a guardrail, just so she could sort out where she was. Everything was happening so fast. Brakes were unused. The stereo remained at full, deafening decibels. There was no time to turn it down. No time to think. No time to sweat. Was there somewhere she could pull off? But that question did not register in the time it took her to sail off the road.

The little-Civic-that-could missed the end of a guardrail, grabbed the bit of gravel just off of the pavement, bulleted her through the small pulloff. The car continued, severing a maple tree that was contemplating the changing leaf colors soon, continuing on to impact the base of a large rock formation. The car came to an immediate halt from the forty-plus miles per hour it was traveling just seconds prior. The rear of the car was the last to learn of the immediate stop being insisted upon by the fixed and rooted boulder. It had no choice but to follow the rest of the cars' lead and jetted into the air, rear tire spinning as it tried to continue beyond the mess. It failed.

The sound of the dance music halted, replaced by the sound of mangling of metal and the pulverizing of bone. The jagged metal sliced through flesh which added to the cacophony of horrific sounds. The macabre series of sounds lasted but a beat, but the devastation would be permanent.

Nothing would be continuing beyond the crash. Not the maple tree, not poor Arelia Diaz formerly of Recife, Brazil and more recently of Wayland, New Hampshire. Where her body existed in the cab, where she was car-dancing to her favorite band, singing as loud as her beautiful lungs could project, was a sick sculpture of metal, plastic, glass, rubber and human organs. The front of the car no longer existed. It was impossible to discern car from body, where the red paint from the Honda started, through all the blood, and the end of the former occupant. Her lifeless face rested, burning on part of the steaming engine; searing what was left of her beautiful features, her head and neck was now where the backseat should have been.

The offending headlights stared onto the wreckage for a time, determining what was already known. The lights crept slowly toward the destruction, attached to the black vehicle that was camouflaged by the dark of the night. They would abandon the devastation they had caused. The upbeat, accordion-based dance music and singing, followed by the horrifying reverberations of the crash were no more. The sounds were replaced by the ticking of the cooling, destroyed engine; the sizzling of flesh; the acceleration of the fleeing murderous vehicle. And crickets.

1

UGLY. THE IMAGE APPEARING back at him in the makeshift mirror was ugly. No other word could summarize the reflection and the atmosphere surrounding it; his every thought and emotion. The stainless steel metal above the all-in-one, Willoughby sink-toilet reflected pure ugliness. The image itself superimposed upon the backdrop of the institutional beige walls, the florescent lighting, the grey concrete floor.

Jacob Grantes had never been considered a hunk, nor an Adonis, he was not a physical specimen for which to lust. He had never been compared to the likes of George Clooney but he had been somewhat attractive, smart, confident. His six foot one inch frame, his square jaw, his sea-green eyes were some of the features that admirers had named when defending him as 'a catch'. The image that had once stared back at him, however, had disappeared, morphing into the figure that was reflected back at him in the polished steel. He was splashing water on his face, one push button at a time, but no matter how much water he applied, how much he washed, and how much he scrubbed his face, he could not cleanse the ugliness inside or out.

Grantes, inmate #437261, had been a guest at the Wayland County House of Corrections for the past six months, having been denied bail. He had not been in trouble with the law prior to the events leading him to this very moment, which made the denial pending trial quite unusual. Jacob was accustomed to living in a large home, family, and the picket fence; which made the current accommodations all the more intolerable. His cell was an eight by twelve foot concrete room with a double bunk, a small desk and a sink-toilet which he had to share with his celly. The space was tight and the nerves were stretched even tighter. Twenty hours per day were spent in this tiny space. Best friends could be put together in such a way and it would not take long to become mortal enemies. To make matters worse, the door to the cells lacked bars, it was a solid door, which allowed little air flow, with a narrow, horizontal slot at waist-high for food trays to be passed through, or to be handcuffed prior to exiting. The small, vertical window was convenient only for the Correctional Officers who had to execute head counts. This solid metal door was manufactured to make the most loud, God-awful clanks and noises when opened and closed. Studies had been done on this; millions spent, to craft an audible assault on inmates in an effort to make them uncomfortable, on edge, and contemplating the actions that had led them to their current place of residence.

The CO had awoken Grantes with a loud, mechanical unlatching, the grinding of metal as his cell door was sliding open at 5:30 AM.

"Grantes. You got 15 minutes to shit, shower 'n shave. Court. You'll get chow on the ride over."

"Yeah," he said between splashes of water on his face.

His grumbled reply indicated his malcontent, as this was to be a real shit day. It was to be a different kind of shit day, but a shit day all the same. All other days had the exact same schedule; filled with misery, meetings with so-called counselors, and a myriad of conversations with fellow inmates all of whom proclaim to be innocent or screwed by their lawyer. This day would be a shit day of a different color but a shade he knew quite well. Jacob Grantes had previously spent most of his adult life immersed in the muck and mire of the legal system, but on the other side of it. As an attorney, he knew exactly what this day would entail. The splashing of water on his face would make none of it go away.

"Jesus Christ, can you shut the fuck up? What time is it, bro?"

The shout came from a lump in the sheets, covering the body laying on the top bunk in his cell. Grantes's celly had a very low tolerance for anything beyond sleeping away his bid. This is known in prison as a bed-bid, and he is not the only one trying desperately to dream away the time.

"It's early. Sorry. I have court today. But it looks like you'll have the cell to yourself for the day."

"Goody." He said this without removing the covers which made him appear as though he was levitating five feet above a filthy concrete floor.

"You'll be able to shit in peace at least. I wish you'd spent a little time out of the cell so I could crap without an audience."

"You really gonna shower?"

"Yeah, I'm getting my shower bag ready now."

"That means that the door is gonna open and close a couple more times. Why you gonna shower anyways? Gonna be front and center with a jumpsuit and shackles anyway, clean ain't gonna matter."

"They'll let me change into a suit."

"Ha - you're funny. You're an idiot, but you're funny. Where are you gonna get a suit asshole?"

"I came here in a suit. My lawyer will have another one if they won't let me have that one out of property."

"You're gonna be in a holding tank, good luck getting one of the courthouse COs to let you change. Lazy assholes might have to do extra work," he said. "Whats today anyway?"

"February fif—"

"— the case moron. What part of the case is it?"

"Oh. Discovery and motions. It's when — "

" — I know what it is. Fifteen minutes tops bro. They're not lettin' you change into a fuckin' suit. Two bus rides and a day in the tank for fifteen minutes. Have fun."

"Shithouse lawyers."

It amazed him how much legal knowledge inmates had. Especially those with high recidivism. Grantes's cellmate had a very vast and intimate knowledge of the law from a certain prospective. He was, therefore, known throughout the prison as a good shithouse lawyer. His celly was of course aware that Jacob was a real lawyer, which only caused that many more passionate discussions.

"We'll see."

2

JACOB GRANTES AND HIS BEST FRIEND, Ryan Wells, had started a law practice together fifteen years prior. They had, over time, cornered the bustling criminal and legal market of nowhereville. The small southern New Hampshire town of Barstone, in Wayland County, was considered to be the other side of the tracks by the more affluent locals. Those elevated locals being the residents of the affluent town of Wayland, which was literally just across the tracks of the commuter rail into Boston, Massachusetts. The clichéd delineation was real. The constituents of Wayland Township made it quite clear to all of the inhabitants of Barstone, and really anywhere else for that matter but less vocally, that they were not welcome. The elected Sheriff of Wayland County, his office located in the town of Wayland by design, was well aware of what would happen if the petty crimes and riff-raff of Barstone were to bleed into the backyards of the wealthy community. And so the two towns within the same county coexisted; the town with the same name of the county reaped all the rewards, while the slums went about being the outcasts.

The law office of Grantes, Wells & Associates was strategically located in Barstone, on the border of the two towns. They needed the criminal element, and therefore the business from the Barstonians, and they wanted the much more civilized legal filings of Wayland. The two townships utilized the same courthouse as they were in the same county. Life was never boring for the two attorneys. Defending the proprietors of a Meth Lab one day; filing an uncontested, fourth divorce on behalf of the scorned trophy-wife on the next.

The *Associates* in the name of the firm was a mistruth. JG, as he was called, and Ryan were the only partners, the only lawyers, and there were no others seeking partnership. None would be sought out either as they were not seeking any new blood for such an arrangement. The associates consisted of their part-time private investigator, Warren Dennihan; and their full-time secretary in Ryan's wife, Angie. Warren had his own thriving business, with his own partner, and was subcontracted by the law firm whenever a top investigator was needed. He was rarely, if ever, in the office. Angie was in the office every business day, much to Ryan's chagrin, and she had almost no legal knowledge. What she lacked in legal prowess, she made up for in organization and efficiency. She was invaluable and JG had said in the past, in plain language to Ryan, that whatever problem he had with the arrangement, to get over it.

The arrangement had been Ryan's doing in the first place. He had hired Angie Grummond, as was her name at the time, without consulting JG on the spot at the first interview. Rather than ask the prospective employee out on a date upon their first meeting, which was ultimately what Ryan wanted to do, he decided to hire her instead. The would-be sexual harassment suit in waiting didn't last long, as they were officially an item by the time she was finished her training. JG didn't mind as much as he had initially let on, not even annoyed if truth be told. The headache of starting a firm was a larger migraine than that of an office romance. Besides, Ryan had been JG's best friend since law school, almost for as long as he could remember, and he had never seen his friend so happy.

The startup capital for the small firm came from the money bestowed to Jacob via his surrogate family. His in-laws had been more than good to him, they had filled a hole left in him by the passing of his natural parents. His wife, Anna, had come from money and while she had married for love, her parents could think of no reason for them to struggle financially. They had made the idle threats to rescind the money once they learned that Ryan was to be made full partner from the outset, but all concerned knew the threats were empty. Their apprehension came from genuine concern as they saw their son-in-law, Jacob, as the much more talented of the partnership. With Jacob viewed as having a much higher potential than his friend, especially since he had no money invested in the venture, they felt Ryan was there for the ride instead of the build.

Ryan was not a bad lawyer. He was no Shapiro either. He was talented but he was also a free-spirit. Wells would get caught up in the spirit of the law rather than the black letter. He took flyers. Rather than take on more legitimate claims, he often went to the hoop with little on evidence and heavy on the liberal sentiment. He would often take on the lost cause that was rejected by JG; acknowledging that he might win some, but he would lose more.

Ryan was an idealist. He was interested in the law for the good it could do. He actually thought the lady with the scales was indeed blind. He still does to this day.

JG had depended on Ryan to bring in fees not necessarily wins. Winning of course would draw the big cases, but with a location in Barstone, New Hampshire, who was he kidding? JG had the wins, Ryan had the passion. But that was all in the past. What JG needed from his friend and partner now was a win. A big win. He needed him to win the case of his life. For Jacob's life.

3

"All RISE. PLEASE COME TO ORDER, court is now in session. The honorable Judge McCaglia presiding." The bailiff shouted with much too much in the way of volume. There were few people in the fourth session of the Wayland County Superior courtroom. It was entirely unnecessary to shout at that level, but Grantes decided that the loud volume coordinated nicely with the loud color of the neon, hazard-orange prison jumpsuit he was wearing.

He had asked the Correctional Officer, politely mind you, if he could change into a suit that his lawyer had brought for him to wear to court. He even bargained to leave on the shackles, but the request didn't warrant any response. He repeated the question in case the officer didn't hear him. The CO had heard the request because he gave the sternest of looks upon hearing it a second time, though he still gave no response. Ryan had then gotten involved when he arrived but the plea to the Deputy Sheriff was in vain. The officer didn't like the hippie lawyer in the linen suit, and never liked any inmate ever. He was appointed to rid the county of these unwanteds, and this nonconformist was working to free them. Chalk one up for the political right, getting one over on the liberal left.

"You may be seated," said the judge. She was the moderately attractive Judge Grace McCaglia. Wearing the usual black robe, matching black hair that may have been colored to do so, and mystic blue eyes that could virtually see through a person. She confidently presided with a no-nonsense efficiency.

In her late forties, she had accomplished more than most attorneys had in the course of their entire career, in a fraction of the time. In the *Live Free or Die* State of New Hampshire; there were rumors of political favoritism, affirmative action, and sleeping her way into a judgeship. Any explanation was more plausible than that she had earned her position. These whispers did not go unnoticed which is why she once prosecuted and now presided strictly but fairly. There would not be any second-guessing her rulings. She would not

317

allow anyone to be justified in criticizing her for not being the right person for the bench.

"Where are we in the matter of the State of New Hampshire v Grantes?"

"Where are Anna and Brady is the better question." JG whispered into Ryan's ear as they sat in their seats at the defendant's table. He looked around the room but with few people in it, it was quite clear that his wife and son were not present.

"No idea. Three messages without a response this morning. Maybe they are giving her a hard time about a four year old in the courtroom?"

Ryan finished whispering the response as he stood to address the judge.

"We would like to request a continuance, your honor."

"On what grounds? This has been ongoing for six months, time is ticking here sir."

"We are still in discovery, judge. Both theirs and ours."

"Theirs? A Grand Jury was convened and subsequent to Rule 8, they found probable cause to sustain an indictment. The 90-day threshold was met. Do you want to weigh in here counselor?"

She swiveled her chair to her right so she could face the prosecuting Assistant District Attorney. 'Weigh in' was a poor choice of words and she immediately realized it.

Pierce La Fontagne was an enormous man. Fat. He was an unhealthy glutton that could blame whatever or whomever he wanted to regarding his obesity, but it was a fact that he tipped the scales at over four hundred-fifty pounds. He was always disheveled and just as disorganized. How he had lasted as an ADA was a mystery, but his nickname was not so mysterious. They called him Jabba, after the enormous creature in *Star Wars*, behind his back. And he knew it. He spoke with as slow a purpose as his metabolism.

"We have. Ah. Given the defense and have enough to provide the state to move. Ah. Forward with the case, Judge. We. Ah. Don't need much, but we do need a little more time." The fat on his neck jiggled when he spoke. He never looked up to face the judge when he spoke to her, as he was still shuffling papers in the disorganized mess he had created at the prosecution table. Besides his disorganization, not making eye contact with her infuriated her. She felt it was a sign of disrespect.

"Does that mean you are ready or not? Kind of late in the game aren't we, counselor? You had enough to sustain the charges, do you have what you need to move forward or don't you?"

"Ah. We feel confident that the current evidence will prove our case beyond the threshold of reasonable doubt."

"I can tell." She had to pause to control her anger. She was a professional to her very core. She swiveled back toward the defendant.

"Mr. Wells. Have you received all of this said evidence? If so, then I'm confused. Speedy trial gentlemen. The defendant has the right to one, he is remanded and sitting in prison awaiting the disposition of this trial. So I would think his lawyer would be more adamant about moving this forward. He pleaded not guilty. ADA La Fontagne and the state requires a speedy trial, and frankly I demand it so I don't get backlogged. Six months gentlemen. This has been going long enough, wouldn't you both agree? We move ahead forthwith." Efficiency experts could learn a thing or two from Judge McCaglia.

"I agree that six months is a long time, your honor. Especially for my client, who was only remanded due to an imminent threat justification, which we will get to in a minute with the other motion you have before you."

Ryan had filed to have the issue of bail revisited. Jabba had used a justification that argued that Jacob Grantes was an immediate danger to society and should be remanded as to allay any danger to the community. She was already disgruntled with the prosecutor, he was hoping to use that to his and therefore his client's advantage.

"But with all due respect, judge, I do not agree with the a forthwith," Ryan continued. "In order to provide a proper defense against the charges, I need to ensure that the burden of proof and all pertaining evidence is met and provided to me by the prosecution. The ADA has just told you and I, after some equivocating I might add, that they now have all the evidence they plan to use when and if this goes to trial. I need time to assemble all the counter-evidence supporting our claim against the charges, and that proving that my client is innocent."

JG nodded his approval. His friend and partner was doing well. Unlike television and movies in Hollywood, the State cannot come out of nowhere in the last minute of the trial with a damning piece of evidence. It was now time for the prosecution to put up or shut up and Ryan had just spoken legalese saying so.

"OK. So we are moving forward to trial with this, correct gentlemen?"

The two opposing men nodded in agreement instead of stating it aloud for the court stenographer. The judge didn't make them, she continued instead.

"I don't see a green sheet with any deals on the table as of yet. So Mr. Wells, how long do you need?"

"We request ninety days your honor."

"Three months for discovery and prep for trial? You are joking right? Nice try. ADA La Fontagne, is there anything else you would like to state before I rule on this?"

"Ah. No your honor. I would just like to reiterate that — "

" - No need to reiterate anything, I heard you the first time. You've got thirty days." She turned toward the clerk to dictate. "Let's set a date for pretrial and jury selection at or about one month from today."

"Your Honor with that being settled, I would like to revisit the issue of bail. The motion should be before you," Ryan said.

He was hoping that since things had not exactly gone his way thus far, Judge McCaglia would throw him, and more importantly JG, a bone on the motion to revisit the issue of bail.

"That has already been denied. I denied it six months ago. Is there anything new to bring forth where I would reconsider?"

"He is a prominent attorney in the area, Judge. He has a family, is a husband, and father. He is the sole breadwinner. This has created an enormous hardship. His driver's license has been reinstated at this point, but we would surrender it again in lieu of incarceration if the State is still concerned that he is an imminent threat. But if we are now talking another thirty days before a trial is to even begin, I see no reason or threat to continue to remand him. He has been a model inmate, never been in trouble with the law prior to this case, and he has — "

"Save it Mr. Wells. You have nothing new here. A woman is dead. The allegation is that she is dead because of your client. Drinking and Driving is serious and a blight on our society. When a child is in the car on top of this, allegedly, it is reprehensible. I continue to believe that he may be an imminent threat. The fact that he is a prominent figure in this community; and that he is an attorney; that has been before me and this court in the past; is not a reason for him to benefit. He cannot garner favor from a court that is supposed to judge his alleged crimes. Any defendant before me with these same allegations would get remanded, remain alcohol-free, surrender their license to drive a motor vehicle, and pending the outcome of the trial matriculate a Substance Abuse Program. I'm sorry Mr. Grantes, but you are to stay at the Wayland County House of Corrections pending trial. Stay in the Substance Abuse Program or there will be consequences, sir. As Mr. Wells just stated it is only thirty more days."

She paused only for a moment while she briefly looked over the rest of the documents regarding this case in front of her.

" So unless there are any other motions, we will resume these proceedings in thirty days. No more delays gentlemen, either one of you. Court is adjourned."

The gavel was only tapped onto the sound block but it sounded as though it was slammed through to the other side by a sledgehammer.

4

THE TRUTH WAS that the hardship the Grantes family was facing was not at all financial. It was Jacob who was suffering the most, but they were all unaccustomed to this torment. Not being able to see his wife and four year old child was all but killing him. Brady was not supposed to be without his father. He hadn't been in his life up to that point. Anna had been distant in recent months but they had dealt with serious difficulty in the past. They would get through it. Their college romance had started blissfully and had some serious downs despite their intense love for one another. Their eventual vows to take each other through good times and bad had taken significant meaning.

Norman and Olivia Craig had done whatever they could to encourage the college romance of their only daughter, Anna. Jacob, not Jake or JG as others called him (his natural parents had taken the time and effort to pick a name for him, and it was rude to bastardize that effort they had said repeatedly), was decidedly the perfect match for their Anna. Especially with the boys she had brought home in previous courtships. True, Jacob's family didn't come from wealth, nor had they built any. They had faith that this legacy would change with Jacob. He had work ethic, was smart, and pre-law. Yes, this is what they had in mind for their girl and they would do whatever they could, financially or otherwise, to support Jacob's goals. As long as Anna was included in the equation.

Jacob was always humbly appreciative, respectful in declining the offers of money or the "just because" expensive gifts, but would relent over time. Anna joined in on the pressure to accept these material tokens of affection for they were deemed as simple manifestations of parental approval. She viewed the entire subject as "only money". Of course it was only money to her, she had been privied to these same gestures and more over the course of her entire life. These were just an extension of her expectations from her wealthy parents.

"You should just get used to it honey, they won't let up. They love you and they just want to show you how much. Besides, you deserve to live a certain lifestyle even if you don't know it yet," she said in one of their more memorable spats on the subject. There had been more discussions regarding this very subject, all of which she won with some version of the same statement.

Jacob's fight for financial independence with her was a broken alliance, however. He would say things like, "I'm used to doing things for myself, babe. It's not that I am unappreciative of it, but there is something honorable in building a life for ourselves, by ourselves. I feel like I am forever indebted to them."

These declarations would fall on deaf ears and would either reluctantly fade or would be the impetus for a battle royale, depending on the value of the gesture and how much Jacob really wanted to press the issue. Eventually Jacob acquiesced, as he did every time. As the relationship developed, the lifestyle became de rigueur. He had lost every battle and the war as well. In truth, he had built up enormous debt and was very thankful for the financial help. Boston University was not cheap, Boston University School of Law even less so. The money, cars, apartments, the ability to go to Law School (only 11% of those applying to BU School of Law get accepted. The competition is stiff, but Mr. Craig was friends with someone on the Board of Trustees, or so he said).

"It's not bribery," Norman Craig had said. "I love Anna," he also said. It was to ensure that they had a strong foundation on which to build their life together. Of that, Jacob was sure.

Jacob's biological parents loved him with all of their hearts, albeit with fewer trinkets to show for it. Actually, there weren't any trinkets. Reginald and Elizabeth Grantes had to work and toil for every nickel of property or possession they owned, and even then the nickels didn't add up to anything of worth. They doled out hugs and kisses the way Norman Craig doled out money. Before the Craigs, Jacob had been a wealthy man. His parents attended or coached every athletic endeavor their only son struggled to perform. Neither parent had attended college but made it a priority for their son to get the education they did't have. They would not, could not, contribute financially. But they were motivating and supportive.

Young Grantes left upstate Vermont to attend Boston University and achieve his and his parent's goals for him. His parents remained there, driving south for visits or sending care packages of sweets to their starving student. They were pleased to learn that as of his sophomore year, their son would no longer struggle financially. The ends would more than meet. Unfortunately, in the end, they would never meet Anna.

******

It was the start of Jacob's second semester, of his second year at BU that Reggie and Liz would drive down to Boston to visit their son for the last time. He had been home for Christmas break and every other sentence was, "Anna this" or "Anna that".

He had been a social mingler in high school, never the most popular kid but was a welcome addition to any clique. He was better than averagely attractive. He was polite, and was familiar with many a female as well, in large part because of his standing in a plethora of social circles. He had many dates, with a few sporadically retained as official girlfriends over the years. He certainly didn't have any that he had prattled on about for days on end.

His freshman year had been new and exciting, but also the most difficult endeavor he had undertaken in his life up to then. There were precious few stories regarding the fairer sex as he said there was no time. That was only half true. The other half was that going to University was not about settling down but about exploring, both academically and socially. It was novel that this Anna would commandeer so much of a conversation, which made necessary the trip to Boston.

Interstate 89 is a long, windy, treacherous highway running north-south over and around the Green Mountains, crisscrossing Vermont and into New Hampshire. This is one of two major highways in Vermont, and is the quickest way south to Boston, Massachusetts. The two lanes of patchy, frost-heaved road are tricky to negotiate any time of year; soft shoulders, ice, elevation changes, with notorious fog make it more so during bad weather.

January brings major snow storms almost every year, often dropping several feet of snow in a relatively few number of hours. This particular *Noreaster* should have postponed the trek south to Boston, the storm well-tracked and advised in advance. But in the Northeast, weather personnel and meteorologists, were wrong as often as correct. Though every weather girl, on every channel, was forecasting the same snow advisory. But the days had been requested off, cashing in vacation and/or personal time, so the show must go on. And so on that January afternoon, Reg and Liz Grantes of Burlington, Vermont embarked on their journey south.

Jacob found it odd that his parents had not called him once they had arrived in Boston. They had a reservation with a late check-in scheduled at the Buckingham Hotel on Commonwealth Avenue, as was customary when they visited. When he had not heard from them, the thought of the big storm resonated in the back of his mind. He almost immediately disregarded it, however; his father had driven in the snow his entire life, had taught him how to drive in the stuff. He called the prepaid cellphone they used only when traveling, as cell phones were not the rage with the senior Granteses back then. He could not get through. Their voicemail was not set up, of course. It was not until he called the hotel and been informed that they had not checked in that he began to worry. More phone calls to their friends and to their places of work without a definitive answer to their whereabouts led to panic.

By 10:00 AM the following morning, panic became horrified shock. The Vermont State Police informed him by telephone that neither had survived a severe car crash. Neither had been alive when authorities had arrived at the scene.

"We hate to inform you over the phone," they said. "How very sorry we are," they also said. "Please come to Montpelier, Vermont to identify your parents."

They had not made it out of their own state. The reports showed that the snowy weather conditions inhibited sight; mixed with the unplowed snow on top of black ice, with an unfamiliar rental vehicle that was not equipped with all-wheel drive, were some of the elements contributing to the disastrous formula. The guard rail was ill-placed, meaning that there wasn't one in place. A guard rail would have at a minimum kept the vehicle on the road. The lack of this safety measure did the opposite and did not keep them on the road. The rental vehicle launched off the elevated highway into the icy ravine below. The final element in their premature demise.

The aftershock of the catastrophe had left Jacob scarred both emotionally and financially. Anna and her parents were there to reassemble the pieces as best they could. The financial piece was easy. Norman took care of the massive debt in one phone call. Anna was there for the emotional part. This was not as easy. But they dealt with it.

Reginald and Elizabeth Grantes, formerly of Burlington, Vermont, had loved life. They cared not for money but for the happiness it could provide from joyous memories. They loved each other and they loved their son, and in that they were rich. Realistically, they were not. They lived paycheck to paycheck and didn't manage those very well at all. There were always events deemed too important to pass up, spending money earmarked for bills; spending in lieu of life insurance, savings, or a 401k. They were upside down on their mortgage in part because of the market, but primarily because of the repeated refinancing and remortgaging.

Without life insurance, in their terrible financial condition, and most recently with the cost of their final expenses, they had left their only son with an enormous financial burden. He was already in debt because of his educational loans and the catastrophe would make him more so without a house or substantial property to sell. And so at the ages of 58 and 56, Reggie and Liz respectively, had left their son broken and broke. Had it not been for the Craigs, he would have been broke for the rest of his life.

5

JG WAS ANXIOUSLY AWAITING the arrival of his lawyer at the table in one of the courthouse conference rooms. He was immediately escorted there after his brief legal fray in the fourth session upstairs. Ryan had worked it out to conduct a meeting with his client before he was bussed back to prison, should he not make bail. Which to his misfortune is exactly what happened. Ryan seemed to be taking a long time doing whatever he was doing in the eyes of JG; leaving him alone in the dark, windowless conference room with a court officer standing watch in the corner. It was an awkward silence which made Ryan's absence seem even longer. He was not in any hurry to get back to his cell, nor his celly, but he was overwrought with how his case was progressing thus far. Or not progressing, which consumed his thoughts every minute of every day in prison.

The large wooden door opened with a start, ending the tension that had been building in the small room, adding a different sort of unease. Ryan moved quickly to a chair opposite his client, setting his leather briefcase down on the oversized table between them.

"I'd like to be alone with my client please," he said over his left shoulder to the officer.

"Sure thing. I'll be outside the door when you're finished."

Once the babysitter had left, the lawyer-client pretense was abandoned. "Well, that didn't go very well." The hearing had not gone well, they both knew it, and neither one would sugarcoat it to say that it had.

"Ya think?"

"Look pal, we have them on the ropes, right where we want them," Ryan said.

"Rope a dope, huh? Who's the dope? They're kicking our asses, Ry."

"Well I don't know what I could have done differently in retrospect. Thoughts? I mean what would the Great Jacob Grantes have done?"

JG's elbows were on the table, head in hands. He needed a lifeline. The sarcasm and mucking it up with his friend needed to cease. He was on the verge of breaking down.

"You did what you did, Ry. I mean you did what I would have done. That woman is a ball-buster."

"McCaglia has always been brutal, you knew that going in. You've been in front of her before. Hell, she was as an ADA, she is now on the bench. She has something to prove, always has, and she doesn't cut breaks unless she absolutely has to. And she doesn't have to here. We don't have anything going for us, and Jabba isn't chomping at the bit to cut a deal either."

"Exactly. So what do we have we going for us?"

"I was just speaking with tons-of-fun upstairs after our hearing. That's what took so long. I've got the 'one and only green sheet' right here. This is the only deal he is offering, or is ever going to offer, he says. It's not a good one, I'll warn you."

He reached into his briefcase on the table, removed the green court document the La Fontagne had given Ryan a few moments prior. It was conveniently on top and quickly slid directly in front of his jumpsuit-clad friend. A green sheet is a bargaining document with legalese and three vertical columns in the middle horizontal third. The form is on No Carbon Required (NCR) paper with three sheets; one for the ADA, one for the defense, and one for the judge. The first column is for the prosecutor, which offers a sentencing recommendation if the defense forgoes the expense of a trial. The middle column is the defense counter offer, which typically chips away at what the State wants. The final column on the right, is the deal formed between the two and goes to the judge. He or she reads the statutory minimums to ensure nobody is ponying up the courthouse, then usually rubber-stamps the deal. When all is said and done, all the judge wants is to clear their docket, keep justice moving just like everyone else. This is called a green sheet for the complicated reason in that the color of the document is a light green. Though it must be signed by all parties, it is only legally binding when and if a formal hearing takes place and agreed to on the record.

"He likes where he is," Ryan continued. "As you can see, the offer is Vehicular Manslaughter, OUI 1 with injury, leaving the scene. He drops the child endangerment, and puts a recommend of eight to ten on the VM, concurrent. Loss of licenses, two years after release on the drivers, law for life because we are talking felonies."

"Not much of a deal."

"You would get fifteen years on the VM alone at trial. Add in the OUI-with, leaving the scene, and indifference would get you another ten-plus separately. Add the child endangerment back into the charges if we go to the hoop, and you would not be able to see your kid without someone watching over your shoulder until he is legally an adult. Eight to ten, to run concurrent means with good time, two years off the minimum. You've been in for six months already, so you would be out in five and half. No child supervision, no probation. It's not good but it is the best we're gonna get I'm afraid."

The drivers license didn't make that much difference to JG. The loss of his ability to practice law could also be dealt with, he had money and he could always find something to occupy his days. Maybe he could teach. The five and a half years away from his family was intolerable. He could not lose his family for any longer than he already had. Supervised visits with Brady was unacceptable also but at least he would be able to see him other than through glass. These thoughts were going through his mind but he wasn't vocal about them, which caused a long pause. He continued to stare at the offer, lost in the ramifications if he agreed to what was written.

"What's going through your mind? Talk to me. There is nothing saying that you can't be behind the scenes at the firm, you just wouldn't be able to take cases when you get out."

"You think that is what's bothering me, Ry? How long have you known me? You really think that is what's hanging me up?"

"No, I don't. I'm just trying to help. But Jabba isn't going to budge. It's this or we go to the hoop. But you have given me nothing to work with on defense. We go to trial? I think unless we come up with something really damned compelling, you're going to go away for a long time."

"Have you been in touch with Anna yet? I'd like to discuss this with her."

"She isn't, nor was she, here today. No answer either. Voicemail is full. I'm really not sure where she is, but I'll keep trying." He pulled out some other documents from the briefcase, spreading out the pile on his side of the table. "What I would like to discuss is all of this circumstantial evidence and see if anything jogs your memory. Anything we can hammer away at. If we weaken anything he has, maybe the deal gets better."

"We've been through this, I don't remember anything about that night. Well, other than Sully's anyway."

"Yeah well we are going to go through it again. You admitted to quote, 'being hammered' when they picked you up at your house. You were passed out by the way. Again, Brady was upstairs asleep but unsupervised."

"I can't believe I drove in that condition, much less with Brady in the car. Then left him on his own like that in the house. I just can't believe it."

"Thats what they're going with. I have a statement from the bartender, Jenna, that you left Sully's between 8:00 and 8:15 PM. You also admitted to being at the bar in the back of the cruiser, which means you had to be really banged up. You, of all people, know better than to say anything to the police after you've been arrested. But anyway, you left and picked up Brady at the Destriers at 8:20 PM; the servant that was watching him told Chamille Destrier that she put him in his carseat in the back of the running car, that you never spoke or left the driver's seat. She said she found it odd behavior, but this is all third hand through Chamille because the servant doesn't speak English, apparently. The police never spoke to her directly to confirm or deny anything. Chamille was at the charity event next to your wife, so we strike the kid being in the car as hearsay. I think that is why the big-boy is dropping child endangerment, the kind soul."

"Yeah, what a sweetheart."

"Right. So you drove away and must have bounced off a tree, veering into the opposite lane where this poor woman happened to be coming right at you. She goes off the road and plays chicken with a big tree and an even bigger rock. She lost and you went home to sleep it off."

"It's not funny, Ry. Please don't make light of the fact that this woman was decapitated by a smoking-hot engine. I feel awful."

"Sorry, just trying to add some levity. Anyway, they have matching paint from the tree, black sapphire pearl, and the scrape on your Volvo has wood and bark all through it. Exact. No real credible argument there, I'm afraid. Furthermore the rubber zig-zagging on Wayland Country Club Road matches the Michelin 235/60R18s on your ride. Cops investigated your tires, they've got you dead to rights there too."

"Match? *Cops* are matching this all up? Can we get experts to refute them? Volvos are a dime a dozen in New England, hell I have two of them."

"Lab techs. This isn't *CSI*, they didn't stop everything they were doing and get top experts from all over the country to fly in on the state's dime, no. But you don't have to be an expert to see that all of this doesn't look good. Picking apart their lab technicians with our expensive ones is not going to win over a jury, if that's what you're thinking."

"That is exactly what I am thinking. The techs are overworked, underpaid, they make mistakes — "

" — this is New Hampshire, JG. They are neither overworked, nor are they underpaid. These aren't MIT grads by any stretch but they don't have a whole lot to investigate, trust me. Just between you and me, I looked at your car, the road, the tree. You killed this poor woman. If you were anybody else — "

" - So what are we doing here then?"

"You're my best friend. I'm trying to mitigate your responsibility here. I'm trying to help. I don't know, find a technicality. What we're doing here is trying to get the best deal we can."

"Great. Just great. You think five and half is the best I can do?"

"We haven't discussed the 911 call yet. Anonymous, but that is how they nailed you. How they knew to go to your house to grab you."

"What is there to discuss? You've already told me to take the deal, right?

Ryan paused. He shuffled the stack of papers containing all the condemning evidence. He really wasn't sure why he was against taking the deal but he was. He knew his friend, knew him better than any other male on the planet, and something was not right. Endangering the life of his only son, the one they had so much trouble conceiving, was not scanning. True, he had been drinking more in the months before the accident, but to get that blackout drunk was not something he would expect from his friend. He was mister safety. People disappointed. But not JG. Not Jacob Grantes. He had never disappointed. Not until now.

"Look, I'm not telling you to take the deal. At least not yet. We finally have all the evidence that fat-body has compiled; so we put Deni on it and see what he comes up with. I mean, the cops didn't pick you up at your house until 9:45 PM, which gives you a huge window to get shattered in the comfort of your own home. If everything comes back the way it looks here, which admittedly is really fucking bad, then we pick away at the bartender and the illegal lady."

"Please leave the vic alone. Arelia, right? Jenna too."

"Look. Jenna is a sweet girl, we go there and knock a few back and she is always good to us, but she over-served you. She claims not, but obviously she screwed up and is covering her ass. As far as the victim, she is dead. Which is unfortunate. But she shouldn't have been in this country to be dead. She was illegal. I feel for her just like you do, but when it comes to my friend or someone who may or may not even pay taxes? I might be a 'hippie' but I look out for my own. We've kinda got a role reversal here, huh? You're usually the cutthroat."

"Prison changes people I guess. Usually for the worse, not more sympathetic. But it is what it is."

"Maybe. But if shit goes south, all the cards lead to what we have before us, then we go after the ladies. The bartender has some responsibility here, and so does the vic. This *is* New Hampshire. We don't like drunk drivers but we don't like illegal aliens more."

"Not very Politically Correct of us, is it?"

"Unfortunately, like you said, it is what it is. Peace, love, and get a green card."

"Well lets hope it doesn't come to that. Just get Deni going because we don't have much time."

"I'm on it. I'm not going anywhere. You need anything?"

"Actually, yes."

"Name it."

"Find Anna."

6

RYAN WELLS WAS JG's longest and closest personal friend. They had both grown up poor but not impovered, had been instilled with a strong work ethic, and were the first in their respective families to go to college. They had met at BU during freshman orientation and were all but inseparable since. Grantes had been a loyal friend in pulling Wells into the fold of the partnership and Ryan had been loyal in many other ways, including during the death of Jacob's parents. They were each the brother to the other.

The two were so alike in so many ways that they could have been biological brothers. Ryan was good looking, tall and had what was once an athletic build. They would both be forty this year and had previously made plans for both families to go on vacation together to celebrate. Until the incarceration, all had looked forward to the time away. The only major difference between them was professionally. They were both strong advocates, but the hippie would live in the shadow of his more talented, leaning to the right, brother.

As Ryan left the courthouse, he pulled his iPhone out of his long winter overcoat to call Warren Dennihan, the firm investigator.

"Deni, how are you?" He immediately regretted not using his bluetooth ear device to make the call as he juggled his briefcase, the phone, and his car keys to open his parked car.

"Same shit, different pile. What's up?" Warren Dennihan was a *Southie*, or from the district of South Boston and had the severe accent to prove it. Bad. Or 'wicked bad, guy'. It was almost like he spoke a different language as *pahk tha cah in hah-vid yahd*, just doesn't quite describe how broken his English really was. He didn't pronounce *r's*, unless of course they were not in the word like *drawr* instead of draw. It was work to hold a conversation with him unless you were familiar with him or his kind.

"I just finished up with JG's hearing. It didn't go well."

"I figured. I got my partner workin' my other shit, so how much time do I gotta clear up?"

"Ah shit," Ryan said. He had dropped his phone while opening his car to get it started and warmed up. He had to retrieve it out of the snow but fortunately it still worked. With the new synthetic oils and the fact that he drove an Audi A6, he didn't need to get the car warmed up for performance reasons, but he couldn't get the winter-fighter to work on his cold body until the engine was pumping warm air at him.

"You ok?"

"Yeah, Yeah. I'm here. Just dropped something. So everything we talked about? That's what they've got. The whole shah-bang. We've gotta work on it."

"By we, ya mean me."

"It's been a tough morning, are you really gonna give me a hard time right now?"

"Always. Hey listen. I've been callin' WHOC, I know a few guys over there. Not much I can do to look after him in there. Its all political. He's a lawyer, so nobody trusts him, and he can't gang up. At least he knew not to PC, just take a beat'n like a man if thats what they wanna do."

"If it was going to happen, it would have happened by now."

"Not necessarily, but we can hope. How much longer?"

"That depends on you, Deni. Thirty days if this goes to the hoop. Trial will be probably about two weeks or so, after that depends on what we get. I was hoping we could get enough to kill a trial, maybe enough to get a deal. They are offering eight to ten, which means five and half when all is said and done."

"All depends on me? No pressure. Who's breakin' balls now?"

Ryan was still sitting in his car, which was starting to kick out the warm seventy-four degree air that was set on his in-dash computer. He still couldn't drive, however; the car had not yet picked up the signal for the phone and you cannot drive and talk on the phone in New Hampshire unless handsfree. "Hey where are you?"

"Around the corner from you, I'll be there in thirty secs or less."

"Good. This might be easier face to face. I have a ton of documents you should look at."

"Do you still drive the silver Audi?"

"Yes, of course. I love this — "

" — I'm behind ya."

"Holy crap. That was fast."

Deni parked his blacked-out Escalade and relocated to the passenger seat of Ryan's vehicle. This was the part that took the thirty-seconds. "Let's see it all," he said without explanation of how or why he was in the immediate area.

"So this is everything."   He handed Warren the stack of evidential material from his briefcase, then continued.   "I know we discussed it when this thing happened, and since, but something just isn't sitting right about this case. You think I'm nuts though don't you?"

"I don't think you're nuts, per se, but would you really go through all this bullsh for anybody but JG? I agree that somethin' isn't stirrin' the kool-aid, but you and I both know he did it. He was drinkin' like a fish for months before this all happened. I was thinkin' family trouble at the time, but who knows? That kid is his life, so I can't see him throwing that away. But we all fuck up, doesn't have to be on purpose for it to do damage."

"So does that mean that you are on board? I gotta know that you are on this."

"Loyal as lab, huh? Yeah, me too. I'm in, and you know it. I just need somethin' to work with here, guy."

"Look I never ask how you do what you do, because I'm not sure I want to know, but we are going to need all you've got on this. We need to dig into; Jenna, the bartender we know from Sully's Tavern, the Destrier servant or au pair or whatever she is, the 911 call is a bit wonky, and if all else fails — we make the vic the most despicable person who has ever illegally entered the borders of this country," Ryan said before pausing. "I was kind of hoping for a sliding scale on this one. I know you have to clear your calendar and this is going to take some time, but with me taking this case, I have all of his cases I have to work, and mine, and of course he isn't in the office taking cases so the firm is really financially tight right now and — "

" — hey relax, buddy. I can't dig up what ain't there, but I'm on it. As legit as possible anyway. As for the fee, don't worry about it. I owe tha kid. He's been good to me over the years."

"So what are you thinking?"

"I've got a couple of ideas. Mostly hunches, but I know people."

"I know you know people, that's why you are so good at what you do. Anyone I know?"

"Stop kissin' my ass Ry. I wanna check out the bar first. Jenna."

"Business or pleasure?"

"Both."

"I've got another project that's just as important."

"I'm listenin'."

"Find Anna and Brady. They didn't show up at court today and she is not answering phones. It's weirding me out, and JG is really freaking out."

"Huh. Lets go over to the house. You drive."

"Right now? Deni, I've got — "

" — you said it's important. Was that fact or bullsh?"

"Fact."

"Then start driving."

CRASH **A Warren Dennihan Novel** is available in print

and in ebook wherever books are sold.

Google Play

amazon.com

iBooks

WWPGroup.webs.com

Createspace.com

and other fine retailers